Hugo Erichsen

The London medical student and other comicalities

Hugo Erichsen

The London medical student and other comicalities

ISBN/EAN: 9783337215101

Printed in Europe, USA, Canada, Australia, Japan

Cover: Foto ©Andreas Hilbeck / pixelio.de

More available books at **www.hansebooks.com**

THE

LONDON MEDICAL STUDENT

AND

OTHER COMICALITIES.

SELECTED AND COMPILED

BY

HUGO ERICHSEN, M. D.,

Recently Professor of Neurology in the Quincy School of Medicine, Medical Department of
Chaddock College; Licentiate of the Royal College of Physicians and Surgeons of
Kingston, Canada; Member of the Detroit Medical and Library Association;
Formerly Assistant Editor of the Detroit Clinic; Recently Associate
Editor of the Western Medical Reporter and the Med.-Chir. Cor-
respondenz-Blatt fuer Deutsch-Amerikanische Aerzte, etc.

MOTTO:—"Fools have a Greater Dread of Laughter than of T.*' .'

DETROIT, MICH.:
DETROIT FREE PRESS PRINTING COMPANY.
1885.

PREFATORY.

PERHAPS the psychology of laughter has never been better expressed than by HAZLITT.

"Man," says HAZLITT, "is the only animal that laughs, for he is the only animal that is struck with the difference between what things are and what they ought to be."

Laughter, then, is one of the distinguishing features of man. In aiding every medical man to assert and show his superiority over other animals, I feel confident that my present effort will receive the same appreciation which was accorded to the "Medical Rhymes."

The LONDON MEDICAL STUDENT is taken from the London Punch, where it was published about a half a century ago. To speak of the merits of Punch were as absurd as to paint the beauty of a rose: it is now, as it was formerly, the representative journal of English wit and humor. Despite my strenuous efforts I could not detect who wrote the sparkling portraiture of medical-student-life in the greatest metropolis of the world, but I was convinced by my investigation that its authorship belongs to HOOD, DICKENS, THACKERAY, MARK LEMON, or DOUGLAS JERROLD. Of one thing, however, I am absolutely certain, that is, that I am the first to introduce my friends, Mr. MUFF and J. RANDALL, Esq., to the medical profession at large. They will not find them to be dull companions.

After an interview with these London students, I fear my brethren in medicine will have to adjust their collars; therefore I suggest that they be taken off before the perusal of this book is begun. If waistcoats should tear during the reading, a copy of this volume sent along with the ruptured garment to the tailor will serve as sufficient apology.

There is nothing that pays a physician better than ready wit and overflowing humor. They are far better matters of capital than a prominent olfactory organ — beg pardon — I was going to say than prompt olfactories and steady nerves. The public entertains the same dislike for long-faced physicians who are as melancholy as a gib cat, that it feels towards funny sextons or jolly clergymen. Smiles have outbidden remedies in many a health purchase; in fact it is well known that "the value of a smile is beyond price." A joke well administered often removes bile better from the body (and soul) of an irritable patient than any of the most potent cathartics. I am sorry to state that the gall of some acrimonious individuals cannot be removed in any way or manner.

When a student begins dissection, when he for the first time faces disease and death in the wards of the hospital, he laughs away the disagreeable, unpleasant feelings he experiences, and this kind of philosophy continues during his novitiate; but the humor once conjured never leaves him, and follows him on his entry into the profession. This, I think, is the reason why we meet with so many good-natured M.D.'s, and why physicians are as a rule long-lived. Indeed, some of the disciples of Hippocrates actually ruin their pocket-prospects by laughing their neighborhood into perpetual health. They are overflowing with generosity, and would stop in a cane-brake to write a gratuitous prescription for the floor-polisher of a roller skating rink, who in a few days may furnish them with a case of compound comminuted fracture.

I do not remember of ever having met with a hypochondriac among medical students. The almost invariable process of training pursued by these gentlemen cultivates wit and humor and banishes the green-eyed monster. When they have graduated and put in most of their time waiting for patients with patience (while time causes hair after hair to

fall from their heads, like leaves from a tree, bringing on pre-
maturely an aged appearance, which after all proves to be
good capital), and for many years the patients of emergency
and the rash encouragers of rising merit deal cautiously with
them; they console hours of weary waiting with the surest
of all hope-revivers — problematical and practical humor.
The habit of youth is but subdued as they climb the ladder
of professional renown, and score increasing thousands at the
banker's. From the desk of the lecture-room, and over the
table of the clinic, the professor has his joke of the hour.
The medical teacher well knows that he can often impress
the point of his lecture better on the mind of the student by
relating a little story or a joke, than by the most eloquent
flight of rhetoric.

The old adage, "laugh and grow fat," well deserves more
than a passing notice, as obese persons are generally considered
jolly and happy, and happiness is the great object of life.
The life of a physician is arduous; he comes constantly in
contact with trouble, pain, and death; to him are confided
the innermost thoughts and the burdens of his patients, so
that the load he carries is often too heavy and bears him
down if his mind is not directed at times into some other
channel. A busy man will soon wear out if he has no recreation. To rest and supply new life to an overworked brain, a
change of reading matter often becomes necessary.

I hope that by compiling the contents of this book I will
meet an existing, though unexpressed, wish of the medical
profession. The anecdotes collected in this volume have
been obtained from many sources. I am principally indebted
to the following medical journals: Obstetric Gazette, Medical
and Surgical Reporter, The Doctor, Louisville Medical News,
Peoria Medical Monthly, Michigan Medical News, The Medical
Age, and others. Some anecdotes have been taken from J. C.
Jeaffreson's "Book about Doctors."

I must here express my thanks to D. Appleton & Co. of

New York City for their kind permission to reprint two anecdotes from their "Cyclopædia of Wit and Humor of Ireland,
England, and America."

H. E.

11 Farmer St., Detroit, Mich.

CONTENTS.

8 CONTENTS.

MEDICAL ANECDOTES.

THE

PHYSIOLOGY

OF THE

LONDON MEDICAL STUDENT,

AND

CURIOSITIES OF MEDICAL EXPERIENCE.

THE

PHYSIOLOGY OF THE LONDON MEDICAL STUDENT.

I.

THE INTRODUCTORY DISCOURSE.

WE are about to discuss a subject as critical and important to take up as the abdominal aorta; for should we offend the class we are about to portray, there are fifteen hundred medical students, arrived this week in London, ripe and ready to avenge themselves upon our devoted cranium, which, although hardened throughout its ligneous formation by many blows, would not be proof against their united efforts. And we scarcely know how or where to begin. The instincts and different phases, under which this interesting race appears, are so numerous, that far from complaining of the paucity of materials we have to work upon, we are overwhelmed by mental suggestions, and rapidly dissolving views, of the various classes from Guy's to the London University, from St. George's to the London Hospital, perpetually crowding upon our brains (if we have any), and rendering our ideas as completely muddled as those of a " new man " who has, for the first week of October, attended every single lecture in the day, from the commencement of chemistry, at nine in the morning, to the close of surgery, at eight in the evening. Lecture ! auspicious word ! we have a beginning prompted by the mere sound. We will address you, medical students, according to the style you are most accustomed to.

Gentlemen,—Your attention is to be this morning directed to an important part of your course on physiology, which your various professors, at two o'clock on Saturday afternoon, will separately tell you is derived from two Greek words, so that we have no occasion to explain its meaning at present. Magendie, Müller, Mayo, Millengen, and various other M's, have written works upon physiology, affecting the human race generally; you are now requested to listen to the demonstration of one species in particular—the Medical Student of London.

Lay aside your deeper studies, then, and turn for a while to our lighter sketches; forget the globules of the blood in the contemplation of red billiard balls; supplant the *tunica arachnoidea* of the brain by a gossamer hat—the *rete mucosum* of the skin by a pea-jacket; the vital fluid by a pot of half-and-half. Call into play the flexor muscles of your arms with boxing-gloves and single-sticks; examine the secreting glands in the shape of kidneys and sweetbreads; demonstrate other theories connected with the human economy in an equally analogous and pleasant manner; lay aside your crib Celsus and Steggall's Manual for our own more enticing pages, and find your various habits therein reflected upon paper, with a truth to nature only exceeded by the artificial man of the same material in the Museum of King's College. Assume for a time all this joyousness. PUNCH has entered as a pupil at a medical school (he is not at liberty to say which), on purpose to note your propensities, and requests you for a short period to look upon him as one of your own lot. His course will commence next week, and "The New Man" will be the subject.

II.

THE NEW MAN.

EMBRYOLOGY precedes the treatise on the perfect animal ; it is but right, therefore, that the new man should have our attention before the mature student.

No sooner do the geese become asphyxiated by torsion of their cervical *vertebræ*, in anticipation of Michaelmas-day; no sooner do the pheasants feel premonitory warnings, that some chemical combinations between charcoal, nitre, and sulphur, are about to take place, ending in a precipitation of lead; no sooner do the columns of the newspapers teem with advertisements of the ensuing courses of the various schools, each one cheaper, and offering more advantages than any of the others; the large hospitals vaunting their extended field of practice, and the small ones ensuring a more minute and careful investigation of disease, than the new man purchases a large trunk and a hat-box, buys a second-hand copy of Quain's Anatomy, abjures the dispensing of his master's surgery in the country, and placing himself in one of those rattling boxes denominated by courtesy second-class carriages, enters on the career of a hospital pupil in his first season.

The opening lecture introduces the new man to his companions, and he is easily distinguished at that annual gathering of pupils, practitioners, professors, and especially old hospital governors, who do a good deal in the gaiter-line, and applaud the lecturer with their umbrellas, as they sit in the front row. The new man is known by his clothes, which incline to the prevalent fashion of the rural districts he has quitted; and he evinces an affection for cloth-boots, or short Wellingtons with double soles, and toes shaped like a toad's mouth, a propensity which sometimes continues throughout the career of his pupilage. He likewise takes off his hat when he enters the dissecting-room, and thinks that beautiful design is shown in the mechanism and structure of the human body—an idea which gets knocked out of him at the end of the season, when he looks upon the distribution of the nerves as "a blessed bore to get up, and no use to him after he has passed." But at first he perpetually carries a "DUBLIN DISSECTOR" under his arm; and whether he is engaged upon a subject or no, delights to keep on his black apron, pockets, and sleeves (like a barber dipped in a blacking-bottle), the making of which his sisters have probably superintended in the country, and which he thinks endows him with an air of industry and importance.

The new man, at first, is not a great advocate for beer; but this dislike may possibly arise from his having been compelled to stand two pots upon the occasion of the first dissection. After a time, however, he gives way to the indulgence, having received the solemn assurances of his companions that it is absolutely necessary to preserve his health, and keep him from getting the collywobbles in his pandenoodles—a description of which obstinate disease he is told may be found in "Dr. Copland's Medical Dictionary," and "Gregory's Practice of Physic," but as to under what head the informant is uncertain.

The first purchase that a new man makes in London is a

gigantic note-book, a dozen steel pens on a card, and a screw inkstand. Furnished with these valuable adjuncts to study, he puts down every thing he hears during the day, both in the theatre of the school and the wards of the hospital, besides many diverting diagrams and anecdotes which his fellow-students insert for him, until at night he has a confused dream that the air-pump in the laboratory is giving a party, at which various scalpels, bits of gums, wax models, tourniquets, and fœtal skulls, are assisting as guests—an eccentric and philosophical vision, worthy of the brain from which it emanates. But the new man is, from his very nature, a visionary. His breast swells with pride at the introductory lecture, when he hears the professor descant upon the noble science he and his companions have embarked upon; the rich reward of watching the gradual progress of a suffering fellow-creature to convalescence, and the insignificance of worldly gain compared with the pure treasures of pathological knowledge; whilst to the riper student all this resolves itself into the truth, that three draughts, or one mixture, are respectively worth four-and-sixpence or three shillings: that the patient should be encouraged to take them as long as possible, and that the thrilling delight of ushering another mortal into existence, after being up all night, is considerably increased by the receipt of the tin for superintending the performance ; i. e. if you are lucky enough to get it.

It is not improbable that, after a short period, the new man will write a letter home. The substance of it will be as follows: and the reader is requested to preserve a copy, as it may, perhaps, be compared with another at a future period.

My dear Parents,—I am happy to inform you that my health is at present uninjured by the atmosphere of the hospital, and that I find I am making daily progress in my studies. I have taken a lodging in —— (Gower place, University-street, Little Britain, or Lant-street, as the case may be), for which I pay twelve shillings a week, including shoes. The mistress of the house is a pious old lady, and I am very comfortable, with the exception that two pupils live on the floor above me, who are continually giving harmonic parties to their friends, and I am sometimes compelled to request they will allow me to conclude transcribing my lecture notes in tranquillity—a request, I am sorry to say, not often complied with.—The smoke from their pipes fills the whole house, and the other night they knocked me up two hours after I had retired to rest, for the loan of the jug of cold water from my washhand-stand, to make grog with, and a 'Little Warbler,' if I had one, with the words of 'The Literary Dustman' in it.

"Independently of these annoyances, I get on pretty well, and have already attracted the notice of my professors, who return my salutations very condescendingly, and tell me to look upon them rather as friends than teachers. The students here, generally speaking, are a dissipated and irreligious set of young men : and I can assure you I am often compelled to listen to language that quite makes my ears tingle. I have found a very decent washerwoman, who mends for me as well; but, unfortunately, she washes for the house, and the initials of one of the students above me are the same as mine, so that I find our things are gradually changing hands, in which I have the worst, because his shirts and socks are somewhat dilapidated, or, to speak professionally, their fibrous texture abounds in organic lesions; and the worst is, he never finds out the error until the end of the week, when he sends my things back, with his compliments, and thinks the washerwoman has made a mistake.

"I have not been to the theatres yet, nor do I feel the least wish to enter into any of the frivolities of the great metropolis. With kind regards to all at home, believe me,

"Yours, affectionately,

"JOSEPH MUFF."

III.

OF HIS GRADUAL DEVELOPMENT.

For the first two months of the first winter session the fingers of the new man are nothing but inkstains and industry. He has duly chronicled every word that has fallen from the lips of every professor in his leviathan note-book; and his desk teems with reports of all the hospital cases, from the burnt housemaid, all cotton-wool and white lead, who set herself on fire reading penny romances in bed, on one side of the hospital, to the tipsy glazier who bundled off his perch and spiked himself upon the area rails, on the other. He becomes a walking chronicle of pathological statistics, and after he has passed six weeks in the wards, imagines himself an embryo Hunter.

To keep up his character, a new man ought perpetually to carry a stethoscope—a curious instrument, something like a sixpenny toy trumpet with its top knocked off, and used for the purpose of hearing what people are thinking about, or something of the kind. In the endeavor to acquire a perfect knowledge of its use he is indefatigable. There is scarcely a patient but he knows the exact state of their thoracic viscera, and he talks of enlarged semilunar valves, and thickened ventricles, with an air of alarming confidence. And yet we rather doubt his skill upon this point; we never perceived any thing more than a sound or a jog, something similar to what you hear in the cabin of a fourpenny steamboat, and especially mistrusted the "metallic tinkling," and the noise resembling a blacksmith's bellows blowing into an empty quart-pot, which is called the *bruit de soufflet.* Take our word, when medicine arrives at such a pitch that the secrets of the human heart can be probed, it need not go any further, and will have the power of doing mischief enough.

The new man does not enter much into society. He sometimes asks a few other juniors to his lodgings, and provides tea and shrimps, with occasional cold saveloys for their refection and it is possible he may add some home-made wine to the banquet. Their conversation is exceedingly professional; and should they get slightly jocose, they retail anatomical paradoxes, technical puns and legendary "catch questions," which from time immemorial have been the delight of all new men in general, and country ones in particular.

But diligent and industrious as the new man may be, he is mortal after all, and, being mortal, is not proof against temptation—at least, after five or six weeks of his pupilage have passed. The good St. Anthony resisted all the endeavors of the Evil One to lure him from the proper path, until the gentleman of the discolored *cutis vera* assumed the shape of a woman. The new man firmly withstands all inducements to irregularity until his first temptation appears in the form of the Cider-cellars—the convivial Rubicon which it is absolutely necessary for him to pass before he can enrol himself as a member of the quiet, hard-working, modest fraternity of the Medical Student of our London Hospitals.

Facilis descensus Averni.—The steps that lead from Maiden-lane to the Cider-cellars are easy of descent, although the return is sometimes attended with slight difficulty. Not that we wish to compare our favorite *souterrain* in question to the "Avernus" of the Latin poet; oh, no! If Æneas had met with roast potatoes and stout during his celebrated voyage across the Styx to the infernal regions, and listened to songs and glees in place of the multitude of condemned souls, "horrendum stridens," we wager that he would have been in no very great hurry to return. But we have arrived at an important point in our physiology—the first launch of the new man into the ocean of his London life, and we pause upon its shore. He has but definite ideas of three public establishments at all intimately connected with his professional career —the Hall, the College, and the Cider-cellars. There are but three individuals to whom he looks with feelings of deference —Mr. Sayer of Blackfriars, Mr. Belfour of Lincoln's-inn-fields, and Mr. Rhodes of Maidenlane. These are the impersonation of the Fates—the arbitrators of his destinies.

As it is customary that an attendance in the Theatre of Lectures should precede the student's determination to "have a shy at the College," or "go up to the Hall," so is it usual for a visit to one of the theatres to be paid before going down to the Cider-cellars. The new man has been beguiled into the excursion by the exciting narratives of his companions, and beginning to feel that he is behind the other "chaps" (a new man's term) in knowledge of the world, he yields to the attraction held out; not because he at first thinks it will give him pleasure so to do but because it will put him on a level with those who have been, on the same principle as our rambling compatriots go to Switzerland and the Rhine. His Mentor is ready in the shape of a third-season man, and under his protecting influence he sallies forth.

The theatres have concluded; every carriage, cab, and "coach 'nhired" in their vicinity is in motion; venders of trotters and ham-sandwiches are in full cry; the bars of the proximate retail establishments are crowded with thirsty gods; ruddy chops and steaks are temptingly displayed in the windows of the supper-houses, and the turnips and carrots in the freshly-arrived market-carts appear astonished at the sudden confusion by which they are surrounded. Amidst this confusion the new man and his friends arrive beneath the beacon which illumines the entrance of the tavern. He descends the stairs in an agony of anticipation, and feverishly trips up the six or eight succeeding ones to arrive at the large room. A song has just concluded, and he enters triumphantly amidst the thunder of applause, the jingling of glasses, the imperious

2

vociferations of fresh orders, and an atmosphere of smoke
that pervades the whole apartment, like dense clouds of incense burning at the altar of the genius of conviviality.

The new man is at first so bewildered, that it would take
but little extra excitement to render him perfectly unconscious as to the probability of his standing upon his *occipito-
frontalis* or *plantar fascia*. But as he collects his ideas, he
contrives to muster sufficient presence of mind to order a
Welsh rabbit, and in the interim of its arrival earnestly contemplates the scene around him. There is the room, which, in
after life, so vividly recurs to him, with its bygone *souve-
nirs* of mirth, when he is sitting up all night at a bad case in
the mud cottage of a pauper union. There are its blue walls,
its wainscot and its pillars, its lamps and ground-glass shades,
within which the gas jumps and flares so fitfully; its two
looking-glasses, that reflect the room and its occupants from
one to the other in an interminable vista. There also is Mr.
Rhodes, bending courteously over the backs of the visitors' chairs, and hoping everybody has got every thing to
their satisfaction, or bestowing an occasional subdued ac-
knowledgment upon an *habitué* who chances to enter; and
the professional gentlemen all laying their heads together at
the top of the table to pitch the key of the next glee; and
the waiters bustling up and down with all sorts of tempting
comestibles; and the gentleman in the Chesterfield wrapper
smoking a cigar at the side of the room while he leans back
and contemplates the ceiling, as if his whole soul was concen-
trated in its smoke-discolored moldings.

The new man is in ecstasies; he beholds the realization of
the Arabian Nights, and when the harmony commences
again, he is fairly entranced. At first, he is fearful of adding
the efforts of his laryngeal "little muscles with the long
names" to swell the chorus; but, after the second glass of stout
and a "go of whiskey," he becomes emboldened, and when
the gentleman with the bass voice sings out the Monks of
Old, what a jovial race they were, our friend trolls out how
"they laughed, ha, ha!" so lustily, that he gets quite red in
the face from obstructed jugulars, and applauds, when it has
concluded, until every thing upon the table performs a curious
ballet-dance, which is only terminated by the descent of the
cruets upon the floor.

The precise hour at which the new man arrives at home,
after this eventful evening, has never been correctly ascer-

tained; having a latch-key, he is the only person that could give any authentic information upon this point; but, unfortunately, he never knows himself. Some few things, however, are universally allowed, namely, that in extreme cases he is found asleep on the rug at the foot of the stairs next morning, with the rushlight that was left in the passage burnt quite away, and all the solder of the candlestick melted into little globules. More frequently he knocks up the people of the neighboring house, under the impression that it is his own, but that a new keyhole has been fitted to the door in his absence; and, in the mildest forms of the disease, he drinks up all the water in his bed-room during the night, and has a propensity for retiring to rest in his pea-coat and Bluchers, from the obstinate tenacity of his buttons and straps. The first lecture the next morning fails to attract him; he eats no breakfast, and when he enters the dissecting-room about one o'clock, his fellow-students administer to him a pint of ale, warmed by the simple process of stirring it with a hot poker, with some Cayenne pepper thrown into it, which he is assured will set to rights the irritable mucous lining of his stomach. The effect of this remedy is, to send him into a sound sleep during the whole of the two o'clock anatomical lecture; and awakened at its close by the applause of the students, he thinks he is still at the Cider-cellars, and cries out "Encore!"

IV.

OF THE MANNER IN WHICH THE FIRST SEASON PASSES.

FROM the period of our last chapter our friend commences to adopt the attributes of the mature student. His notes are taken as before at each lecture he attends, but the lecturers are few, and the notes are never fairly transcribed; at the same time they are interspersed with a larger proportion of portraits of the lecturer, and other humorous conceits. He proposes at lunch-time every day that he and his companions should "go the odd man for a pot;" and the determination he had formed at his entry to the school, of working the last session for all the prizes, and going up to the Hall on the Thursday and the College on the Friday without grinding, appears somewhat difficult of being carried into execution. It is at this point of his studies that the student commences a steady course of imaginary dissection: that is to say, he keeps a chimerical account of extremities whose minute structure he has deeply investigated (in his head), and received in return various sums of money from home for the avowed purpose of paying for them. If he really has put his name down for any heads and necks or pelvic viscera at the commencement of the season, when he had imbibed and cherished some lunatic idea " that dissection was the sheet-anchor of safety at the College," he becomes a trafficker in human flesh, and disposes of them as quickly as he can to any hard-working man who has his examination in perspective.

He now assumes a more independent air, and even ventures to chalk odd figures on the black board in the theatre. He has been known, previously to the lecture, to let down the skeleton that hangs by a balance weight from the ceiling, and, inserting its thumb in the cavity of its nose, has there secured it with a piece of thread, and then, placing a short pipe in its jaws, has pulled it up again. His inventive faculties are likewise shown by various diverting objects and allusions cut with his knife upon the ledge before him in the lecture-room, whereon the new men rest their note-books and the old ones go to sleep. In vain do the directors of the school, order the ledge to be coated with paint and sand mixed together—nothing is proof against his knife; were it adamant he would cut his name upon it. His favorite. position at lecture is now the extremity of the bench, where its horseshoe form places him rather out of the range of the lecturer's vision; and, ten to one, it is here that he has cut a cribbage-board on the seat, at which he and his neighbor play during the lecture on Surgery, concealing their game from common eyes by spreading a Mackintosh cape on the desk before them. His conversation also gradually changes its tone, and instead of mildly inquiring of the porter, on his entering the school of a morning, what is for the day's anatomical demonstration, he talks of "the regular lark he had last night at the Eagle, and how jolly screwed he got!"—a frank admission, which bespeaks the candor of his disposition.

Careful statistics show us that it is about the end of November the new man first makes the acquaintance of his uncle; and observant people have remarked, as worthy of insertion in the Medical Almanac, amongst the usual phenomena of the calendar—" About this time dissecting cases and tooth-instruments appear in the windows, and we may look for

watches towards the beginning of December." Although
this is his first transaction on his own account, yet his property
has before ascended the spout, when some unprincipled student, at the beginning of the season, picked his pocket of a
big silver lancet-case, which he had brought up with him from
the country; and having pledged it at the nearest money-
lender's, sent him the duplicate in a polite note, and spent the
money with some other dishonest young men, in drinking their
victim's health in his absence. And, by the way, it is a general rule that most new men delight to carry big lancet-cases,
although they have about as much use for them as a lecturer
upon practice of physic has for top-boots.

Thus gradually approaching step by step towards the perfection of his state, the new man's first winter-session passes;
and it is not unlikely that, at the close of the course, he may
enter to compete for the anatomical prize, which he sometimes
gets by stealth, cribbing his answers from a tiny manual of
knowledge, two inches by one-and-a-half in size, which he
hides under his blotting-paper. This triumph achieved, he
devotes the short period which intervenes before the commencement of the summer botanical course to various hilarious pastimes; and as the watch and dissecting-case are both
gone, he writes the following despatch to his governor:

LETTER NO. II.—(*Copy.*)

MY DEAR FATHER—You will, I am sure, be delighted to
learn that I have gained the twenty-ninth honorary certificate
for proficiency in anatomy, which you will allow is a very
high number when I tell you that only thirty are given. I
have also the satisfaction of informing you that the various
professors have given me certificates of having attended their
lectures *very diligently* during the past courses.

I work very hard, but I need not inform you that, with all
my economy, I am at some expense for good books and instruments. I have purchased *Liston's Surgery*, Anthony Thomp-
son's *Materia Medica*, Burns and Merriman's *Midwifery*,
Graham's *Chemistry*, Astley Cooper's *Dislocations*, and
Quain's *Anatomy*, all of which I have read carefully through
twice. I also pay a private demonstrator to go over the bones
with me of a night; and I have bought a skeleton at Alexander's—a great bargain. This, when I " pass," I think of presenting to the museum of the hospital, as I am under great
obligations to the surgeons. I think a ten-pound note will

clear my expenses, although I wish to enter to a summer course of dissections, and take some lessons in practical chemistry in the laboratories with Professor Carbon, but these I will endeavor to pay for out of my own pocket. With my best regards to all at home, believe me,

Your affectionate son,   JOSEPH MUFF.

As soon as the summer course begins, the Botanical Lectures commence with it, and the polite Company of Apothecaries courteously request the student's acceptance of a ticket of admission to the lectures, at their garden at Chelsea. As these commence somewhere about eight in the morning, of course he must get up in the middle of the night to be there ; and consequently he attends very often, of course. But the botanical excursions that take place every Saturday from his own school are his especial delight. He buys a candle-box to contain all the chickweed, chamomiles, and dandelions he may collect, and slinging it over his shoulder with his pocket-handkerchief, he starts off in company with the Professor and his fellow-herbalists to Wandsworth Common, Battersea Fields, Hampstead Heath, or any other favorite spot which the cockney Flora embellishes with her offspring.

The conduct of medical students on botanical excursions generally appears in various phases. Some real lovers of the study, pale men in spectacles, who wear shoes and can walk forever, collect every weed they drop upon, to which they assign a most extraordinary name, and display it at their lodgings upon cartridge paper, with penny pieces to keep the leaves in their places as they dry. Others limit their collections to stinging-nettles, which they slyly insert into their companions' pockets, or long-bulrushes, which they tuck under the collars of their coats; and the remainder turn into the first house of public entertainment they arrive at on emerging from the smoke of London to the rural districts, and remain all day absorbed in the mysteries of ground billiards and knock-'em-downs, their principal studies being confined to lettuces, spring onions, and water-cresses. But all this is very proper—we mean the botanical part of the story—for the knowledge of the natural class and order of a buttercup must be of the greatest service to a practitioner in after-life in treating a case of typhus fever or ruptured blood-vessel. At some of the Continental Hospitals, the pupil's time is wasted at the bedside of the patient, from which he can only get practical information. How much better is the primrose-investigating *curriculum* of study observed at our own medical schools?

V.

OF HIS MATURITY AND LATIN EXAMINATION.

THE second season arrives, and our pupil becomes " a medical student " in the fullest sense of the word. He has an indistinct recollection that there are such things as wards in the hospital as well as in a key or the city, and a vague wandering, like the morning's impression of the dreams of the preceding night, that in the remote dark ages of his career he took some notes upon the various lectures, the which have long since been converted into pipe-lights or small darts, which, twisted up and propelled from between the forefingers of each hand, fly with unerring aim across the theatre at the lecturer's head, the slumbering student, or any other object worth aiming at—an amusing way of beguiling the hour's lecture, and only excelled by the sport produced, if he has the good luck to sit in a sunbeam, from making a tournament of " Jack-o'-lanthorns " on the ceiling. His locker in the lobby of the dissecting-room has long since been devoid of apron, sleeves, scalpels, or forceps; but still it is not empty. Its contents are composed of three bell-pull handles, a valuable series of shutter-fastenings, two or three broken pipes, a pewter " go " (which, if everybody had their own, would in all probability belong to Mr. Evans, of Covent Garden Piazza), some scraps of biscuit, and a round knocker, which forcibly recalls a pleasant evening he once spent, with the accompanying anecdotes of how he "bilked the pike" at Waterloo Bridge, and poor Jones got " jug'd " by mistake.

It must not, however, be supposed that the student now neglects visiting the dissecting-room. On the contrary, he is unremitting in his attendance, and sometimes the first there of a morning, more especially when he has, to use his own expression, been "going it rather fast than otherwise" the evening before, and comes to the school very early in the morning to have a good wash and refresh himself previously to snatching a little of the slumber he has forgotten to take during the night, which he enjoys very quietly in the injecting-room down stairs, amidst a heterogeneous assemblage of pipkins, subjects, deal coffins, sawdust, inflated stomachs, syringes, macerating tubs, and dried preparations. The dissecting-room is also his favorite resort for refreshment, and he broils sprats and red-herrings on the fire-shovel with consummate skill, amusing himself during the process of his culinary arrangements by sawing the corners off the stone mantel-piece, throwing cinders at the new man, or seeing how long it takes to bore a hole through one of the stools with a red-hot poker. Indeed, these luckless pieces of furniture are always marked out by the student as the fittest objects on which to wreak his destructive propensities; and he generally discovers that the readiest way to do them up is to hop steeple-chases upon them from one end of the room to the other—a sporting amusement which shakes them to pieces, and irremediably dislocates all their articulations, sooner than anything else. Of course these pleasantries are only carried on in the absence of the demonstrator. Should he be present, the industry of the student is confined to poking the fire in the stove and then shutting the flue, or keeping down the ball of the cistern by some abdominal hooks, and then, before the invasion of smoke and water takes place, quietly joining a knot of new men who are strenuously endeavoring to dissect the brain and discover the *hippocampus major*, which they expect to find in the perfect similitude of a sea-horse, like the web-footed quadrupeds who paw the "reality" in the "area usually devoted to illusion," or tank, at the Adelphi Theatre.

If one of the professors of his medical school chances to be addicted to making anti-Martin experiments on animals, or the study of comparative anatomy, the pursuits offer an endless fund of amusement to the jocose student. He administers poison to the toxicological guinea-pigs; hunts the rabbit kept for galvanism about the school; lets loose in the theatre, by accident, the sparrows preserved to show the rapidly fatal action of *choke-damp* upon life; turns the bladders, which have been provided to tie over bottles, into footballs; and makes daily contributions to the plate of pebbles taken from the stomach of the ostrich, and preserved in the museum to show the mode in which these birds assist digestion, until he quadruples the quantity, and has the quiet satisfaction of seeing exhibited at lecture, as the identical objects, the heap of small stones which he has collected from time to time in the garden of the school, or from any excavation for pipes or pav-ing which he may have passed in his route from his lodgings.

The second or middle course of the three winter sessions which the medical student is compelled to go through, is the one in which he most enjoys himself, and indulges in those lit-tle outbreaks of eccentric mirth which so eminently qualify him for his future professional career. During the first course he studies from novelty—during the last from compulsion; but the middle one passes in unlimited sprees and perpetual half-and-half. The only grand project he now undertakes is "going up for his Latin," provided he had not courage to do so upon first coming to London. For some weeks before this period he is never seen without an interlined edition of Celsus and Gregory; not that he debars himself from joviality dur-ing the time of his preparation, but he judiciously combines study with amusement—never stirring without his translation in his pocket, and even, if he goes to the theatre, beguiling the time between the pieces by learning the literal order of a new paragraph. Every school possesses circulating copies of these works: they have been originally purchased in some wild moment of industrious extravagance by a new man; and when he passed, he sold them for five shillings to another, who, in turn, disposed of them to a third, until they had run nearly all through the school. The student grinds away at these un-til he knows them almost by heart, albeit his translation is not the most elegant. He reads—"*Sanus homo,* a sound man; *qui,* who; *et,* also; *bene valet,* well is in health; *et,* and; *suæ spontis,* of his own choice; *est,* is," &c. This, however, is quite suffi-cient; and, accordingly, one afternoon, in a rash moment, he makes up his mind to "go up." Arrived at Apothecaries' Hall—a building which he regards with a feeling of awe far beyond the Bow street Police Office—he takes his place amongst the anxious throng, and is at last called into a room, where two examiners politely request that he will favor them by sitting down at a table adorned with severe-looking ink-stands, long pens, formal sheets of foolscap, and awfully-sized copies of the light entertaining works mentioned above. One of the aforesaid examiners then takes a pinch of snuff, coughs, blows his nose, points out a paragraph for the student to translate, and leaves him to do it. He has, with a prudent forethought, stuffed his cribs inside his double-breasted waistcoat, but, unfortunately, he finds he cannot use them; so when he sticks at a queer word he writes it on his blotting-paper, and shoves it quietly on to the next man. If his neighbor is a brick, he returns an answer; but if he is not, our friend is compelled to take shots of the meaning and trust to chance—a good plan when you are not certain what to do, either at billiards or Apothecaries' Hall. Should he be fortunate enough to get through, his schedule is endorsed with some hieroglyphics explanatory of the auspicious event; and, in gratitude, he asks a few friends to his lodgings that night, who have legions of sausages for supper, and drink gin-and-water until three o'clock in the morning. It is not, however, absolutely necessary that a man should go up himself to pass his Latin. We knew a student once who, by a little judicious change of appearance—first letting his hair grow very long, and then cutting it quite short—at one time patronizing whiskers, and at another shaving himself perfectly clean—now wearing spectacles, and now speaking through his nose—being, withal, an excellent scholar, passed a Latin examination for half the men in the hospital he belonged to, receiving from them, when he had succeeded, the fee which, in most cases they would have paid a private teacher for preparing them.

The medical student does not like dining alone; he is gregarious and attaches himself to some dining-rooms in the vicinity of his school, where, in addition to the usual journals, they take in the Lancet and Medical Gazette for his express reading. He is here the customer most looked up to by the proprietor, and is also on excellent terms with "Harriet," who confidentially tells him that the boiled beef is just up; indeed, he has been seen now and then to put his arm around her waist and ask her when she meant to marry him, which question Harriet is not very well prepared to answer, as all the second season men have proposed to her successively, and each stands equally well in her estimation, which is kept up at the rate of a penny *per diem*. But Harriet is not the only waiting domestic with whom he is upon friendly terms. The Toms, Charleses, and Henrys of the supper-taverns enjoy equal familiarity; and when Nancy, at Knight's, brings him oysters for two and asks him for the money to get the stout, he throws down the shilling with an expression of endearment that plainly intimates he does not mean to take back the fourpence change out of the pot. Should he, however, in the course of his wanderings, go into a strange eating-house, where he is not known, and consequently is not paid becoming attention, his revenge is called into play, and he gratifies it by the simple act of pouring the vinegar into the pepper-castor, and emptying the contents of the salt-cellar into the water-bottle before he gets up to walk away.

VI.

OF THE GRINDER AND HIS CLASS.

ONE fine morning, in the October of the third winter session, the student is suddenly struck by the recollection that at the end of the course the time will arrive for him to be thinking about undergoing the ordeals of the Hall and College. Making up his mind, therefore, to begin studying in earnest, he becomes a *pro tempore* member of a temperance society, pledging himself to abstain from immoderate beer for six months; he also purchases a coffee-pot, a reading-candle-stick, and Steggall's Manual; and then, contriving to accumulate five guineas to pay a "grinder," he routs out his old note-books from the bottom of his box, and commences to "read for the Hall."

Aspirants to honors in law, physic, or divinity, each know the value of private cramming—a process by which their brains are fattened, by abstinence from liquids and an increase of dry food (some of it *very* dry), like the livers of Strasbourg geese. There are grinders in each of these three professional classes; but the medical teacher is the man of the most varied and eccentric knowledge. Not only is he intimately acquainted with the different branches required to be studied, but he is also master of all their minutiæ. In accordance with the taste of the examiners, he learns and imparts to his class at what degree of heat water boils in a balloon—how the article of commerce, *Prussian blue*, is more easily and correctly defined as the *Ferrosesquicyanuret of the cyanide of potassium*—why the nitrous oxide, or laughing gas, influences people to make such asses of themselves; and, especially, all sorts of individual inquiries, which, if continued at the present rate, will range from " Who discovered the use of the spleen ?" to " Who killed Cock Robin ?" for aught we know. They ask questions at the Hall quite as vague as these.

It is twelve o'clock at noon. In a large room, ornamented by shelves of bottles and preparations, with varnished prints

of medical plants and cases of articulated bones and ligaments, a number of young men are seated round a long table
covered with baize, in the centre of whom an intellectual-
looking man, whose well-developed forehead shows the amount
of knowledge it can contain, is interrogating by turns each
of the students, and endeavoring to impress the points in
question on their memories by various diverting associations.
Each of his pupils, as he passes his examination, furnishes
him with a copy of the subjects touched upon; and by studying these minutely, the private teacher forms a pretty correct
idea of the general run of the "Hall questions."

"Now, Mr. Muff," says the gentleman to one of his class,
handing him a bottle of something which appears like speci-
mens of a chestnut colt's coat after he had been clipped;
"what's that, sir?"

"That's cow-itch, sir," replies Mr. Muff.

"Cow what? You must call it at the Hall by its botanical
name—*Dolichos pruriens*. What is it used for?"

"To strew in people's beds that you owe a grudge to," replies Muff; whereat all the class laugh, except the last comer,
who takes it all for granted, and makes a note of the circumstance in his interleaved manual.

"That answer would floor you," continues the grinder.
"The *dolichos* is used to destroy worms. How does it act,
Mr. Jones?" going on to the next pupil—a man in a light
cotton cravat and no shirt-collar, who looks very like a butler
out of place.

"It tickles them to death, sir," answers Mr. Jones.

"You would say it acts mechanically," observes the grinder.
"The fine points stick into the worms and kill them. They
say 'Is this a dagger which I see before me?' and then die.
Recollect the dagger, Mr. Jones, when you go up. Mr. Manhug, what do you consider the best sudorific, if you wanted
to throw a person into a perspiration?"

Mr. Manhug, who is the wag of the class, finishes, in rather
an abrupt manner, a song he was humming, *sotto voce*, having
some allusion to a peer who was known as Thomas, Lord
Noddy, having passed a night at a house of public entertainment in the Old Bailey previous to an execution. He then
takes a pinch of snuff, winks at the other pupils as much as to
say, "See me tackle him, now;" and replies, "The gallery
door of Covent Garden on Boxing-night."

"Now, come, be serious for once, Mr. Manhug," continues the teacher; "what else is likely to answer the purpose!"

"I think a run up Holborn-hill, with two Ely-place knockers on your arm, and three policemen on your heels, might have a good effect," answers Mr. Manhug.

"Do you ever think you will pass the Hall, if you go on at this rate?" observes the teacher, in a tone of mild reproach.

"Not a doubt of it, sir," returns the imperturbable Manhug. "I've passed it twenty times within this last month, and did not find any very great difficulty about it; neither do I expect to, unless they block up Union-street and Water-lane."

The grinder gives Mr. Manhug up as a hopeless case, and goes on to the next. "Mr. Rapp, they will be very likely to ask you the composition of the *compound gamboge pill:* what is it made of?"

Mr. Rapp hasn't the least idea.

"Remember, then, it is composed of cambogia, aloes, ginger, and soap—C, A, G, S,—*cags.* Recollect Cags, Mr. Rapp, What would you do, if you were sent for to a person poisoned by oxalic acid?"

"Give him some chalk," returns Mr. Rapp.

"But suppose you had not got any chalk, what would you substitute?"

"Oh, anything; pipeclay and soapsuds."

"Yes, that's all very right; but we will presume you could not get any pipeclay and soapsuds; in fact, that there was nothing in the house. What would you do then?"

Mr. Manhug cries out from the bottom of the table—"Let him die and be——!"

"Now, Mr. Manhug, I really must entreat of you to be more steady," interrupts the professor. "You would scrape the ceiling with the fire-shovel, would you not? Plaster contains lime, and lime is an antidote. Recollect that, if you please. They like you to say you would scrape the ceiling, at the Hall: they think it shows a ready invention in emergency. Mr. Newcome, you have heard the last question and answer?"

"Yes, sir," says the fresh arrival, as he finishes making a note of it.

"Well, you are sent for, to a man who has hung himself. What would be your first endeavor?"

"To scrape the ceiling with the fire-shovel," mildly observes Mr. Newcome; whereupon the class indulges in a hearty laugh, and Mr. Newcome blushes as deep as the red bull's-eye of a New-road doctor's lamp.

"What would *you* do, Mr. Manhug? perhaps you can inform Mr. Newcome."

"Cut him down, sir," answers the indomitable *farceur.*

"Well, well," continues the teacher; "but we will presume he has been cut down. What would you strive to do next?"

"Cut him up, sir, if the coroner would give an order for a *post mortem* examination"

"We have had no chemistry this morning," observes one of the pupils.

"Very well, Mr. Rogers; we will go on with it if you wish. How would you endeavor to detect the presence of gold in any body!"

"By begging the loan of a sovereign, sir," interrupts Mr. Manhug.

"If he knew you as well as I do, Manhug," observes Mr. Jones, "he'd be sure to lend it—oh, yes!—I should rather think so, certainly," whereupon Mr. Jones compresses his nostril with the thumb of his right hand, and moves his fingers as if he was performing a concerto on an imaginary one-handed house flageolet.

"Mr. Rapp, what is the difference between an element and a compound body?"

Mr. Rapp is again obliged to confess his ignorance.

"A compound body is composed of two or more elements," says the grinder, "in various proportions. Give me an example, Mr. Jones."

"Half-and-half is a compound body, composed of the two elements, ale and porter, the proportion of the porter increasing in an inverse ratio to the respectability of the public-house you get it from," replies Mr. Jones.

The professor smiles, and taking up a Pharmacopœia, says, "I see here directions for evaporating certain liquids 'in a water-bath.' Mr. Newcome, what is the most familiar instance of a water-bath you are acquainted with?"

"In High Holborn, sir; between Little Queen street and Drury lane," returns Mr. Newcome.

"A water-bath means a vessel placed in boiling water, Mr. Newcome, to keep it at a certain temperature. If you are asked at the Hall for the most familiar instance, they like you to say a carpenter's glue-pot."

And in like manner the grinding-class proceeds.

VII.

OF VARIOUS OTHER DIVERTING MATTERS CONNECTED WITH GRINDING.

From experience we are aware that the invention of the useful species of phrenotypics, alluded to in our last chapter, does not rest with the grinder alone. We once knew a medical student (and many even now at the London hospitals will recollect his name without mentioning it), who when he was grinding for the Hall, being naturally of a melodious and harmonic disposition, conceived the idea of learning the whole of his practice of physic by setting a description of the diseases to music. He had a song of some hundred and twenty verses, which he called "The Poetry of Steggall's Manual;" and this he put to the tune of the "Good Old Days of Adam and Eve." We deeply lament that we cannot produce the whole of this lyrical pathological curiosity. Two verses, however, linger on our memory, and these we have written down, requesting that they may be said or sung to the air above mentioned, and dedicating them to the gentlemen who are going up next Thursday evening. They relate to to the symptoms, treatment, and causes of Hæmoptysis and Hæmatemesis; which terms respectively imply, for the benefit of the million unprofessional readers who weekly gasp for our fresh number, a spitting of blood from the lungs and a vomiting of ditto from the stomach. The song was composed of stanzas similar to those which follow, except the portion relating to *Diseases of the Brain*, which was more appropriately separated into the old English division of *Fyttes*.

HÆMOPTYSIS.

A sensation of weight and oppression at the chest, sirs;
With tickling at the larynx, which scarcely gives you rest, sirs;
Full hard pulse, salt taste, and tongue very white, sirs;
And blood brought up in coughing, of color very bright, sirs;
It depends on causes three—the first's exhalation;
The next a ruptured artery—the third, ulceration.
In treatment we may bleed, keep the patient cool and quiet,
Acid drinks, digitalis, and attend to a mild diet.
     Sing hey, sing ho, we do not grieve
     When this formidable illness takes its leave.

HÆMATEMESIS.

Clotted blood is thrown up, in color very black, sirs,
And generally sudden, as it comes up in a crack, sirs.
It's preceded at the stomach by a weighty sensation;
But nothing appears ruptured upon examination.
It differs from the last, by the particles thrown off, sirs.
Being denser, deeper colored, and without a bit of cough, sirs.
In plethoric habits bleed, and some acid draughts pour in, gents,
With Oleum Terrebinthinæ (small doses) and astringents.
    Sing hey, sing ho; if you think the lesion spacious,
    The Acetate of Lead is found very efficacious.

Thus, in a few lines a great deal of valuable professional information is conveyed, at the same time that the tedium of much study is relieved by the harmony. If poetry is yet to be found in our hospitals—a queer place certainly for her to dwell, unless in her present feeble state the frequenters of Parnassus have subscribed to give her an in-patient's ticket —we trust that some able hand will continue this subject for the benefit of medical students generally; for, we repeat, it is much to be regretted that no more of this valuable production remains to us than the portion which Punch has just immortalized, and set forth as an apt example for cheering the pursuit of knowledge under difficulties. The gifted hand who arranged this might have turned Cooper's First Lines of Surgery into a tragedy; Dr. Copeland's Medical Dictionary into a domestic melodrama, with long intervals between the acts; and the Pharmacopœia into a light one-act farce. It strikes us if the theatres could enter into an arrangement with the Borough Hospitals to supply an amputation every evening as the finishing *coup* to an act, it would draw immensely when other means failed to attract.

The last time we heard this poem was at an harmonic meeting of medical students, within twenty shells' length of the —— School dissecting-room. It was truly delightful to see these young men snatching a few Anacreontic hours from their harassing professional occupations. At the time we heard it, the singer was slightly overcome by excitement and tight boots; and, at length, being prevailed upon to remove the obnoxious understandings, they were passed round the table to be admired, and eventually returned to their owner, filled with half-and-half, cigar-ashes, broken pipes, bread-crusts, and gin-and-water. This was a jocular pleasantry, which only the hilarious mind of a medical student could have conceived.

As the day of examination approaches, the economy of our friend undergoes a complete transformation, but in an inverse entomological progression—changing from the butterfly into the chrysalis. He is seldom seen at the hospitals, dividing the whole of his time between the grinder and his lodgings; taking innumerable notes at one place, and endeavoring to decipher them at the other. Those who have called upon him at this trying period have found him in an old shooting-jacket and slippers, seated at a table, and surrounded by every book that was ever written upon every medical subject that was ever discussed, all of which he appears to be reading at once —with little pieces of paper strewn all over the room, covered with strange hieroglyphics and extraordinary diagrams of chemical decompositions. His brain is just as full of temporary information as a bad egg is of sulphuretted hydrogen; and it is a fortunate provision of nature that the *dura mater* is of a tough fibrous texture—were it not for this safeguard, the whole mass would undoubtedly go off at once like a too tightly-rammed rocket. He is conscious of this himself, from the grinding information wherein he has been taught that the brain has three coverings, in the following order:—the *dura mater*, or Chesterfield overall; the *tunica arachnoidea*, or "dress coat of fine Saxony cloth;" and, in immediate contact, the *pia mater*, or five-and-sixpenny long cloth shirt with linen wristbands and fronts. This is a brilliant specimen of the helps to memory which the grinder affords, as splendid in its arrangement as the topographical methods of calling to mind the course of the large arteries, which define the abdominal aorta as Cheapside, its two common iliac branches, as Newgate-street and St. Paul's Churchyard, and the medio sacralis given off between them, as Paternoster-row.

Time goes on, bringing the fated hour nearer and nearer; and the student's assiduity knows no bounds. He reads his subjects over and over again, to keep them fresh in his memory, like little boys at school, who try to catch a last bird's-eye glance at their book before they give it into the usher's hands to say by heart. He now feels a deep interest in the statistics of the Hall, and is horrified at hearing that "nine men out of thirteen were sent back last Thursday!" The subjects, too, that they were rejected upon, frighten him just as much. One was plucked upon his anatomy; another, because he could not tell the difference between a daisy and a chamomile; and a third, after "being in" three hours and a

3

quarter, was sent back, for his inability to explain the process of making malt from barley,—an operation, whose final use he so well understands, although the preparation somewhat bothered him.   And thus, funking at the rejection of a clever man, or marvelling at the success of an acknowledged fool— determining to take prussic acid in the event of being refused —reading fourteen hours a-day—and keeping awake by the combined influence of snuff and coffee—the student finds his first ordeal approach.

VIII.

OF THE EXAMINATION AT APOTHECARIES' HALL.

THE last task that devolves upon our student before he goes up to the Hall is to hunt up his testimonials of attendance to lectures and good moral conduct in his apprenticeship, to- gether with his parochial certificate of age and baptism.   The first of these is the chief point to obtain; the two last he gen- erally writes himself, in the style best consonant with his own feelings and the date of his indenture.   His "morality ticket" is as follows:—

(Copy.)

"I hereby certify, that during the period Mr. Joseph Muff served his time with me, he especially recommended himself to my notice by his studious and attentive habits, highly moral and gentlemanly conduct, and excellent disposition. He always availed himself of every opportunity to improve his professional knowledge."

(Signed.)

According to the name on the indenture.

The certificate of attendance upon lectures is only obtained in its most approved state by much clever manœuvring.   It is important to bear in mind that a lecturer should never be asked whilst he is loitering about the school, for his signature of the student's diligence.   He may then have time to recollect his ignorance of his pupil's face at his discourses.   He should always be caught flying—either immediately before or after his lecture—in order that the whole business may be too hur- ried to admit of investigation.   In the space left for the de- gree of attention which the student has shown, it is better that he subscribes nothing at all than an indifferent report; because, in the former case, the student can fill it up to his own satisfaction. He usually prefers the phrase—"with unremitting diligence."

And having arrived at this important section of our Physiology, it behoves us to publish, for the benefit of medical students in general, and those about to go up in particular, the following

CODE OF INSTRUCTIONS

TO BE OBSERVED BY THOSE PREPARING FOR EXAMINATION AT THE HALL.

1. Previously to going up, take some pills and get your hair cut. This not only clears your faculties, but improves your appearance. The Court of Examiners dislike long hair.

2. Do not drink too much stout before you go in, with the idea that it will give you pluck. It renders you very valiant for half an hour, and then muddles your notions with indescribable confusion.

3. Having arrived at the Hall, put your rings and chains in your pocket, and, if practicable, publish a pair of spectacles. This will endow you with a grave look.

4. On taking your place at the table, if you wish to gain time, feign to be intensely frightened. One of the examiners will then rise to give you a tumbler of water, which you may, with good effect, rattle tremulously against your teeth when drinking. This may possibly lead them to excuse bad answers on the score of extreme nervous trepidation.

5. Should things appear to be going against you, get up a hectic cough, which is easily imitated, and look acutely miserable, which you will probably do without trying.

6. Endeavor to assume an off-hand manner of answering; and when you have stated any pathological fact—right or wrong—*stick to it;* if they want a case for example, invent one, "that happened when you were an apprentice in the country." This assumed confidence will sometimes bother them. We knew a student who once swore at the Hall, that he gave opium in a case of concussion of the brain, and that the patient never required anything else. It was true—he never did.

7. Should you be fortunate enough to pass, go to your hospital next day and report your examination, describing it as

the most extraordinary ordeal of deep-searching questions ever undergone. This will make the professors think well of you, and the new men deem you little less than a mental Colossus. Say, also, "you were complimented by the Court." This advice is, however, scarcely necessary, as we never knew a student pass who was not thus honored—according to his own account.

All things being arranged to his satisfaction, he deposits his papers under the care of Mr. Sayer, and passes the interval before the fatal day much in the same state of mind as a condemned criminal. At last Thursday arrives, and at a quarter to four, any person who takes the trouble to station himself at the corner of Union street will see various groups of three and four young men wending their way towards the portals of Apothecaries' Hall, consisting of students about to be examined, accompanied by friends who come down with them to keep up their spirits. They approach the door, and shake hands as they give and receive wishes of success. The wicket closes on the candidates, and their friends adjourn to the "Retail Establishment" opposite, to *go the odd man* and pledge their anxious companions in dissector's diet-drink— *vulgo*, half-and-half.

Leaving them to their libations, we follow our old friend Mr. Joseph Muff. He crosses the paved court-yard with the air of a man who has lost half-a-crown and found a half-penny; and through the windows sees the assistants dispensing plums, pepper, and prescriptions, with provoking indifference. Turning to the left, he ascends a solemn-looking staircase, adorned with severe black figures in niches, who support lamps. On the top of the staircase he enters a room, wherein the partners of his misery are collected. It is a long narrow apartment, commonly known as "the funking-room," ornamented with a savage-looking fireplace at one end, and a huge surly chest at the other; with gloomy presses against the walls, containing dry moldy books in harsh, repulsive bindings. The windows look into the court; and the glass is scored by diamond rings, and the shutters pencilled with names and sentences, which Mr. Muff regards with feelings similar to those he would experience in contemplating the inscriptions on the walls of a condemned cell. The very chairs in the room look overbearing and unpleasant; and the whole locality is invested with an overallishness of unanswerable questions and intricate botheration. Some of the students are marching up and down the room in feverish restlessness; others, arm in arm, are worrying each other to death with questions; and the rest are grinding away to the last minute at a manual, or trying to write minute atomic numbers on their thumb-nail.

The clock strikes five, and Mr. Sayer enters the room, exclaiming—"Mr. Manhug, Mr. Jones, Mr. Saxby, and Mr. Collins." The four depart to the chamber of examination, where the medical inquisition awaits them, with every species of mental torture to screw their brains instead of their thumbs, and rack their intellects instead of their limbs,—the chair on which the unfortunate student is placed being far more uneasy than the tightest fitting "Scavenger's daughter" in the Tower of London. After an anxious hour, Mr. Jones returns, with a light bounding step to a joyous extempore air of his own composing: he has passed. In another twenty minutes Mr. Saxby walks fiercely in, calls for his hat, condemns the examiners *ad inferos*, swears he shall cut the profession, and walks away. He has been plucked; and Mr. Muff, who stands sixth on the list, is called on to make his appearance before the awful tribunal.

IX.

OF THE SEQUEL TO THE HALL EXAMINATION.

Whilst Mr. Muff follows the beadle from the funking-room to the Council Chamber, he scarcely knows whether he is walking upon his head or his heels; if any thing, he believes that he is adopting the former mode of locomotion; nor does he recover a sense of his true position until he finds himself seated at one end of a square table, the other three sides whereof are occupied by the same number of gentlemen of grave and austere bearing, with all the candles in the room apparently endeavoring to imitate that species of eccentric dance which he has only seen the gas-lamps attempt occasionally as he has returned home from his harmonic society. The table before him is invitingly spread with pharmacopæias, books of prescriptions, trays of drugs, and half-dead plants; and upon these subjects, for an hour and a half, he is compelled to answer questions.

We will not follow his examination: nobody was ever able to see the least joke in it; and therefore it is unfitted for our columns. We can but state that after having been puzzled, bullied, "caught," quibbled with, and abused, for the above space of time, his good genius prevails, and he is told he may retire. Oh! the pleasure with which he re-enters the funking-room—that nice, long, pleasant room, with its cheerful fire-place and good substantial book-cases, and valuable books, and excellent old-fashioned furniture; and the capital tea which the worshipful company allows him—never was meal so exquisitely relished. He has passed the Hall! won't he have a flare-up to-night!—that's all.

As soon as all the candidates have passed, their certificates are given them, upon payment of various sovereigns, and they are let out. The first great rush takes place to the "re-tail establishment" over the way, where all their friends are assembled—Messrs. Jones, Rapp, Manhug, &c. A pot of "Hospital Medoc" is consumed by each of the thirsty candi-dates, and off they go, jumping Jim Crow down Union-street, and swaggering along the pavement six abreast, as they sing several extempore variations of their own upon a glee which details divers peculiarities in the economy of certain small pigs, pleasantly enlivened by grunts and whistles, and the occasional asseveration of the singers that their paternal par-ent was a man of less than ordinary stature. This insensibly changes into "Willy brewed a Peck of Malt," and finally settles down into "Nix my Dolly," appropriately danced and chorused, until a policeman, who has no music in his soul, stops their harmony, but threatens to take them into charge if they do not bring their promenade concert to a close.

Arrived at their lodgings, the party throw off all restraint. The table is soon covered with beer, spirits, screws, hot water, and pipes; and the company take off their coats, unbutton their stocks, and proceed to conviviality. Mr. Muff, who is in the chair, sings the first song, which informs his friends that the glasses sparkle on the board and the wine is ruby bright, in allusion to the pewter-pots and half-and-half. Hav-ing finished, Mr. Muff calls upon Mr. Jones, who sings a ballad, not altogether perhaps of the same class you would hear at an evening party in Belgrave-square, but still of in-finite humor, which is applauded upon the table to a degree that flirps all the beer out of the pots, with which Mr. Rapp draws portraits and humorous conceits upon the table with his finger. Mr. Manhug is then called upon, and sings

THE STUDENT'S ALPHABET.

Oh, A was an Artery, fill'd with injection;
And B was a Brick, never caught at dissection.
C were some Chemicals—lithium and borax;
And D was a Diaphragm, flooring the thorax.
Chorus (taken in short-hand with minute accuracy.)
Fol de rol lol,
Tol de rol lay,
Fol de rol, tol de rol, tol de rol, lay.

E was an Embryo in a glass case;
And F a Foramen, that pierced the skull's base.
G was a Grinder, who sharpen'd the fools;
And H means the Half-and-half drunk at the schools.
Fol de rol lol, &c.

I was some Iodine; made of sea-weed.
J was a Jolly Cock, not used to read.
K was some Kreosote, much over-rated;
And L were the Lies which about it were stated
Fol de rol lol, &c.

M was a Muscle—cold, flabby, and red;
And N was a Nerve, like a bit of white thread.
O was some Opium, a fool chose to take;
And P were the Pins used to keep him awake.
Fol de rol lol, &c.

Q were the Quacks, who cure stammer and squint.
R was a Raw from a burn, wrapp'd in lint.
S was a Scalpel, to eat bread and cheese;
And T was a Tourniquet, vessels to squeeze.
Fol de rol lol, &c.

U was the Unciform bone of the wrist.
V was the Vein which a blunt lancet miss'd.
W was Wax, from a syringe that flow'd.
X, the Xaminers, who may be blow'd!
Fol de rol lol, &c.

Y stands for You all, with best wishes sincere;
And Z for the Zanies who never touch beer.
So we've got to the end, not forgetting a letter;
And those who don't like it may grind up a better
Fol de rol lol, &c.

This song is vociferously cheered, except by Mr. Rapp, who during its execution has been engaged in making an elaborate piece of basket-work out of wooden pipe-lights, which having arranged to his satisfaction, he sends scudding at the chairman's head. The harmony proceeds, and with it the desire to assist in it, until they all sing different airs at once; and the lodger above, who has vainly endeavored to get to sleep for the last three hours, gives up the attempt as hopeless, when he hears Mr. Manhug called upon for the sixth time to do the cat and dog, saw the bit of wood, imitate Macready, sing his own version of "Lur-lie-e-ty," and accompany it with his elbows on the table.

The first symptom of approaching cerebral excitement from the action of liquid stimulants is perceived in Mr. Muff himself, who tries to cut some cold meat with the snuffers. Mr. Simpson, also a new man, who is looking very pale, rather overcome with the effects of his elementary screw in a first essay to perpetrate a pipe, petitions for the window to be let down, that the smoke, which you might divide with a knife, may escape more readily. This proposition is unanimously negatived, until Mr. Jones, who is tilting his chair back, produces the desired effect by overbalancing himself in the middle of a comic medley, and causing a compound, comminuted, and irreducible fracture of three panes of glass by tumbling through them. Hereat, the harmony experiencing a temporary check, and all the half-and-half having disappeared, Mr. Muff finds there is no great probability of getting any more, as the servant who attends upon the seven different lodgers has long since retired to rest in the turn-down bedstead of the back kitchen. An adjournment is therefore determined upon; and, collecting their hats and coats as they best may, the whole party tumble out into the streets at two o'clock in the morning.

"Whiz-z-z-z-t!" shouts Mr. Manhug, as they emerge into the cool air, in accents which only Wieland could excel; "there goes a cat!" Upon the information a volley of hats follow the scared animal, none of which go within ten yards of it, except Mr. Rapp's, who, taking a bold aim, flings his own gossamer down the area, over the railings, as the cat jumps between them on to the water-butt, which is always her first leap in a hurried retreat. Whereupon Mr. Rapp goes and rings the house-bell, that the domestics may return his property; but not receiving an answer, and being assured of the absence of a policeman, he pulls the handle out as far as it will come, breaks it off, and puts it in his pocket. After this they run about the streets, indulging in the usual buoyant recreations that innocent and happy minds so situated delight to follow, and are eventually separated by their flight from the police, from the safe plan they have adopted of all running different ways when pursued, to bother the crushers. What this leads to we shall probably hear next week, when they are once more *réunis* in the dissecting-room to recount their adventures.

X.

THE TERMINATION OF THE HALL EXAMINATION.

THE morning after the carousal reported in our last chapter, the parties thereat assisting are dispersed in various parts of London. Did a modern Asmodeus take a spectator to any elevated point from which he could overlook the Great Metropolis of Mr. Grant and England just at this period, when Aurora has not long called the sun, who rises as surlily as if he had got out of bed the wrong way, he would see Mr. Rapp ruminating upon things in general, whilst seated on some cabbages in Covent Garden Market; Mr. Jones taking refreshment with a lamplighter and two cabmen at a promenade coffee-stand near Charing Cross, to whom he is giving a lecture upon the action of veratria in paralysis, jumbled somehow or other with frequent asseverations that he shall at all times be happy to see the aforesaid lamplighter and two cabmen at the hospital or his own lodgings; Mr. Manhug, with a pocket-handkerchief tied round his head, not clearly understanding what has become of his latch-key, but rather imagining that he threw it into a lamp instead of the short pipe which still remains in the pocket of his pea-jacket, and, moreover, finding himself close to London Bridge, is taking a gratuitous doze in the cabin of the Boulogne steamboat, which he ascertains does not start until eight o'clock; whilst Mr. Simpson, the new man, with the usual destiny of such green productions—thirsty, nauseated, and "coming round"—is safely taken care of in one of the small private, unfurnished apartments which are let by the night on exceedingly moderate terms (an introduction by a policeman of known respectability being all the reference that is required) in the immediate neighborhood of the Bow-street Police-office. Where

Mr. Muff is—it is impossible to form the least idea; he may probably speak for himself.

The reader will now please to shift the time and place to two o'clock P. M., in the dissecting-room, which is full of students, comprising three we have just spoken of, except Mr. Simpson. A message has been received that the anatomical teacher is unavoidably detained at an important case in private practice, and cannot meet his class to-day. Hereupon there is much rejoicing amongst the pupils, who gather in a large semicircle round the fire-place, and devise various amusing methods of passing the time. Some are for subscribing to buy a set of four-corners to be played in the museum when the teachers are not there, and kept out of sight in an old coffin when they are not wanted. Others vote for getting up sixpenny sweepstakes, and raffling for them with dice—the winner of each to stand a pot out of his gains, and add to the goodly array of empty pewters which already grace the mantelpiece in bright order, with the exception of two irregulars, one of which Mr. Rapp has squeezed flat to show the power of his hand; and in the bottom of the other Mr. Manhug has bored a foramen with a red hot poker in a laudable attempt to warm the heavy that it contained. Two or three think they had better adjourn to the nearest slate table and play a grand pool; and some more vote for tapping the preparations in the museum, and making the porter of the dissecting-room intoxicated with the grog manufactured from the proof spirit. The various arguments are, however, cut short by the entrance of Mr. Muff, who rushes into the room, followed by Mr. Simpson, and throwing off his Mackintosh cape, pitches a large fluttering mass of feathers into the middle of the circle.

"Halloo, Muff! how are you, my bean—what's up?" is the general exclamation.

"Oh, here's a lark!" is all Mr. Muff's reply.

"Lark!" cries Mr. Rapp; "you're drunk, Muff—you don't mean to call that a lark!"

"It's a beautiful patriarchal old hen," returns Mr. Muff, "that I bottled, as she was meandering down the mews; and now I uote we have her for lunch. Who's game to kill her?"

Various plans are immediately suggested, including cutting her head off, poisoning her with morphia, or shooting her with a little cannon Mr. Rapp has got in his locker; but at last the majority decide upon hanging her. A gibbet is speedily prepared, simply consisting of a thigh-bone laid across two high stools; a piece of whip cord is then noosed round the victim's neck; and she is launched into eternity, as the newspapers say—Mr. Manhug attending to pull her legs.

"Depend upon it that's a humane death," remarks Mr. Jones. "I never tried to strangle a fowl but once, and then I twisted its neck bang off. I know a capital plan to finish cats though."

"Throw it off—put it up—let's have it," exclaim the circle.

"Well, then; you must get their necks in a slip-knot and pull them up to a key-hole. They can't hurt you, you know, because you are the other side the door."

"Oh, capital—quite a wrinkle," observes Mr. Muff. "But how do you catch them first?"

"Put a hamper outside the leads with some valerian in it, and a bit of cord tied to the lid. If you keep watch, you may bag half-a-dozen in no time; and strange cats are fair game for everybody—only some of them are rum 'uns to bite."

At this moment, a new Scotch pupil, who is lulling himself into the belief that he is studying anatomy from some sheep's eyes by himself in the Museum, enters the dissecting-room, and mildly asks the porter "what a heart is worth?"

"I don't know, sir," shouts Mr. Rapp; "it depends entirely upon what's trumps;" whereupon the new Scotch pupil retires to his study as if he was shot, followed by several pieces of cinders and tobacco-pipe.

During the preceding conversation, Mr. Muff cuts down the victim with a scalpel; and, finding that life has departed, commences to pluck it, and perform the usual post-mortem abdominal examinations attendant upon such occasions. Mr. Rapp undertakes to manufacture an extempore spit from the rather dilapidated umbrella of the new Scotch pupil, which he has heedlessly left in the dissecting-room. This being completed, with the assistance of some wire from the ribs of an old skeleton that had hung in a corner of the room ever since it was built, the hen is put down to roast, presenting the most extraordinary specimen of trussing upon record. Mr. Jones undertakes to buy some butter at a shop behind the hospital; and Mr. Manhug, not being able to procure any flour, gets some starch from the cabinet of the lecturer on Materia Medica, and powders it in a mortar which he borrows from the laboratory.

"To revert to cats," observes Mr. Manhug, as he sets himself before the fire to superintend the cooking; "it strikes

me we could contrive no end of fun if we each agreed to
bring some here one day in carpet-bags. We could drive in
plenty of dogs, and cocks, and hens, out of the back streets,
and then let them all loose together in the dissecting-room."

"With a sprinkling of rats and ferrets," adds Mr. Rapp.
"I know a man who can let us have as many as we want.
The skrimmage would be immense, only I shouldn't much
care to stay and see it."

"Oh, that's nothing," replies Mr. Muff. "Of course, we
must get on the roof and look at it through the sky-lights.
You may depend upon it, it would be the finest card we ever
played."

How gratifying to every philanthropist must be these
proofs of the elasticity of mind peculiar to a Medical Student! Surrounded by scenes of the most impressive and
deplorable nature — in constant association with death, and
contact with disease — his noble spirit, in the ardor of his
search after professional information, still retains its buoyancy
and freshness; and he wreaths with roses the hours which he
passes in the dissecting-room, although the world in general
looks upon it as a rather unlikely locality for those flowers to
shed their perfume over!

"By the way, Muff, where did you get to last night after
we all cut?" inquires Mr. Rapp.

"Why, that's what I am rather anxious to find out myself," replies Mr. Muff; "but I think I can collect tolerably
good reminiscences of my travels."

"Tell us all about it, then," cry three or four.

"With pleasure—only let's have in a little more beer; for
the heat of the fire in cooking produces rather too rapid an
evaporation of fluids from the surface of the body."

"Oh, blow your physiology!" says Rapp. "You mean to
say you've got a hot copper—so have I. Send for the precious
balm, and then fire away."

And accordingly, when the beer arrives, Mr. Muff proceeds
with the recital of his wanderings.

XI.

HOW MR. MUFF CONCLUDES HIS EVENING.

ESSENTIAL as sulphuric acid is to the ignition of the platinum in an hydropneumatic lamp, so is half-and-half to the proper illumination of a Medical Student's faculties. The Royal College of Surgeons may thunder and the lecturers may threaten, but all to no effect; for, like the slippers in the Eastern story, however often the pots may be ordered away from the dissecting-room, somehow or other they always find their way back again with unflinching pertinacity. All the world inclined towards beer knows that the current price of a pot of half-and-half is fivepence, and by this standard the Medical Student fixes his expenses. He says he has given three pots for a pair of Berlin gloves, and speaks of a half-crown as a six-pot piece.

Mr. Muff takes the goodly measure in his hand, and decapitating its "spuma" with his pipe, from which he flings it into Mr. Simpson's face, indulges in a prolonged drain, and commences his narrative—most probably in the following manner:—

"You know we should all have got on very well if Rapp hadn't been such a fool as to pull away the lanthorns from the place where they are putting down the wood pavement in the Strand, and swear he was a watchman. I thought the crusher saw us, and so I got ready for a bolt, when Manhug said the blocks had no right to obstruct the footpath; and, shoving down a whole wall of them into the street, voted for stopping to play at *duck* with them. Whilst he was trying how many he could pitch across the Strand against the shutters opposite, down came the *pewlice* and off we cut."

"I had a tight squeak for it," interrupts Mr. Rapp; "but I beat them at last, in the dark of the Durham-street arch. That's a dodge worth being up to when you get into a row near the Adelphi. Fire away, Muff—where did you go?"

"Right up a court to Maiden-lane, in the hope of bolting into the Cider-cellars. But they were all shut up, and the fire out in the kitchen, so I ran on through a lot of alleys and back-slums, until I got somewhere in St. Giles's, and here I took a cab."

"Why, you hadn't got an atom of tin when you left us," says Mr. Manhug.

"Devil a bit did that signify. You know I only took the *cab*—I'd nothing at all to do with the driver; he was all right in the gin-shop near the stand, I suppose. I got on the box, and drove about for my own diversion—I don't exactly know where; but I couldn't leave the cab, as there was always a crusher in the way when I stopped. At last I found myself at the large gate of New Square, Lincoln's Inn, so I knocked until the porter opened it, and drove in as straight as I could. When I got to the corner of the square, by No. 7, I pulled up, and, tumbling off my perch, walked quietly along to the Portugal-street wicket. Here the other porter let me out, and I found myself in Lincoln's Inn Fields."

"And what became of the cab?" asks Mr. Jones.

"How should I know?—it was no affair of mine. I dare say the horse made it right; it didn't matter to him whether he was standing in St. Giles's or Lincoln's Inn, only the last was the most respectable."

"I don't see that," says Mr. Manhug, refilling his pipe.

"Why, all the thieves in London live in St. Giles's."

"Well, and who live in Lincoln's Inn?"

"Pshaw! that's all worn out," continues Mr. Muff. "I got to the College of Surgeons, and had a good mind to scud some oyster-shells through the windows, only there were several people about—fellows coming home to chambers, and the like; so I pattered on until I found myself in Drury-lane close to a coffee-shop that was open. There I saw such a jolly row!"

Mr. Muff utters this last sentence in the same ecstatic accents of admiration with which we speak of a lovely woman or a magnificent view.

"What was it about?" eagerly demanded the rest of the circle.

"Why, just as I got in, a gentleman of a vivacious turn of mind, who was taking an early breakfast, had shied a soft-boiled egg at the gas-light, which didn't hit it, of course, but flew across the tops of the boxes, and broke upon a lady's head."

"What a mess it must have made?" interposes Mr. Manhug. "Coffee-shop eggs are always so very albuminous."

"Once I found some feathers in one, and a fœtal chick," observes Mr. Rapp.

"Knock that down for a good one!" says Mr. Jones, taking the poker and striking three distinct blows on the mantelpiece, the last of which breaks off the corner. "Well, what did the lady do?"

"Commenced kicking up an extensive shindy, something between crying, coughing, and abusing; until somebody in a fustian coat, addressing the assailant, said, 'he was no gentleman, whoever he was, to throw eggs at a woman; and that if he'd come out he'd pretty soon butter his crumpets on both sides for him, and give him pepper for nothing.' The master of the coffee shop now came forward and said, 'he wasn't a going to have no uproar in his house, which was very respectable, and always used by the first of company, and if they wanted to quarrel, they might fight it out in the streets.' Whereupon they all began to barge the master at once,—one saying 'his coffee was all snuff and chickweed,' or something of the kind; whilst the other told him 'he looked as measly as a mouldy muffin;' and then all of a sudden a lot of half-pint cups and pewter spoons flew up in the air, and the three men began an indiscriminate battle all to themselves, in one of the boxes, 'fighting quite permiscus,' as the lady properly observed. I think the landlord was worst off though; he got a very queer wipe across the face from the handle of his own toasting-fork."

"And what did you do, Muff?" asks Mr. Manhug.

"Ah, that was the finishing card of all. I put the gas out, and was walking off as quietly as could be, when some policemen who heard the row outside met me at the door, and wouldn't let me pass. I said I would, and they said I should not, until we came to scuffling, and then one of them calling to some more, told them to take me to Bow-street, which they did; but I made them carry me though. When I got into the office they had not any especial charge to make against me, and the old bird behind the partition said I might go about my business; but, as ill luck would have it, another of the unboiled ones recognized me as one of the party who had upset the wooden blocks—he knew me again by my d—d Taglioni."

"And what did they do to you?"

"Marched me across the yard and locked me up; when, to my great consolation in my affliction, I found Simpson, crying and twisting up his pocket-handkerchief, as if he was wringing it; and hoping his friends would not hear of his disgrace through the *Times*."

"What a love you are Simpson!" observes Mr. Jones patronizingly. "Why, how the deuce could they, if you gave a proper name? I hope you called yourself James Edwards."

Mr. Simpson blushes, blows his nose, mutters something about his card-case and telling an untruth, which excites much merriment; and Mr. Muff proceeds:—

"The beak wasn't such a bad fellow after all, when we went up in the morning. I said I was ashamed to confess we were both disgracefully intoxicated, and that I would take great care nothing of the same humiliating nature should occur again; whereupon we were fined twelve pots each, and I tossed sudden death with Simpson which should pay both. He lost and paid down the dibs. We came away, and here we are."

The mirth proceeds, and, ere long, gives place to harmony; and when the cookery is finished, the bird is speedily converted into an anatomical preparation,—albeit her interarticular cartilages are somewhat tough, and her lateral ligaments apparently composed of a substance between leather and caoutchouc. As afternoon advances, the porter of the dissecting-room finds them performing an incantation dance round Mr. Muff, who, seated on a stool placed upon two of the tressels, is rattling some halfpence in a skull, accompanied by Mr. Rapp, who is performing a difficult concerto on an extempore instrument of his own invention, composed of the Scotchman's hat, who is still grinding in the Museum, and the identical thigh-bone that assisted to hang Mr. Muff's patriarchal old hen!

XII.

OF THE COLLEGE, AND THE CONCLUSION.

OUR hero once more undergoes the process of grinding before he presents himself in Lincoln's-Inn Fields for examination at the College of Surgeons. Almost the last affair which our hero troubles himself about is the Examination at the College of Surgeons; and as his anatomical knowledge requires a little polishing before he presents himself in Lincoln's-Inn Fields, he once more undergoes the process of grinding.

The grinder for the College conducts his tuition in the same style as the grinder for the Hall—often they are united in the same individual, who perpetually has a vacancy for a resident pupil, although his house is already quite full; somewhat resembling a carpet-bag, which was never yet known to be so crammed with articles, but you might put something in besides. The class is carried on similar to the one we have already quoted; but the knowledge required does not embrace the same multiformity of subjects; anatomy and surgery being the principal points.

Our old friends are assembled to prepare for their last examination, in a room fragrant with the amalgamated odors of stale tobacco-smoke, varnished bones, leaky preparations, and gin-and-water. Large anatomical prints depend from the walls, and a few vertebræ, a lower jaw, and a sphenoid bone, are scattered upon the table.

"To return to the eye, gentleman," says the grinder; "recollect the Petitian Canal surrounds the cornea. Mr. Rapp, what am I talking about?"

Mr. Rapp, who is drawing a little man out of dots and lines upon the margin of his "Quain's Anatomy," starts up and observes—"Something about the Paddington Canal running round the corner, sir."

"Now, Mr. Rapp, you must pay me a little more attention," expostulates the teacher. "What does the operation for cataract resemble in a familiar point of view?"

"Pushing a boat-hook through the wall of a house to pull back the drawing-room blinds," answers Mr. Rapp.

"You are incorrigible," says the teacher, smiling at the simile, which altogether is an apt one. "Did you ever see a case of bad cataract?"

"Yes, sir, ever-so-long ago—the Cataract of the Ganges at Astley's. I went to the gallery, and had a mill with—"

"There, we don't want particulars," interrupts the grinder; "but I would recommend you to mind your eyes, especially if you get under Guthrie. Mr. Muff, how do you define an ulcer!"

"The establishment of a raw," replies Mr. Muff.

"Tit! tit! tit!" continues the teacher with an expression of pity. "Mr. Simpson, perhaps you can tell Mr. Muff what an ulcer is?"

4

"An abrasion of the cuticle produced by its own absorption," answers Mr. Simpson, all in a breath.

"Well, I maintain its easier to say a *raw* than at all," observes Mr. Muff.

"Pray, silence. Mr. Manhug, have you ever been sent for to a bad incised wound?"

"Yes, sir, when I was an apprentice: a man using a chopper cut off his hand."

"And what did you do?"

"Cut off myself for the governor, like a two-year old."

"But now you have no governor, what plan would you pursue in a similar case?"

"Send for the nearest doctor—call him in."

"Yes, yes, but suppose he wouldn't come?"

"Call him out, sir."

"Pshaw! you are all quite children," exclaims the teacher. "Mr. Simpson, of what is bone chemically composed?"

"Of earthy matter, or *phosphate of lime*, and animal matter, or *gelatine*."

"Very good, Mr. Simpson. I suppose you don't know a great deal about bones, Mr. Rapp?"

"Not much, sir. I haven't been a great deal in that line. They give a penny for three pounds in Clare Market. That's what I call popular osteology."

"Gelatine enters largely into the animal fibres," says the leader, gravely. "Parchment, or skin, contains an important quantity, and is used by cheap pastry-cooks to make jellies."

"Well, I've heard of eating your *words*," says Mr. Rapp, "but never your *deeds*."

"Oh! oh! oh!" groan the pupils at this gross appropriation, and the class getting very unruly is broken up.

The examination at the College is altogether a more respectable ordeal than the jalap and rhubarb botheration at Apothecaries' Hall, and *par conséquence*, Mr. Muff goes up one evening with little misgivings as to his success. After undergoing four different sets of examiners, he is told he may retire, and is conducted by Mr. Belfour into "Paradise," the room appropriated to the fortunate ones, which the curious stranger may see lighted up every Friday evening as he passes through Lincoln's-Inn Fields. The inquisitors are altogether a gentlemanly set of men, who are willing to help a student out of a scrape, rather than "catch question" him into one: nay, more than once the candidate has attributed his success to a whisper prompted by the kind heart of the venerable and highly-gifted individual—now, alas! no more—who until last year assisted at the examinations.

Of course, the same kind of scene takes place that was enacted after going up to the Hall, and with the same results, except the police office, which they manage to avoid. The next day, as usual, they are again at the school, standing innumerable pots, telling incalculable lies, and singing uncounted choruses, until the Scotch pupil, who is still grinding in the Museum, is forced to give over study, after having been squirted at through the keyhole five distinct times, with a reversed stomach-pump full of beer, and finally unkennelled. The lecturer upon chemistry, who has a private pupil in his laboratory learning how to discover arsenic in poisoned people's stomachs, where there is none, and make red, blue, and green fires, finds himself locked in, and is obliged to get out at the window; whilst the professor of medicine, who is holding forth, as usual, to a select very few, has his lecture upon intermittent fever so strangely interrupted by distant harmony and convivial hullaballoo, that he finishes abruptly in a pet, to the great joy of his class. But Mr. Muff and his friends care not. They have passed all their troubles—they are regular medical men, and, for aught they care, the whole establishment may blow up, tumble down, go to blazes, or any thing else in a small way that may completely obliterate it. In another twelve hours they have departed to their homes, and are only spoken of in the reverence with which we regard the ruins of a by-gone edifice, as bricks who were.

Our task is finished. We have traced Mr. Muff, from the new man through the almost entomological stages of his being, to his perfect state; and we take our farewell of him as the "general practitioner." In our Physiology we have endeavored to show the medical student as he actually exists—his reckless gayety, his wild frolics, his open disposition. That he is careless and dissipated we admit, but these attributes end with his pupilage; did they not do so spontaneously, the up-hill struggles and hardly-earned income of his laborious future career would, to use his own terms, "soon knock it all out of him;" although, in the after-waste of years, he looks back upon his student's revelries with an occasional return of old feelings, not unmixed, however, with a passing reflection upon the lamentable inefficacy of the present course of medical education pursued at our schools and hospitals, to fit a man for future practice.

We have endeavored in our sketches so to frame them, that the general reader might not be perplexed by technical or local allusions, whilst the students of London saw they were the work of one who had lived amongst them. And if in some places we have strayed from the strict boundaries of perfect refinement, yet we trust the delicacy of our most sensitive reader has received no wound. We have discarded our joke rather than lose our propriety; and we have been pleased at knowing that in more than one family circle our Physiology has, now and then, raised a smile on the lips of the fair girls, whose brothers were following the same path we have traveled over at the hospitals.

We hope with the new year to have once more the gratification of meeting our friends. Until then, with a hand offered in warm fellowship,—not only to those composing the class he once belonged to, but to all who have been pleased to bestow a few minutes weekly upon his chapters—the Medical Student takes his leave.

XIII.

A LETTER FROM AN OLD FRIEND, SHOWING HOW HE IS GETTING ON.

CLODPOLE, Dec. 23, 1841.

My dear Punch,

Here I am, you see, keeping Christmas, and having no end of fun amongst the jolly, innocent grubs that vegetate in these rural districts. All I regret is that you are not here. I would give a ten-pound note to see you, if I had it;—I would, indeed—so help me several strong men and a steam-engine!

We had a great night in London before I started, only I got rascally screwed: not exactly sewed up, you know, but hit under the wing, so that I could not very well fly. I managed to break the window on the third-floor landing of my lodgings, and let my water-jug fall slap through the wash-hand basin upon a looking-glass that was lying face upwards underneath; but as I was off early in the morning it did not signify.

The people down here are a queer lot; but I have hunted up two or three jolly cocks, and we contrive to keep the place alive between us. Of course, all the knockers came off the first night I arrived, and to-morrow we are going to climb out upon the roof of my abode, and make a tour along the tops of the neighboring houses, putting turfs on the tops of all prac-ticable chimneys. Jack Randall—such a jolly chick! you must be introduced to him—has promised to tie a cord across the pavement at the corner, from the lamp-post to a door-scraper; and we have made a careful estimate that, out of every half-dozen people who pass, six will fall down, four cut their faces more or less arterially, and two contuse their foreheads. I, you may imagine, shall wait at home all the evening for the crippled ones, and Jack is to go halves in what I get for plas-tering them up. We may be so lucky as to procure a case of concussion—who knows? Jack is a real friend: he cannot be of much use to me in the way of recommendation, because the people here think he is a little wild; but as far as seriously injuring the parishioners goes, he declares he will lose no chance. He says he knows some gipsies on the common who have got scarlet-fever in their tent; and he is going to give them half-a-crown if they can bring it into the village, to be paid upon the breaking out of the first undoubted case. This will fag the Union doctor to death, who is my chief opponent, and I shall come in for some of the private patients.

My surgery is not very well stocked at present, but I shall write to Ansell and Hawke after Christmas. I have got a pickle-bottle full of liquorice-powder, which has brought me in a good deal already, and assisted to perform several won-derful cures. I administer it in powder, two drachms in six, to be taken morning, noon, and night; and it appears to be a valuable medicine for young practitioners, as you may give a large dose, without producing any very serious effects. Some-body was insane enough to send to me the other night for a pill and draught; and if Jack Randall had not been there, I should have been regularly stumped, having nothing but Epsom salts. He cut a glorious calomel pill out of pipeclay, and then we concocted a black-draught of salts and bottled stout, with a little patent boot-polish. Next day, the patient finding him-

self worse, sent for me, and I am trying the exhibition of lin-
seed-meal and rose-pink in small doses, under which treatment
he is gradually recovering. It has since struck me that a
minute portion of sulphuric acid enters into the composition
of the polish, possibly causing the indisposition which he describes " as if he was tied all up in a double-knot, and pulled
tight."   .

I have had one case of fracture in the leg of Mrs. Pinkey's
Italian greyhound, which Jack threw a flower-pot at in the
dark the other night. I tied it up in two splints cut out of a
clothes-peg in a manner which I stated to be the most popular
at the Hotel Dieu at Paris; and the old girl was so pleased
that she asked me to keep Christmas-day at her house, where
she burns the Yule log, makes a bowl of wassail, and all manner of games. We are going to bore a hole in the Yule log
with an old trephine, and ram it chuck full of gun-powder;
and Jack's little brother is to catch six or seven frogs, under
pain of a severe licking, which are to be put into one of the
vegetable dishes. The old girl has her two nieces home for
the holidays—devilish handsome, larky girls—so we have determined to take some mistletoe, and give a practical demonstration of the action of the *orbicularis oris* and *levatores
labiæ superioris et inferioris*. If either of them have got any
tin, I shall try and get all right with them; but if the brads
don't flourish I shall leave it alone, for a wife is just the worst
piece of furniture a fellow can bring into his house, especially
if he inclines to conviviality; although to be sure a medical
man ought to consider her as part of his stock in trade, to be
taken at a fair valuation amidst his stopple-bottles, mortars,
measures, and pill-rollers.

If business does not tumble in well, in the course of a few
weeks, we have another plan in view; but I only wish to resort to it on emergency, in case we should be found out. The
railway passes at the bottom of my garden, and Jack thinks,
with a few pieces of board, he can contrive to run the engine
and tender off the line, which is upon a tolerably high em-
bankment. I need not tell you all this is in strict confidence;
and if the plan does not jib, which is not very probable, will
bring lots of grist to the mill. I have put the engineer and
stoker at a sure guinea a head for the inquest; and the concussions in the second class will be of unknown value. If
practicable, I mean to have an elderly gentleman "who must

not be moved under any consideration;" so I shall get him into my house for the term of his indisposition, which may possibly be a very long one. I can give him up my own bed-room, and sleep myself in an old harpsichord, which I bought cheap at a sale, and disembowelled into a species of deceptive bed. I think the hint might put "people about to marry" up to a dodge in the way of spare beds. Everybody now sees through the old chiffonier and wardrobe turn-up impositions, but the grand piano would beat them; only it should be kept locked, for fear any one given to harmony might commence playing a fantasia on the bolster.

Our parishioners have very little idea of the Cider-cellars and Coal-hole, both of which places they take in their literal sense. I think that, with Jack's assistance, we can establish something of the kind at the Swan, which is the principal inn. Should it not succeed, I shall turn my attention to getting up a literary and scientific institution, and give a lecture. I have not yet settled on what subject, but Jack votes for Astronomy, for two reasons; firstly, because the room is dark nearly all the time; and secondly, because you can snug in some pots of half-and-half behind the transparent orrery. He says the dissolving views in London put him up to the value of a dark exhibition. We also think we can manage a concert, which will be sure of a good attendance if we say it is for some parish charity. Jack has volunteered a solo on the *cornet-à-piston;* he has never tried the instrument, but he says he is sure he can play it, as it looks remarkably easy hanging up in the windows of the music-shops. He thinks one might drill the children and get up the Macbeth music.

It is turning very cold to-night, and I think will turn to a frost. Jack has thrown some water on the pavement before my door; and should it freeze, I have given strict orders to my old housekeeper not to strew any ashes, or sand, or saw-dust, or any similar rubbish about. People's bones are very brittle in frosty weather, and this may bring a job. I hope it will.

If, in your London rambles, as you seem to be everywhere at once, you pitch upon Manhug, Rapp, or Jones, give my love to them, and tell them to keep their powder dry, and not to think of practicing in the country, which is after all a species of social suicide. And with the best compliments of the season to yourself, and "through the medium of the

columns of your valuable journal" to your readers, believe me
to remain,

My dear old beau, yours very considerably,

JOSEPH MUFF.

XIV.

A FEW LINES FROM MR. JOSEPH MUFF

CLODPOLE, Feb. 20, 1842.

MY DEAR OLD PUNCH,

It is now two months since I last wrote to you, so I thought
you would not object to see what I have been about. I know
you take an interest in all my proceedings.

I got my surgery a little into order soon after Christmas,
and hung up a lamp at my door; such a stunner—with red
and blue shades, and a pestle and mortar on the top. The
very first evening I put it up, Jack Randall took it down
again, and carried it on to the railroad, where it stopped the
down mail-train, the engineer mistaking the red bull's-eye for
the signal at the station. Jack's a splendid chick, but a little
too larky. He fills my leech jar with tadpoles and water-efts;
and the fellows he brings to see me have walked into all my
Spanish liquorice and Confection of Roses. He likewise never
passes my house, as he comes home late from a party, but he
pulls the night-bell almost clean away, and when I put my head
out of the front second floor to know what's the matter, expecting nothing short of a guinea case, he sings out "Lur-li-e-ty,"
and asks if I have got any beer in the house. I am, however,
obliged to put up with this, for he is a prime chap at heart,
and will do anything for me. He quite lived on the ice during the frost, tripping everybody up he could come near; and
whether he injured them seriously or not, I know the will was
good, and was therefore much obliged to him.

Of course, at present, my patients are rather select than
numerous, but I think the red lamp and brass-plate may en-
tice a few. I had a glorious case of dislocation of the shoulder last week, and nearly pulled the fellow in half, with the
assistance of two or three bricklayers who were building next
door, and a couple of jack-towels. I have not been paid for

it; but the best of the matter is, the other doctor tried first and couldn't reduce it, because he had no bricklayers at hand. This has got my name up rather.

I see a correspondent of yours, L. S. B. Bart., has been very irritated at my calling the country people *grubs*. What would he have me to term them? I'm sure he is a tolerably fair specimen of the class. They are terrible Goths down here. Not one in twenty can read or write; and so all my dispensing labels which I tie on the bottles are quite thrown away. A small female toddled into the surgery the other day and horrified me by drawling out—

"If you please, sir, mother's took the lotion, and rubbed her leg with the mixture!" This might have been serious, for the lotion contained a trifle of poison; but Jack and I started off directly; and as it happened very luckily to be washing-day, we drenched the stupid woman with soapsuds and pearl-ash, until every thing was thrown off the stomach, including, I expect, a quantity of the lining membrane. This taught me a lesson that a medical man should always have the instruments in order; for, if Jack had not borrowed my stomach-pump to squirt at the cats with, a good deal of bother might have been avoided.

As soon as I can get a little settled, you shall hear from me again. In the mean time, believe me,

Yours rather much than otherwise,

JOSEPH MUFF.

CURIOSITIES OF MEDICAL EXPERIENCE.

I.

SINCE our last despatches received overland from Clodpole, and bearing date March 2, 1842, we learn that our old friend Mr. Joseph Muff has at length got his surgery tolerably in order. The majority of the bottles and jars literally contain what they profess by their labels; we may except the one inscribed *Aqua Distill.*, which is filled with Hodges' best. A carboy ticketed *Syrup. Papav.* yields some very fine home-brewed ale upon drawing the cork; and, as the surgery is cooler than the parlor closet, he keeps his fresh butter in the jar assigned to *Ceratum cetacei.* He has moreover, invested twelve shillings in six dozen phials, a gross of corks, two quires of outside demy, and a ball of red string. In fact, he wants nothing now but patients.

As he has nothing to do, he has taken Jack Randall to live with him as an assistant, and finds him very useful in dispelling the *ennui* naturally attendant upon waiting for practice, by his diverting and eccentric flights of hilarity. His inventive genius has procured Mr. Muff the best haul of victims he has had since he commenced business. He crawled out of his garret window along the gutter to the roof of the adjoining house a few evenings ago, and tied down the ball of the cistern with some packthread, in consequence of which the water overflowed in the night and percolated all the ceilings of the upper rooms, providentially dripping exactly over the beds of some of the inmates. This has given rise to one intermittent fever, and three capital cases of rheumatism, which he is in hopes may eventually prove chronic. He is at present hard at work endeavoring to introduce the ringworm into Miss Trimkid's preparatory school, through the medium of the day-scholars. Jack was apprenticed for two years to a surgeon who failed, and subsequently emigrated to Port Adelaide, so that he knows a little of his profession, and is moreover exceedingly anxious to improve himself, readily undertaking all operations that chance throws in his way. He is represented as particularly clever at keeping people awake who have taken laudanum; which he accomplishes by inserting needles under their finger-nails, and blowing grains of cayenne pepper up their nostrils through a quill. It struck Mr. Muff that his friend produced lockjaw in one case by these means; but as the patient died "from the effects of the opium," the slight error was never discovered. He succeeds, perhaps, best in tooth-drawing. The great power of his wrist enables him to extract anything; and whether the jaw breaks or is dislocated, the sufferer is certain to be relieved from his torture. He carefully saves all the carious teeth he extracts, and is preparing a curious arabesque of decayed molars and eye-teeth upon black velvet whereon he is going to frame the intimation, "*Charges regulated according to circumstances.*"

Our two friends employ their leisure hours, which amount to twenty-three and a half out of twenty-four, in smoking birdseye and telling various anecdotes connected with their past career. As these legends furnish much valuable information relative to the state of existing medical concerns, we have, by some reason of our intimacy with Mr. Muff, procured notes of their conversations. These we intend to present weekly, until our readers are tired of them or our file is exhausted. We shall adopt the narrative style, and avail ourselves of such illustrations as may tend to throw additional interest over our sketches. And taking an old friend by the hand, we begin by a faint attempt to describe

MR. RAPP'S FAREWELL FEAST.

Next to imprisonment for debt there are few positions in life more cheerfully exhilarating than that of house-surgeon to a hospital; especially if it be one where "accidents are received night and day without letters of recommendation." Constantly surrounded by scenes of the most pleasant and mirth-inspiring description; breathing the purest atmosphere in the world; revelling at lunch upon hospital cheese, which is a relish apparently prepared, with the nicest culinary art, from bees-wax, yellow soap, and doubtful eggs; faring sump-

tuously withal every day at the board-room dinner-table, in
company with the matron, house-apothecary, secretary, and
other choice spirits, who delight in the sunshine of humor or
wit; and never depressed by the wearisome monotony of lying
in bed all night long, his existence is, indeed, enviable. So
thought Mr. Rapp; who having been house-surgeon to the St.
Tourniquet's Hospital for one year, evinced his gratitude at
the close of his duties, by inviting some of his friends to an
extensive spread. Medical students are not in the habit of
refusing invitations (more especially, if there is a faint hope
thrown out of unlimited half-and-half, inexhaustible tobacco-
jars, or uncounted pipes), and accordingly some sixteen or
eighteen accepted, including the majority of our old acquaintances. The immortal Muff himself left all his patients to his
"assistant," and, having locked up the croton oil and prussic
acid for fear of accidents, and provided Randall with a
quart of black draught and a screw of parochial pills, came
up from Clodpole by an evening train. Mr. Manhug and Mr.
Jones did not wait to be asked, but sent word to say that they
meant to come. Mr. Newcome, the last new pupil, wrote the
following note in reply:—

"Mr. Newcome presents his compliments to Mr. Rapp, and
will have much pleasure in accepting his polite invitation,
but hopes it will not be a late party, as he is anxious to follow
up the sober and temperate course recommended by Vincent
Priessnitz."

And the other visitors having heard it reported that there
was to be no end of rumpsteaks and oyster-sauce, went without their dinners, to the great astonishment of the proprietor
of the Rupert Street Dining-rooms; and as soon as the four
o'clock lecture was over, and the professor evaporated, played
with their subscription skittles in the dissecting-room until it
was quite dark, when they adjourned to the house-surgeon's
parlor, where the company was expected to assemble.

Most rooms appropriated by the kindness of hospital governors to house-surgeons, are very much alike; we may say
(for the benefit of those who have passed their Latin), *ex uno
disce omnes.* The apartment has an odor of tobacco, the furniture is fashionable, inasmuch as it is remarkably old, and
the paper is of that elaborate pattern, which you see stamped
before your eyes in the window of a shop in St. Giles, and
afterwards labelled "three farthings;" additionally ornamented on each side of the fire-place by legends, inscriptions,

and diverting diagrams, in pencil. When any house-surgeon of former times possessed a diamond ring, which appears to have been by no means a common occurrence, he signed his name therewith amongst the archives of the window panes; if he were not addicted to jewelry, he simply cut his initials upon the panels of the shutters with a scalpel. Aged men with grey hair, who have been attached as messengers to the hospital for the last sixty years, speak vaguely of persons coming to whitewash the ceiling, and paint the wainscoat when they were boys; but these traditions are ascribed more to the garrulity of age than the remembrance of such a proceeding having actually occurred.

II.

MR. RAPP'S FAREWELL FEAST.—(*Continued.*)

NINE o'clock was the time named for supper; and, unlike the false appointments of worldly society, as the hospital clock chimed that hour, every man had assembled. The appearance of the room was most imposing. The long table had been brought up from the board-room, and was lighted by four mould-candles, inserted respectively in a plated, brass, japanned, and flat tin candlestick, whilst an elegant *épergne* graced the centre of the table, formed by a round galvanic battery full of celery. The whole derived additional beauty from the circumstance of no two articles of glass or crockery being alike; whilst before the gentleman upon whom the task devolved of carving the six baked fowls was placed a double-edged catlin and a metacarpal saw—the technical names of two instruments which would be of great service in the event of the poultry turning out tough or ligamentous. The old skeleton, that generally hung down with a balance-weight from the roof of the theatre, was also brought up and placed in a classical attitude on the small table behind the "vice;" and the base of a skull, presumed to be the same from which all the house-surgeons ever since the dark ages ground up the *foramina*, formed an appropriate and professional tobacco-box, proving that medical students, in their most idle moments, never lose sight of their studies.

We will not describe the actual feeding. It will simply be
necessary to state that the dissections of the *glutœi bovis*
(*vulgo* rump-steaks) were carried on with praiseworthy application, and that the fowls were speedily converted into anatomical preparations. The guests evinced indefatigable perseverance in perpetually taking wine with each other; and
Coke, the porter, who waited, showed his knowledge of his
business, by continually walking round the table, filling every
glass he saw empty with half-and-half, from a can which
somewhat resembled a two-gallon water-pot without a spout.

At length, when the appetites were appeased and the things
removed, the real business of the evening commenced.

"Gentlemen," said Mr. Rapp, "I have the pleasure of informing you that there is nothing in the wards over our head
but broken arms and convalescent dislocations; you can therefore kick up as much row as you please. I beg to propose
'The Queen, Prince Albert, the Prince of Wales, the Princess
Royal, and the rest of the Royal Family.' As none of them
are here to return thanks, pass the wine, Manhug, and sing a
song."

The toast being first greeted with musical honors, which in-
timated that the Queen was "a jolly good fellow," strength-
ened by the affirmation that all of them said so, Mr. Manhug
proceeded to sing, tucking his thumbs into the arm-holes of
his waistcoat, balancing himself on the hind-legs of his chair,
clearing the trachea of some imaginary obstacle, and looking
rather vicious at a crack in the ceiling.

MR. MANHUG'S SONG.—An Assistant Wanted.

WANTED a gentleman fitted to fill
The post of assistant with competent skill
To a country practitioner highly genteel,
With a Union of paupers to physic and heal;
Where against all petitions his heart he must steel,
Nor ever presume their distresses to feel,
For a medical man should be always genteel,—
          So extraordinarily genteel.

He's expected to know all the different branches
Into which proper medical science now launches;
He must bleed with precision, ne'er missing a vein,
And draw double teeth without fracture or pain.
The parish is small—ten miles by sixteen—
With some commons and gravel-pits scattered between;

And, respecting the cases—to state 'tis perhaps right,
That they always occur in the dead of the night.
        Wanted a gentleman, &c.

The Pharmacopœia by heart he must know,¦
And ne'er seem reluctant—when sent for—to go;
He must learn to write labels in different styles,
And wash all the bottles—flats, mixtures, and phials.
If well educated he chances to be,
He may come in the parlor to dinner and tea;
But when the meal's over, must put by his chair,
And back to the surgery counter repair.
        Wanted a gentleman, &c.

These are the principal matters—*au reste*—
He must always appear *comme-il-faut* and well-dressed;
And, since with much practice his mind will be stored,
The salary offer'd is—lodging and board.

Wanted a gentleman, fitted to fill
The tooth of a patient, with gold leaf and skill,
Who can walk like a postman, nor ever feel ill,
Nor beyond seven minutes expect to sit still,
But always be making draught, mixture or pill,
And post every ledger, and write every bill,
And sleep in a garret, small, dreary, and chill,
And succumb to a country practitioner's will.
        Who is most particularly genteel.

"That's all, gentlemen," said Mr. Manhug, thinking it was time for the applause to begin, as he made an inclination of his head, intended half for a bow to his auditors, and half to bring his head into his wine-glass—it being a fixed rule at all convivial parties, that a person, having sung, should immediately on the conclusion of his indiscretion make a pretense of drinking, which implies that there is no more to come. This is a wholesome practice, as nothing is more awkward than to thank one for a song, when only two out of the five verses have been got through.

Mr. Manhug's lyrical attempt was applauded to a degree which caused a short divertisement of candlesticks and tumblers, and woke seven patients in the next ward. The sentiment which followed was an expression of regret that the earthquake did not take place immediately under Apothecaries' Hall on an examination night; and then the chairman, after the manner of a gentleman who does the bass before the looking-glass at Evan's, knocked on the table, and said, "Gentlemen, I have to call your attention to a song from Mr. Jones."

Mr. Jones readily complied, and somewhat pluming himself on his voice, commenced informing the company that the glasses sparkled on the board ("room-table," added *sotto voce* by Mr. Rapp), and that the reign of pleasure had begun —finishing by a threat to drown some imaginary intruder in a bowl if he dared to make his appearance. The great point of the song was the execution of the "bowl." The nearest idea we can give the reader of its deliverance is to beg he will separate the word in bo and ole, and put three distinct o's between them, each one lower than the other, until the last appeared to emanate from some organized ophicleide fixed in the pit of the stomach. The song appeared very popular and admitted of a general chorus, which swelled as it proceeded, until one of the night-nurses put her head into the door, and mildly hinted that the sciatica case in No. 12 did not appear to enter equally into the hilarity of the song, but was lying awake, and grumbling; at which Mr. Rapp felt exceedingly indignant, having imagined that he had perfectly provided against any such occurrence, by administering an extra ten minims of Tr. Spir. in the night draught of No. 12.

By degrees the company attained a high state of conviviality. Mr. Jones did the "cats," and imitated Macready; Mr. Manhug sawed the piece of wood; and Mr. Muff sang an extempore song, which sent the new man into a state of astonished paralysis, and very much amused everybody else. This was the style of

MR. MUFF'S EXTEMPORE.

AIR.—"*There is nae luck about the house.*"

The gent who sits upon my left
  Hath stock around his throat,
His trousers they are black, and the
  Same color is his coat.
He weareth broach, but if I have
  On breeding good encroached
I'm really very sorry that
  I have the subject broached.
       Tol lol de lol, tol liddle lol, &c.

There is a gent I now behold
  A drinking of his wine,
He is a regular jolly cove

And that—that—(I beg your pardon gentlemen)—
(*Cries of "Try back," "Never mind, old fellow," "Go ahead," &c.*)
He is a regular jolly cove
And—('pon my word I'm hard up)—
And is a friend of mine.
Loud chorus of charitable students.
Tol lol de lol, tol liddle lol, &c.

"Bravo! Muff; famous! capital! you never did it better," resounded from various mouths as our friend concluded.

"Now, Mr. Newcome, what's your opinion of the ancient Greeks?" said Manhug briskly.

Mr. Newcome started as if he was shot, and replied, "Upon my word, Mr. Manhug, I hardly know. I've never thought about them."

"Well, then, sing a song."

Mr. Newcome blushed exceedingly, and said he really would if he could, but he never knew one, or else he should be most happy.

"Oh, humbug!" continued Manhug: "come fire away; something mentisental, if you don't know a comic one."

After intense confusion, Mr. Newcome was prevailed upon to murmur "Gaily the troubadour;" which was rendered additionally amusing by Mr. Muff always shouting "Singing from Palestine" everywhere but in the right place.

"There, that'll do, Newcome," cried Mr. Jones, who was evidently a little hazy, at the end of the second verse. "We know 'all the rest; it's as stale as a Monday bun, and much more filling at the price."

Thus burked, Mr. Newcome relapsed into silence, and after several more songs and pleasantries, Mr. Rapp voted an adjournment to Evans's in several cabs. Who went with him, and how they fared, remains to be told in the next number.

III

THE DESTINIES OF MR. RAPP'S GUESTS.

REGULAR dramatists, in writing plays, appear to bear in view the various adventures of certain parties, who are separ-

5

ated during the progress of the plot, and eventually brought together again at the conclusion. So must we frame the present section of our experiences; for as all the visitors did not adopt the same course, it will be necessary to follow each party singly.

"Gentlemen,"said Mr. Rapp, with rather indistinct declamation, "the day is gone—the night's our own, and bright are the beams of the morning sky; so who'll have some punch? and then we'll be off. Mr. Jones will first give his imitation of the *cornet-à-pistons*, and play something from 'Norma' with the chill off. Order!"

This command was accompanied by so sharp a rap on the table with the hammer, that it made a large dent and broke the handle. The shock restored a temporary silence with all except Mr. Newcome, who was found, upon Mr. Manhug's endeavoring to ascertain the source of certain plaintive wailings which he heard, seated under the table, and singing, "The brave old oak," in a most melancholy key, crying between the verses, but apparently with the idea that he was contributing in an important manner to the conviviality. Not heeding him, Mr. Jones twisted a piece of paper round a pocket-comb, and gave the desired imitation, which was a kind of variation of the duet, "Yes, we together will live, will die," merging by a very clever graduation into "Nix my Dolly;" upon the introduction of which popular air all the party who were capable to do so rose from their seats, and stamped and twirled about the room, after the most approved manner of Mr. Paul Bedford, until the night-nurse again made her appearance. But just as she was about to speak, Mr. Muff threw a fifteen-shilling pea-coat at her, which repelled her into the passage, and she was never seen again.

On the proposal of the adjournment to Evans's being repeated, the party rose, and with some difficulty routed out their own Chesterfields and hats, which last were more or less contused from the superincumbent wrappers. Then, having corked Mr. Newcome's face, laid him on Mr. Rapp's bed, and hid the looking-glass, they turned out into the open air.

"Cab, sir?" cried the leader of the nearest stand to the hospital, as he saw our friends approach.

"How many can you take, old fireworks?" asked Mr. Rapp.

"Many as you like, sir. Regler ingey-rubber cab mine is —stretch to anythink!"

Whereupon four gentleman immediately rushed inside, put up the windows, and began to smoke; Mr. Muff climbed on to the box, by the driver, with one of the dressers, whose name was Tanks; and Mr. Manhug persisted in riding upon the back, until finding the spikes made rather an uneasy seat, he scaled the roof, and seated himself upon it. Messrs. Rapp and Jones said they would walk to Knight's for some oysters, and join them afterwards; and the others went home, did worse,or talked about setting off to walk to Hampstead for some country air.

"Where would you like to go, gentlem'n?" asked the driver, having reached the box by the succession of violent efforts peculiar to cabmen.

"Hold your row," politely interposed Mr. Manhug; "Go to Evans's and look sharp about it."

Their progress was not very rapid, for the horses in night-cabs are not over-brilliant; but at length the vehicle stopped at the end of the Piazza in Covent-garden, and disgorged its contents. Rather a fierce argument ensued respecting the fare, which Mr. Manhug offered to toss the cabman for first, and fight him afterwards; but it was at length amicably adjusted, and the party descended to the tavern. Elbowing their way through the guests, they pushed up to the top of the room, followed by one of the waiters.

"Pray order, gentleman!" cried the chairman, as they adjusted themselves with some little noise.

"Well, we're doing it as fast as we can," replied Mr. Manhug, giving directions; "I declare I've got perfectly peckish again."

The room was very full of company, and the various characteristics of the guests would have afforded much amusement to a quiet observer. A large proportion of them were evidently visitors from the country, who thought going to the theatre and Evans's afterwards was "the thing." At the end of the room, a tall gentleman in a white Taglioni, large whiskers, and an overpowering shawl-scarf adorned with some gold posts-and-chains, having ascertained that everybody was looking at him, shook hands patronizingly with the singers, which proceeding he made sure stamped him a man about town, and the star of the assembly. Lower down, four "gents," (there is no mistaking the appellation) in cut-away coats and fierce stocks, were attempting the aristocratic, in which they might possibly have succeeded had their hands been less coarse, and their finger-nails less *dubby ;* and in the alcove of one of the windows was another visitor, who, after various "goes" of grog, was half asleep, and half lost in apparent and unchanging admiration of some cigar-ashes that lay on the table before him.

"Herr Von Joel will oblige us with a song, gentlemen," cried the chairman.

"Bravo, Joel!" cried Mr. Muff, from the end of the room; "fire away, old boy. Lully-lully-lully-lully-liety!"

A sharp rap from the chairman's hammer cut short our friend's falsetto imitation, and the good-humored German, who was at a table in the centre, began his own version of "The Swiss Boy." But here Mr. Muff's unhappy propensity to assist in social melody once more became apparent; and after singing the choruses with his customary exuberance of voice and style, he broke out in the middle of one of the verses, using his own dialect as he had picked it up by ear—

> "To shlingalang, to shlungalong, for blatz a dun aloy
> Stch ner ofe, stch ner ofe ——."

"Order, sir!" cried the proprietor. "We cannot have the harmony of the room disturbed by one party."

"I beg to say I was contributing to the harmony," replied Mr. Muff.

It seemed that other persons entertained a different opinion, for the song stopped, and the attention of the room was immediately drawn towards the cause of the interruption. But our friend's steam was well up; and, nothing abashed, he rose gravely from his chair, and spoke as follows:—

"Mr. Evans, gentlemen, and waiters."

"Sit down, Muff, and don't be an ass," gently observed Mr. Manhug.

"I shan't. I came here to enjoy conviviality, and I mean to do it. Mr. Evans, I repeat, and gentlemen," he continued gravely, "I ask you, is it possible to discuss a roast potato, or enjoy a song, with such a small piece of butter as one of your waiters has brought me? Look here, sir!" And hereupon he exhibited on his fork a pat about the size and thickness of a crown.

"I am very sorry it does not meet your approbation, sir," said Evans, half angry, half smiling; "you had better speak to the waiter."

"I *have* spoken to the waiter, Mr. Evans," replied Muff with emphasis; "and he told me, although small in size, yet its flavor was most delicate, which caused it to go twice as far as pats in ordinary."

"I must beg of you to be silent, sir, and sit down," said the proprietor. "You are disturbing the company."

"The company may go ―― "

What he was about to say was never known, for Mr. Manhug interrupted the speech, by pulling the speaker forcibly down into his chair, in which proceeding he knocked over one of the pewter vases of hot water, which deluged the table, and slightly scalded the knees of two nice young gentlemen, with very clean exuberant collars and no whiskers, who were sitting on the other side, and trying to smoke cigars, without looking poorly. Possibly there would have been a riot; but Manhug apologized as well as he was able, and a comic song commenced immediately, in which an Irishman was made to bless the Lord Mayor, and offer a wish "that his red nose might never set fire to the powder in his wig and blow his brains out." By the conclusion, Mr. Muff's equanimity was completely restored, but Mr. Manhug fearing he would plunge into more alcoholic beverage if he staid—having already imbibed quite enough—ventured to persuade him to depart, in which he at length succeeded. But, before going, he insisted upon giving each of the vocalists his card, as well as an invitation to come and stay a fortnight with him at Clodpole when the shooting season came on, or indeed whenever, and for as long as they liked; and he also shook hands affectionately with Evans, and hoped he was not offended, as what he said was this, that he never meant to insult anybody, but would be happy to see him at breakfast the next morning, and begged he would say what he would like to have. Then, favoring the company present with a slight extemporary solo variation of his own, upon a theme furnished by the last song, he accompanied Manhug to the door, the other students remaining behind. A slight altercation arose upon payment, Mr. Muff protesting against his friend's paying tenpence for two poached eggs, which he affirmed was sevenpence clear profit, and which he was about to turn back and expostulate with Evans upon, if Manhug had not coaxed and overruled him. But having, at last, relieved his indignation, by recommending the waiter to study the "Ready Reckoner" in

Punch's Almanack, he blundered upstairs to the Piazza, where
they met Rapp and Jones, just on the point of descending.

IV.

THE DESTINIES OF MR. RAPP'S GUESTS.—(*Continued.*)

LOUNGING out of Evans's, the first proceeding of the quar-
tette was to form a council under the Piazza to consider what
should be done next; and here, as is usual in the deliberations
of medical students, much confusion prevailed.   Mr. Manhug
proposed an adjournment to his lodgings, where "they could
light a fire and have some more grog."   Mr. Rapp voted for
going to a ball at the Lowther Rooms, having ascertained,
from an imposing gas star in King William street, that such
a festivity was being perpetrated.   Mr. Jones appeared inclined to follow the first proposal; and Mr. Muff, whose excitement was considerably increased by coming out into the
fresh air, leant back against one of the columns and said " he
wasn't going to put up with humbug from anybody; and that
if they intended to insult him, or break friends, they would
find themselves in the wrong box."

"Well, come along then, old fellow," said Mr. Rapp, per-
suasively.

"I shan't come along," was the firm response.

"Then stay where you are," rejoined Mr. Rapp.

"I shall do just as I please," answered Mr. Muff, gravely.
"If I like to go to sleep amongst the turnip-tops in the market, I shall do it."

"Nobody wants to hinder you," said Mr. Manhug; and
knowing their friend's obstinacy was rather peculiar, when he
was at all elevated, the other three walked off, leaving Mr.
Muff gazing at a gas lamp: his condition being not inaptly
described by the inscription over the door of the tavern—
"Evans's late Joys;" which was equally applicable to the by-
gone pleasures and the time of night.

Leaving him for a while to his meditations, we will follow
his three companions.   By Mr. Manhug's persuasion they decided upon going to his lodgings in Alfred-street, Bedford-

square: and accordingly proceeded in that direction, varying the usual route by going through the Rookery, where Mr. Jones informed them they would see some life.

For the benefit of the upper classes, we may state that "the Rookery" is the name applied to a portion of St. Giles's which may be comprised in an irregular quadrangle, bounded by Great Russel-street, Tottenham Court Road, High-street, and a small thoroughfare whose name we know not, down which the unsleeping eye of Grimstone never ceases to watch from the snuff-manufactory. Ladies and gentlemen who visit Meux's Brewery, to see the vats, partake of stout and biscuits, and occasionally break their necks, or tumble into the malt bins, may obtain a glimpse of the Rookery from some of the upper windows of that establishment. They will discover some narrow dirty streets, into which the scavenger's cart has apparently never penetrated, choked up with rubbish of every description, amidst which, a tribe of ragged infants are tumbling about, so intimately assimilated to it, that the unpractised eye at first mistakes them for animated dirt heaps. Tattered articles of wearing apparel are displayed on poles, here and there projecting from the windows, deluded into the belief that they have been washed; and if a view could be gained of the interiors, similar things, patched and ragged, might be discovered upon lines stretched across the apartment; but for this purpose the casements must be opened, as the greater part of its panes have brown paper and pieces of board substituted for glass.

No animals, except the aborigines, are seen in the streets; nor is there a single bird-cage hung out from any of the houses; for the inhabitants are so miserably poor that they can scarcely keep themselves. A ragged hen from Tottenham Court Road once misguidedly ventured within the precincts of the Rookery, and was immediately massacred by the natives in a savage and blood-thirsty manner; since which time poultry has been considered as an apocryphal genus in the district. As evening approaches, dull lights gleam from each of the windows, and a few gaunt cats, with grizzled coats and hungry eyes, occasionally make their appearance, darting like spectres past the startled passenger who has dared to invade this wretched spot; whilst one or two dead rats lying in the road, crushed and mangled, prove that they are sometimes found by chance in the houses; but even this is a rare occurrence, for the very vermin would starve, in such a locality.

Not until after nightfall does the vitality of the Rookery spring into full action. Many of its inhabitants, who live perpetually in dark cellars, are distressed, like bats and owls, with the daylight; many more dare not face it. It is then that a few wretched females, shoeless and unbonneted,—their matted hair twisted carelessly round their heads, and a coarse, dirty shawl hugged over their shoulders,—emerge into the nearest thoroughfare, in the hope of gaining a half-quartern from some idle frequenter of the gin-shops. Squalid children also creep out, in search of what they may purloin— children who never knew what childhood was, but who grew up at once from the baby to the adult, cunning and precocious.

"Now, my ancients," said Mr. Jones, as they turned out of Broad-street, "button your coats, and put your handkerchiefs in your hats."

"I attended my first case somewhere about here," observed Mr. Rapp, "and didn't exactly know what to do; so I stood some whiskey to the lot, and can't help thinking that we all got exceedingly drunk."

"And what became of your patient?" inquired Mr. Manhug.

"Oh, I followed the advice of a celebrated professor, and left everything to nature. That's my general plan in all cases that I don't clearly understand."

Which assertion, not being at all doubted, provoked no reply; the other two merely thinking what a very active partner nature must have proved in Mr. Rapp's practice.

They had not proceeded a great way, when a terrific riot in a house on their right attracted their attention. As the portal was open, (there being no door, in common with the other mansions), Mr. Rapp plunged into the passage, expressing his admiration of a "jolly shindy" of any kind, and was of course followed by the two others. As they entered the back parlor, from which spot the popular indignation burst, a curious scene presented itself. The miserable chamber was packed full of Irish,—all screaming and shouting at the top of their voices; and in the thickest part of the throng, various quart pots were observable, with arms attached to them, wheeling round in eccentric figures before they descended on the heads of unseen individuals. Several ladies were stationed on boxes and other articles of furniture round the room, gazing at the *mêlée*, like spectators at a tournament, whom they perhaps resembled, from the extreme antiquity of their costumes; and it was pleasing to see them encouraging their professed champions with their voices, or occasionally throwing a guerdon of their affections, in the shape of a flat iron or broken candlestick, into the lists; not with any avowed aim, but feeling sure, like a cockney with his eyes shut, that something must be hit out of the lot.

"What's the row?" inquired Mr. Rapp of a gentleman next to him, in a livery of blue blanket, turned up with dirt and whitewash.

"Vot's the hods?" was the reply; "are you crushers in disguise?" Not deigning to reply, Mr. Rapp, by dint of extreme muscular exertion, elbowed his way into the centre of the combatants, Messrs. Manhug and Jones being "the creatures who followed in his lee."

"Ooraw for the svells!" cried one of the insurgents, as he tried to bonnet Mr. Rapp, smashing in his gossamer like a strawberry-pottle; whereupon that gentleman put his *flexores digitorum* into a state of extreme contraction, and, by the sudden extension of the elbow-joint and fore-arm, dealt a violent blow on the face of this aggressor, which eventually ruptured a small branch of one of the vessels which accompany the first pair, or olfactory nerves.

This was the signal for a general change in the attack; and it would have been an awkward affair for our friends, had not a policeman providentially appeared at the door. Beating the mob away with his staff, he immediately pounced upon Mr. Rapp, who was throwing his fists about in wild convolutions, something like a dislocated windmill, hitting whoever came first.

"Who are you?" cried the ex-house-surgeon, as he found himself seized.

"I'll pretty soon show you who I am," returned the policeman: "come out of that and let's see what sort of a story you'll tell the inspector."

Forcing his way to the door, he pulled Mr. Rapp after him; and with the other two at his side, they gained the street—the policeman looking about him for a companion, in the wistful manner which these functionaries assume when one man wishes to take three into custody.

Those conversant with street-rows must be aware of the supernatural manner in which policemen appear at any *émeute*. Nobody sees them approach, and yet there they always are, as if they came up traps in the pavement, or dropped down from the skies. We should incline to the latter opinion, only we never saw them on the wing.

In another minute an additional member of the F division marched round the corner; and as the first turned to summons him, Mr. Rapp took advantage of the circumstance, and with a sudden spring jerked himself from the clutch of his detainer.

"Cut like bricks, and bilk the jug," he cried, in one of those speeches which bother the French authors so much when they try to translate our works. In an instant the three were off, whilst the policeman started after them.

"The street—splits—into—three—at the top," gasped Mr. Rapp, as they darted along the centre of the road. "I'll take—the—middle one—Jones, right—Manhug—left. Now—don't—jib."

The value of this advice was soon visible; for the policemen were so confused at the division of their chase, that they actually stopped for two or three minutes before they could make up their minds which to follow; and this space was sufficient to place the three students out of danger.

No. V.

WHICH RE-UNITES OUR FRIENDS.

ALFRED-STREET, Bedford-square, is a small arterial branch of the great aorta of London vitality, situated amidst the central squares of the metropolis. To describe it surgically, we should say, that, in the event of a gas-pipe aneurism in Tottenham Court Road, which required the pavement of that route to be "taken up," Alfred-street, by communicating with certain other thoroughfares, would carry on the circulation. This is the only accident that could cause a bustle in its usually tranquil purlieus, as at ordinary times no one is seen in it but those who lodge therein; except wandering organists, and retailers of tumbling dolls, chickweed, ground-sel, and water-cresses. First and second floors to let, furnished, varying from twenty to thirteen shillings hebdomadal rent, with six-pence a day for fire, and a shilling a week for boots, abound in its mansions, the eastern range of which is *dos-à-dos* with the western line of Gower-street, separated by a rich valley abounding in coach-houses and horses, chickens, carriages, and clothes-lines, termed a Mews.

Several medical students—principally those attached to the University College—reside in Alfred-street. To discover their residences, it is merely necessary to watch the peregrinations of the boy attached to the public-house at the corner, when he calls for the empty pewters. From some of the abodes he only reclaims a modest pint, from others three or four quarts, with the tops squeezed together as if by a powerful grasp, the handles distorted, and the general contour of the vessel battered and disarranged. There is no doubt concerning the occupiers of these latter houses, which have all apertures for latch-keys in their doors, stands for rushlights in their passages, and attenuated carpets on the stairs. Therein do the sucking Galens set up their *Lares* and *Penates*—their preparations and tobacco-jars.

By some kind of instinctive coincidence, the students who betook themselves to flight at the end of the last chapter, arrived within a few minutes of each other at the door of Mr. Manhug's lodgings in Alfred-street. The occupier himself was the first who got there; and, being slightly elevated by the fresh excitement of the chase, he was found trying very hard to let himself in with a short pipe, whilst he was at the same time insanely endeavoring to smoke his latch-key, which he found would not draw at all, after having used up all his German-tinder *allumettes*, and burnt his nail with the phosphorus in the attempt to light it. The arrival of Messrs. Jones and Rapp put all things to rights; but on entering the passage they found that the rushlight had long since given its last sputter, and all was wrapped in obscurity.

"What's to be done now?" asked Mr. Rapp, in a tone of vexation.

"Ring up the servant," rejoined Manhug, seizing the handle of the area-bell, and pulling it down violently. Fortunately, however, for the slumbers of the domestics, none of the area-bells in Alfred-street are available, or it would go hard with the servants of the lodging-houses, in whatever part of the house those useful menials repose—a point, we believe, which has never yet been correctly ascertained, beyond the suppositions of the most vague hypothesis; unless it be in the long drawers of the kitchen-dressers.

"I'm game to climb up the lamp-post," exclaimed Mr. Rapp, with Spartan heroism.

"Well, go on, then," said Mr. Jones; "Manhug and I will help you."

Aided by various thrusts and heaves from his two friends, Mr. Rapp contrived to catch hold of the projecting ladder rest; and, by a sudden muscular exertion, seated himself across it, and opened the door of the lamp; the accomplishment of which feat so delighted his *amour propre*, that he gave vent to his satisfaction in a few selections from the Macbeth music, as performed at Drury Lane Theatre and the Cider Cellars, under the management of Messrs. Macready and Rhodes. He had got through the "*Many more, many more*," and had broken out in a fresh place with "*We fly by night, midst troo-oo-oo-oops of spirits*," which he was shouting most lustily, taking all the parts himself, when an outline appeared at the corner of the street, whose form there was no mistaking. Seeing which, and not anxious for an interview with another policeman, Messrs. Manhug and Jones—we almost blush to chronicle the retreat—slunk quietly into the passage, and closed the door, leaving Mr. Rapp in his elevated situation, totally unconscious of the new arrival, and chanting, with all due emphasis and effect,

"My little, little, airy spirit—see, see—see, see,
Sits on a foggy cloud, and waits for me!"

"Now, just come down from that," exclaimed a voice from below, which stopped the singer as if he had been shot.

Mr. Rapp looked from his post, and saw the policeman. A close observer might have observed that a slight shock convulsed his frame; 'twas but an instant, for speedily his pride ran crimson to his heart, until he recovered his self-possession; the next moment he boldly uttered, in reply,

"I shan't. Come up and take me down yourself, and when I am down, you may take me up."

This speech evidently puzzled the policeman, who, for the space of half a minute, was perfectly silent, considering how

he should proceed. Then, assuming an air of double importance, he cried out,

"I order you in the Queen's name to come down."

"Oh, nonsense, man," resumed Mr. Rapp, in chiding accents
—"you mustn't take the Queen's name in vain in that way.
I'm sure Albert wouldn't like it, if he heard you; he's remarkably particular upon those points."

"Come down, sir," roared the policeman, getting very
angry.

"Hush! now, don't you," replied Rapp; "I must say with
Mr. Evans, 'I can't have the harmony of the street disturbed
by one party.' I am certain your inspector would not ap-
prove of your kicking up a row like this in the middle of the
night."

"Wait a minute," cried the policeman, moving off in extreme wrath toward the centre of the street.

"I should think so, rather," said Mr. Rapp, taking a
manual observation of his retreating form; "Oh, of course, I
shall stay till you return."

Turning off the gas from the jet of the lamp, which threw
his locality into complete darkness—for the Alfred-street
lamps somewhat resemble the complimentary calls of cheru-
bims—Mr. Rapp twisted himself off from his perch, and slid
down the post. Jones and Manhug, who had been on the
watch the whole time, directly admitted him, and then as rapidly closed the door. In two minutes the policeman returned,
when they heard additional footsteps and much grumbling.
Then, waiting in breathless suspense until the evidence of
their presence grew fainter and fainter, they crept up-stairs, not
deeming it safe to venture out again after their hair-breadth
escapes. Mr. Manhug, with true English hospitality, gave up
his bed to Jones and Rapp; then ingeniously forming a temporary couch for himself, out of carpet-bags, pea-coats, boots,
and sofa-cushions, he also retired to rest, with his intellects
still somewhat confused, but withal conscious of his double
escape, and exceedingly rejoiced thereat. And here then we
will leave them—merely informing you, courteous reader, as
Francis Moore would say, that the next morning the sun rose
many hours before they did.

*   *   *   *   *   *   *

What on earth Mr. Muff did after his friends left him, or
where he passed the night, still remains a mystery. From

careful inquiries, however, made by his friends, rather than from any particulars disclosed by himself (for he appears to have been completely ignorant of all the circumstances), it was learned that a gentleman, answering his description, was found sleeping in a temporary erection of orange chests and nut sacks, which occupied a portion of the eastern end of Covent Garden market. It further seems that the said individual subsequently treated two aged basket-women to a pint of coffee each in a neighboring coffee-house, and afterwards had a bottle of soda water in Long Acre. This was presumed to have been Mr. Muff, who appeared at the Hospital next day in any thing but robust health; and, after contriving to swallow a few oysters, returned back to Clodpole, sleeping nearly the whole way down, which betokened a previous want of rest—the more so, as he travelled in a second-class carriage, where, under ordinary circumstances, any thing like sleep is out of the question.

VI.

HOW JACK RANDALL GOT ON DURING MR. MUFF'S ABSENCE.

POSSIBLY our readers may remember that when Mr. Muff quitted Clodpole to be present at Mr. Rapp's farewell banquet, he left his devoted friend, Jack Randall, to take care of his practice during his absence, having locked up the more powerful medicines and dangerous instruments. That ingenious gentleman acquitted himself admirably, both with respect to the patients and the exchequer; as we shall learn from his own mouth.

It was the evening of Mr. Muff's return; and he was seated in his back parlor with Mr. Randall, in company also with some gin and water, pipes, and the day-book.

"Well," said Mr. Muff, "now tell us how you have managed."

"Oh, uncommonly well to be sure," replied Jack. "You hadn't been gone half an hour before the surgery bell was seized with a violent attack of *delirium tremens*, and a gasping page informed me that old Miss Withers had such a fit of hysterics that they thought she would die before anybody got there. So I bolted off directly, taking a tourniquet and two cupping-glasses with me."

"Why, what on earth did you do that for?"

"Because it looked imposing and professional; when I got there I found the old girl crying, and laughing both at once, and talking an immense deal of unconnected rubbish to six or seven old women who were gathered round her. It is remarkable the propensity old women have to get together, when anything like illness is going on. I soon saw how Miss Withers was, you know."

"How do you mean?" inquired Mr. Muff.

"Oh, all right." The remainder of Mr. Randall's reply was simply pantomimic. His tumbler being empty, he took a copious draught of atmospheric air therefrom, and winked his right eye; after which he tapped the quart stopple bottle that contained the gin with his pipe, and then winked his left eye: the import of these combined actions being that Miss Withers had taken too much of "something which had disagreed with her."

"Well, and what did you do?"

"Why, I said you were from home, having been obliged to meet Sir Henry Halford and Sir James Clark, concerning the Archbishop of Canterbury's rheumatism, but that I knew her constitution and usual medicine, from your books. I put the cupping-glasses on her head, and the tourniquet on her arm, telling the old women these measures would counteract the photographic circulation, caused by too much excitement of the tariff and system in general; and that they must keep her perfectly quiet, or a severe attack of missouri leviathan might supervene—in the mean time I would send her something very efficacious. When I got home I made her three such prime draughts."

"What did you give her then?"

"You see I was not exactly certain about the proper doses of the drugs in the surgery, so I made up the physic after a receipt of my own. I recollected the tub of elder wine that turned sour, so I drew a small quantity, and finding it a little too sharp, mixed up some soda with it, which made a great phizzing, and——"

"Excuse me, Jack: 'phizzing' is not a professional term —you should say, it 'effervesced.'"

" Well, you know what I mean. The soda turned it quite green, and exceedingly nasty—so much so that when I went to see her in the evening, she was quite well. Do you charge her visits?"

"Of course, I do."

"Very good—two visits at half a crown are five shillings, and three draughts, four and six—that's nine and sixpence to begin with ; not quite so bad, I think."

"No, indeed; I call it capital. Did any one else come?"

"Oh, lots. I took out two teeth and broke two in; but they all paid—only a shilling a-piece ; I put the money in the desk. Then one of the Browns, the farmers, hurt himself, and came to be bled, and I think I did it rather."

"You don't mean Jack, you were fool enough to try—why it's a most delicate operation."

"I know that—I felt his pulse, and told him he mustn't think of losing blood from the arm; but if he would take my advice he would go home to bed, put a blister on his back, and a dozen leeches on his side, and you would come and see him in the morning. He did as I told him and now he is laid up safe for three or four days, and the bleeding would only have been a shilling. Is he good pay?"

"We must chance that. At all events we can take it out in geese and turnips."

"What a splendid general practitioner you would have made, Jack!" said Mr. Muff, lost in admiration at these proofs of his friend's genius.

"I believe you," was the reply. "I think now, eventually, that I shall turn to it. Well, I had not been in bed twenty minutes, before I was called up to go to the Union Workhouse. A tipsy tramp had disposed of himself in one of the outbuildings."

"Nonsense! "

"So it was; but he had; so I tried to open one of his jugulars."

"My dear Jack! how on earth did you know where the jugular was?"

"I had not got the least idea, only that it was somewhere in the neck. But it didn't matter—it couldn't hurt him, and there must be an inquest: and that's some consolation."

"I think it would answer to run up to London again, and leave you here, if you go on at this rate," said Mr.

Muff; "have some more grog, old chap. Did any thing else come?"

"Yes—the best joke of all. About four in the morning I was awoke by another ring, and a gentleman in a smockfrock told me that the wife of a cottager, at the other end of the common, was expecting an immediate addition to the last census."

"But you didn't surely go there, Jack?"

"Oh, no—not quite. I said you were not at home, but there was a very clever doctor a few doors off; so he went and rung up old Binks, and he has been there ever since. I would advise you to keep in the way, because if any of his patients send for him in a hurry, you will get the job."

"I do not exactly think that would be etiquette, Jack."

"Pshaw! did you ever imagine that medical men know what etiquette meant? Go into any town where four or five doctors are all struggling for the same living—you cannot think what a generous, liberal-minded, open-hearted set of men they are."

Mr. Muff ruminated on his opinion, with his pipe in his mouth, until he had made out a satisfactory view of the cavern in the Miller and his Men amongst the embers of the fireplace. Then ringing the bell to know what there was in the house for supper, and receiving for a reply from the old woman who looked after his domestic comforts, "that there was nothing," if indeed we may except half a lemon and some cold potatoes, he sent out for some oysters; and half an hour after, he was busily engaged with Jack Randall, endeavoring to scallop them in the tin top of the tamarind jar.

VII.

AN IMPORTANT REVELATION.

WE are compelled, as faithful chroniclers, to state that our friend Mr. Muff has been "done"—regularly sold, and swindled out of five pounds one, at Clodpole Races.

We hasten to report the transaction, in hopes that it may be of service to our subscribers; for, although our Number

will not refresh the universe until the Derby is over, yet the
Oaks, Ascot, and Mousley are still to come.

Accompanied by Jack Randall, Mr. Muff locked up his surgery on the "cup day" at the above place of resort; and leaving word that if anything required his attendance, he should
be found at the winning-post after each race, set off to the
race-course, about half a mile distant.   He has not been there
half an hour before the swindle took place, of which we are
indebted to Mr. Randall for the particulars—Mr. Muff evidently feeling ashamed of his simplicity.

It appears that although Joseph was "well up" in London
diversions and impositions, he had not sufficiently studied the
Physiology of the Race-course.   Randall had left him, to ar-
range with some sporting friends about riding a jibbing mare
in the hurdle-race; and as Mr. Muff was sauntering about the
course, his attention was drawn to a little knot of people who
were crowding round a slight three-legged table, upon which
a man was exhibiting the mysteries of the pea and thimble.
As he had frequently heard of this game, coupled with the
parliamentary proceedings of the House of Commons, he
joined the circle, and, by the politeness of the two bystanders,
who saw he was anxious to inspect the game, and politely
made way for him, got close to the table.

A bird's-eye inspection of the company satisfied him that
he was in proper company.   There was an honest farmer in
spectacles, with a pocket-book in his hand, full of notes, and
a very superior gentleman's servant, in clean top-boots, with a
whip; with two young men of fashion, in blue satin stocks,
brown cut-away coats, with conservative brass buttons, and
patent leather boots, with long toes; and a respectable gentleman in black, who looked something between a butler out of
place and a methodist parson; and lastly, such a dashing,
handsome lady, in a lemon-colored linen muslin dress, beauti-
fully embroidered with sprigs and trimmed with green bows,
wearing a flat gold watch at her waist, not at all afraid of the
pick-pockets, and wafting a perfume of verbena from the
laced handkerchief that could be perceived all the way
up the course — also sporting one of the celebrated twenty-
shilling bonnets which have caused so great an excitement in the Royal Drawing-rooms and the fashionable
world at large.

"Gentlemen, and noble sportsmen," said the professor of
the game, who was a very pleasant-looking man, in a shoot-

ing-coat and freckles: "the condishuns of this curious game is very easy to be taught and to be learnt. If you have a quick eye to trace my movements, which is all the chance I have, and diskiver which thimble the little *pay* is under, you wins; otherwise you loses quite different and per-miskus."

"Now, here's little Jack, the dodger, in his round-house, that never pay no taxes. Here he goes again—vun, two, three, and never say die; right round the corner out of that vun, up the middle, down again, and slap into this vun. Here's the thimbles as loses, and that vun's the vinner, and who says done for a fi' pun note! Come farmer, say the five."

The farmer put his hands in his pocket, and inspected the thimbles—the money was laid on the table, and Mr. Muff looked on in breathless excitement. The right thimble was lifted up, and the farmer pocketed the money, which our friend thought he might just as well have had himself, for he should have lifted up the same; so he resolved to keep a sharp look out.

"Well, gentlemen, continues the man, "I never grumbles at losing, but I'd rather win. Them as don't see don't tell, and them as do, hold their tongues, for luck's the real sports-man. Here goes agin—vun, two, three; it's my place to hide, and yours to find; out of this vun, and who's afraid ? Differ-ent people has different opinions, but it's not unkivered now for any sum you like—who says a flimsy ?"

"I think it is under the one nearest to us," observed one of the conservative cut-aways to Mr. Muff.

"No; I think it's the middle one," remarked Joseph in re-ply.

"I'll go you two," said the gentleman to the player.

"Say the five sir," replied the man, touching his hat.

"No, two;" repeated the gentleman, putting down the money.

"Pull away, sir," answered the player. The cut-away lifted up the nearest thimble, and lost.

"Well, I shouldn't have thought it," exclaimed the gentle-man to Mr. Muff; "what a wonderfully quick eye you must have!"

"I could guess it every time," said Mr. Muff; "wait till he begins again."

"Now, then, for another turn," said the man; "if you've

got no money, you can't play; but if you have, you may win a fortune. Here he is, and there he is, and now he's everywhere. Vun, two, three—out of this vun slick into the t'other. Now, you boys, keep back—I only plays with gentlemen."

As the thimble-man turned to disperse the crowd behind him, the conservative cutaway lifted up the thimble, and showed the pea to the spectators, covering it rapidly again as the player resumed his occupation.

"It's not found out for a ten pun' note," said he.

"It's been seen," exclaimed the honest farmer.

"I know that," said the man; I always shows it to the company. Who's game to bet?"

"Take him, sir," whispered the cutaway to Mr. Muff; "you're sure to win, and I'll go your halves."

Mr. Muff was in an agony of desperation, but he would not bet ten pounds. He therefore wagered the five, and, by so doing, nearly emptied his exchequer.

"I'll move them round once more, sir, if you like," said the player, touching the thimbles.

"No, no," cried the cutaway; "I know your cheaty ways; let the gentleman choose for himself."

With nervous haste, Mr. Muff placed the amount of the bet on the table, and lifted up the thimble under which the "little pay" had been seen. What was his consternation and horror to find it was gone!

"Bless me!" said the cutaway, "what a mistake. Look here, sir, this is the thimble you ought to have lifted; you chose the wrong one."

Maddened with anger at being thus gloriously taken in, "downey" as he imagined himself to be, Mr. Muff raised his heavy stick, and smashed the table with one blow, at the same time seriously damaging the shins of the cutaway; and then rushed from the spot, in the vain hope of finding a policeman.

It is really remarkable, that year after year, victims are still found for the thimble-rig—in many instances, clear-headed and intelligent persons. The whole of the ruffianly gang who compose the party are keen adepts at legerdemain, coarse and horny as are all their hands—the chief marks that betray them. There is no cobbler's wax in the thimbles, neither is the pea magnetic or adhesive: the whole swindle is comprised in an adroit use of the nail of the second finger, whilst the thimble is lifted by the forefinger and thumb. After it has once been covered over you are never sure of it, even if the thimbles are not again moved; for it can be taken up or dropped with the slightest visible motion. In Mr. Muff's case, which is a very common one, the transfer was effected when the man asked "if he should move them again."

Were it a fair, straightforward game, the chances are two to one against you; but played as it is, no one can possibly win. Many of our readers may say, that is all very well, but they knew it before. Probably they may; yet it is evident there are some who do not, or the thimble men would not succeed as they do, year after year, in catching new fools—for fools, and downright idiotic ones, they are.

We must refer our friends to the next number, in order that they may learn what steps Mr. Muff took to retrieve his losses, and how he succeeded—the minute anatomy of which speculation we shall also lay open, with any admonition we may think it advisable to give.

VIII.

AN IMPORTANT REVELATION.—(*Continued.*)

How fortunate it was that no one met Mr. Muff immediately after his loss, recorded in the last chapter, or they would have fared but badly. As he left the thimble-table he rushed off the course and plunged into the alley of canvas pavilions appropriated to the amateurs of E. O., whence proceeded unceasing announcements of "Walk in, gentlemen!—the real French Hap-hazard!—no bars, blanks, or apreas!"—"Roulette! roulette!"—"Rouge-et-noir!" "Mechanical horse-racing, my noble sportsmen!" and the like attractions. He had, however, little inclination for any more heavy bets; yet, in the true gaming spirit, hoping to recruit his fortunes, he was anxious for another speculation of a minor character. Mistrusting the chances of the "Dimunt, Star, Hanker, Crown, Club, and Feather," he paused before a table which held out considerable inducements.

The board that formed it was covered with an elaborately

painted canvas divided into forty or fifty squares, and garnished with artistic representations of hands with frilled wristbands, or rich bracelets, like those whilom used in "The White Cat" at Covent Garden, throwing guineas about as if they were button-moulds, sacks of crown pieces being shot like coals, and purses of red gold that literally appeared to be bursting with repletion. The divisions were all numbered, and corresponding to the number was a prize of money, also pictorially represented, or a prominent NO, symbolical of a blank. The presiding genius of the table was a very grand lady, who stood upon a small stool, under an enormous red umbrella, the chief use of which seemed to be, to shade her bonnet from the sun, and protect its feathers, which were severally colored red, blue, and yellow, the bonnet being green. Before her lay a quantity of money, more or less counterfeit, together with a cash-box of notes and a glass of brandy-and-water; and she wielded an instrument somewhat resembling the "rest" of a billiard-table, with which she raked up the money, pointed to the numbers, and counted the ten dice used in the game. The display of wealth, both real and represented, riveted Mr. Muff to the spot; and as he rested at the side of the table, the lady thus harangued her company:

"The mint, the mine, the raffle, the cornycopy, the springing fountain of gold and silver; venture a shilling, and you may get a guinea. There is thirty-two prizes on the table, and sixteen blanks, and no two numbers alike, and every number as is on the dice is on the table. There is ten dice and fifty numbers—a faint heart never won a fair lady, but as I say, so I do."

"Well," thought Joseph to himself, "this seems fair enough. I'll have a shy at all events."

"Keep off my gold," continued the lady; "my silver I do not vally. I've a wagon-load of this stuff just come in, and I expect another to-morrow night, for my grandmother died this week and left me five hundred pounds, and she means to die again next week and leave me five hundred more. Venture the first lucky shilling, and if you don't get a prize of half-a-crown, a crown, three crowns, or a pound, I'll give you the chance over again or treat you with something to drink."

Overcome by the persuasive eloquence of the lady, and the tempting pile of gold before her, Mr. Muff threw down a shilling, and seized the leather quart-pot which formed the dice-box. Rattling them well up for luck, he cast them out on the table, and the woman proceeded to display her powers of calculation in the following style, separating each die from its fellow, as she enumerated it, with the rake:—

"Two and two is four, and five is nine—nine and two is eleven and four is fifteen, and one is sixteen—sixteen and three is nineteen, and four is twenty-three—twenty-three and five is twenty-eight, and three is thirty-one. Look on the table for thirty-one, young man. Twenty-one is a prize of two sovereigns, but thirty-one is a friend of mine—a blank. Try your luck, win a prize, and give the table a fair name."

Nothing disconcerted, Mr. Muff took another chance, and another, and another, but uniformly with the same unfortunate result. The dice were not loaded, the numbers were all on the table and fairly reckoned—he counted them himself—and yet he never could get a prize. At last, when he had completely emptied his pockets, he vented some oaths at the woman which partook more of condemnation than compliment, and left the table to rejoin Jack Randall.

In placing these two instances of race-horse chicanery before the reader, we wish him to understand that we have not been so much influenced by the idea that a detail of the common slang pertaining to the blackguard *clique* of gamblers who infest our race courses would amuse him, as by perusing it, he might be put on his guard against being caught in the same style as our old friend Mr. Muff. Possibly there may be many who will purchase our number to beguile the journey down to those races about to take place; our *exposé* may cause them to reflect a minute before they play, and look upon the entire range of the games as open, and apparently licensed, robberies, rather than mere games of chance. The one we have just alluded to is, perhaps the most dangerous, because it is the most plausible—let us remark it, as Jack Randall did to Mr. Muff when they got home in the evening; and when you comprehend it, your purchase-money of threepence will not have been altogether an idle investment.

The fifty divisions of the table embrace every number from ten to sixty inclusive—such being the range that can be produced by ten dice. These numbers are not put in regular succession on the board, but run irregularly, as 27, 42, 13, and so on, for a reason which we will render obvious. No. 10 is a prize of 100 guineas—so is No. 60; but to make either of

then crossed over Chobham Common, and got on the Heath the night before the race. We had a little table inside, and played whist and smoked all night. The next day, when we dined, we let down the calash and fed under it. Uncommon good fun it was, too; and the people who hadn't been to the sea-side couldn't exactly make it out, and thought it was a show, which they tried to explore by climbing up the wheels and looking in at the little windows, until we closed the shutters."

And with the like diverting reminiscences they beguiled the journey, until the train stopped at Slough, some forty minutes from the time of starting.

*

No. X.

THE WINDSOR EXPEDITION.—(*Continued.*)

UNHESITATINGLY we hasten to contradict a palpable blunder in our last chapter, which we can only account for, by presuming that Mr. Rapp, from whom we received the report, must have been in a state of extreme ale—for which beverage Windsor is justly famed—and must therefore have *seen double*, which circumstance alone could have brought about the curious jumble made between the Birmingham and Great Western Railroad. If the reader will have the goodness to substitute "the large archway at the side of the Edgeware-road," for "the two tall chimneys at the foot of Primrose-hill," this will bring him once more "in the right train" to go on.

There were several conveyances waiting at the station to transport our friends to Windsor; and they immediately appropriated the greater part of one of the omnibuses to themselves. Manhug and a select few stormed the roof, according to custom; whilst Mr. Rapp persisted in standing on the steps behind, and treating the company generally, and those near the door in particular, with some extempore variations upon a theme of his own composing, on a tin horn which he had brought with him. They crossed the main street of Slough, and then passing through a turnpike and over a bridge, ar-

rived at the commencement of Eton, attracting a little attention from the inhabitants by their antics; whilst the appearance of Mr. Newcome, who still kept his candle-box slung
over his shoulders, provoked a few remarks, less courteous
than comical, from the Eton boys, who were sitting on the
low wall before the college.

After crossing the river, and climbing up the steep hill of
Thames street, the omnibus stopped at the White Hart, and
began to descend its load. Dr. Wurzel immediately called a
council as to what should be the order of the day. Some
were for seeing the Castle—others voted for collecting plants
in the Park—Manhug and Rapp proposed something to eat—
and Mr. Newcome, not knowing exactly what to do, acquiesced
with everybody in turn, and thought their plan by far the
best.

As they were rather hungry, a feed was ultimately determined upon, and they proceeded along the street in quest of
a suitable establishment, thinking the White Hart a little too
aristocratic for medical students.

"Halloo! old fellow! how are you?" cried a well-known
voice as they passed the top of Peascod street.

"Jones, my boy!" exclaimed Mr. Rapp, as he recognized
his old fellow-pupil; "why, who would have thought of seeing
you here?"

"Oh, I am assistant to one of the doctors, and have been
here the last three months," replied Jones.

"The deuce you have: and what sort of a place is this?"
inquired Manhug.

"Um—I don't know exactly—rather rummy and very slow
generally, only to-day happens to be market-day. The Queen
doesn't visit much amongst the towns-people."

"Is there a theatre?"

"I believe you—under the management of Eton College—
and chiefly patronized by the mayor and the military. It
pays very well—I've known as much as ten shillings taken at
the doors."

"Where can my flock get anything to eat, Mr. Jones?"
asked Dr. Wurzel, who was a young man, and, apart from the
school, very fond of fun.

"I'll show you, sir," replied Jones; "close by—try our
fourpenny meat pies, strongly recommended by the faculty.
Jolly shop,—not very ornamental, but uncommonly clean, and
commanding a splendid view of the Town-hall."

"Are the things good?" asked Mr. Newcome.

"I believe they are, too," replied Jones. "You should see Prince Albert walk into the buns here now and then."

"Does he come here, then!" inquired Mr. Newcome.

"Oh, frequently. I've gone odd man with him, many a time, for ginger-beer. This is the place."

Acting upon Mr. Jones's advice, they turned into a shop opposite the market-place, with an eagerness that caused much alarm to a young man who was violently making pies at a dresser, as if his life depended upon it, and who, in allusion to his name, Mr. Jones designated as "The Earl of Lester." Passing into a back room, they were soon supplied with eatables, and whilst at lunch, determined upon their proceedings, one party going with the doctor, to botanize in the Park, and the other remaining to see the town, and Castle, with a promise to rejoin them near the statue, in the Long Walk.

"We term this shop the Windsor Exchange," said Jones. "Everybody that comes to market drops in here to inquire after everybody else; and nobody with large families thinks of going away without a load of new buns to choke their children with when they get home."

As soon as the meal was finished, the two divisions separated, and Mr. Jones having bolted home to give the apprentice directions about certain draughts to be sent out, marshalled Rapp and Manhug towards the Castle. Mr. Newcome also joined them, upon the self-promise of collecting a double lot of plants when he joined the others in the Park.

"Newcome is a great card to draw out," whispered Rapp to their conductor: "try it on."

"All right," said Mr. Jones, winking. "These are the Poor Knights' houses," he continued, pointing to a row of dwellings on their right, as they entered the gate.

"Why are they called poor knights?" asked Mr. Newcome, who was exceedingly anxious for information upon every point.

"I don't know," replied Jones, "unless it is because, like summer nights, they are rather short."

"Ah," said Mr. Newcome gravely, "I never thought of that. Where are we going first?"

"To St. George's Chapel: one of the vergers in black breeches will let us in."

"A virgin in black breeches," murmured Mr. Newcome, not exactly hearing the remark: "how very funny!"

Having entered the Chapel, Mr. Jones got the fresh man into a regular line. First he showed them the stalls, "used," he said, "by the knights for their horses in the desecrating times of the Middle Ages;" and then he stated that all the helmets and banners over them had been hired at a great expense by Mr. Bunn, when he brought out "The Jewess" at Drury-Lane. Then he pointed out the exact spot marked by an illegible inscription, where Thomas à Becket was killed by Quentin Matsys, the blacksmith of Antwerp, who shot the apple from William Tell's head. And, having explained a few more curiosities, they moved off to the Round Tower, "called," as Mr. Jones observed, "The Keep, from being formerly used to lock people up in—a kind of preserve, on a large scale, for human game."

"What a magnificent view!" exclaimed Mr. Newcome, as they reached the top.

"I believe you," said Jones: "there are twelve distinct countries to be seen from here, and more than a thousand invisible."

"Law!" replied Newcome; "and which are the twelve?"

"Let's see. Europe, Asia, Africa, Salt-hill, Virginia Waters, Boulogne, Ditton-marsh, Uxbridge, Jellalabad, Ascot-heath, Tottenham-court-road, and Stoke Pogis," replied his companion all in a breath.

Mr. Newcome did not exactly know what to make of this rhapsody, but he was not inclined to contradict it; so he kept on admiring the prospect, exclaiming, before long, "There is a review going on in the Park!"

"Yes," said Manhug, taking his turn at the chaff, "they have them every three months; but the Parks are a good deal torn about by them. They are the quarterly reviews which cut up things so, that you have heard of."

"Yes—which is Virginia Water?"

"That's it," said Rapp, pointing to a pond in the Park.

"And where is the fishing temple?"

"Oh, it's behind the trees—you can't see it."

"Wasn't it built by George the Fourth?" asked Newcome.

"Yes," continued Manhug, "and considering he was a king, and not used to that kind of work, he did it very well. Do you see that spire? Well—that's the church of Egg-ham, so called from the supper King John made there the night

before his great battle with Sir Magna Carter—you've heard
of him, you know."

"Well," remarked Manhug to Jones and Rapp, as they followed Mr. Newcome down-stairs, "I have met many pumps,
but—now, then, Jones, we'll see the State apartments."

XI.

WHICH IS UNEXPECTEDLY CONCLUSIVE.

DEAR READER—To our utter astonishment—for, like a
pleasant journey, we have been unconscious of our rapid progress—the Editor has reminded us that the last number of
the volume has arrived; an unlooked for circumstance,—
which compels us to finish our subject, like a traveller's dressing-case, "in the smallest possible compass!"

Had we space left, we could have set forth the whole particulars of the Windsor expedition. We could have told
how Messrs. Manhug, Rapp, Newcome, and Jones joined their
companions at the top of the Long Walk, and how they hired
a little boy to carry a good can of ale after them, to promote
their festivity. We could have shown how Mr. Rapp scaled
the pedestal of the statue, and proceeded to scratch his name
on the horse's foot, in which situation he was discovered by a
park-keeper; together with the pleasant dialogue that passed
between them, including how Mr. Rapp called the park-keeper
"an overgrown grasshopper in green plush breeches;" which
so incensed him that he would have proceeded to extremities,
had not Mr. Manhug drawn off his attention by chevying a
large herd of deer all about the pasture, drumming in his hat
with his fist while he ran. How, also, to make up for lost
time, Mr. Jones assisted Mr. Newcome to collect some rare
weeds, until his candle-box was quite full, and wrote most
extraordinary names on the slips of paper attached to them;
such as "*Megalanthropogenesia Grandifolia*," the *Batrach-
omyomachia Longwalkensis*," and the *Gossamer Breadstreeti-
una;* all of which Mr. Newcome treasured up in his mind,
and copied out fairly when he got home the next-day.

Neither should we have omitted to tell how Dr. Wurzel,
having to attend an evening meeting at the College of Physicians, departed by an early train, leaving his pupils behind

him, who kept up the conviviality with such liberality, that they spent nearly all their money, and could not raise sufficient to pay the rail back to London; in consequence of which they walked to Slough, and stowed themselves in a Reading wagon, which deposited them in Friday-street, Cheapside, at an early hour the next morning. These entertaining adventures on the road, and the amusing acquaintance they formed with a man who was traveling to Hampton Court Races with sticks and snuff-boxes, would, we are certain, have caused much diversion. How the man was a disciple of Sir Isaac Newton, and filled his boxes with dirt, that they might fall in the hole by the mere power of gravity; and also how it was a great point to have the throwing-sticks slightly—almost imperceptibly curved—that when flung they deviated from the line intended, and hit the shins of the next snuff-boxman but one, or knocked off an alien Jack-in-the-box or pincushion, on the principle of the Australian crooked lath with the out-of-the-way name, whilom sold at the toy-shops, which had the diverting property, when thrown away, of whirling back, and going through a window behind you, or knocking your eyes out.

All this we could have related, and more; but we must now part company. The wish to render each volume, in a manner, complete in itself, is our sole plea for this hasty termination. Our friends, the medical students, with whom we have been acquainted, on and off, for nine or ten months, have assembled to wish the reader good-by. Mr. Joseph Muff is slightly affected, in spite of a glass of cold brandy-and-water recommended and administered by Jack Randall. He begs to assure the subscribers to "PUNCH" that should their affairs lead them to Clodpole, he shall be only too happy to receive them, when he may tell them, *viva voce*, some more anecdotes of Medical Experience.

The summer session of lectures has nearly concluded; the anatomical theatres are deserted, and the preparations repose in the scientific dust of the museums; whilst the majority of the students are realizing the anticipations of rural frolics and country merry-makings, which they formed during the gloom and fog of the winter course; let us wish them every happiness. And, finally, with gratitude for the kind reception already experienced, and humble solicitations for future patronage, the author of these papers respectfully makes his parting bow.

7

THE

LONDON MEDICAL STUDENT.

SECOND SERIES.

.

INTELLIGENCE OF SOME OLD ACQUAINTANCES.

WITH the return of the anatomical session at our medical schools have also arrived some of our old friends to prosecute their studies. The introductory lecture at our own establishment took place toward the end of the past week, and the majority of our ancient students attended to hear Dr. Wurzel deliver it.

Mr. Muff, on the strength of being appointed surgeon to the Clodpole Union, has established an assistant at twenty pounds a-year. He was therefore enabled to come up from Clodpole with comfort to himself, and brought Jack Randall with him, who has determined upon being a medical man, and as such has entered to the lectures. We may from time to time give a few notices of his career.

At present he is settled, through Mr. Muff's advice, in what he terms a very jolly crib, on the third floor—bedroom and parlor all in one. He pays for what fire he burns, and uses his own blacking and brushes—the former of which he purchases at a penny a pot in the form of paste, thus abolishing the long tolerated imposition of a shilling a-week for boots and shoes. On Mr. Muff's recommendation, also, he buys his own coals at a potato-shed near his dwelling; he fetches and keeps them in his carpet-bag, which looks very respectable, only it makes the lining rather dirty.

By the hour appointed for the lecture every seat in the school theatre was filled. The regular teachers of course occupied the bottom row, and immediately over them the usual ring of old gentlemen with large noses, red faces, and grey hair, who attend all introductory lectures, and are supposed to be governors of the hospital, or house-surgeons of the dark ages. Then there were a great many good young men, raw from the country, accompanied by their fathers, who had determined upon going round to all the schools in succession, and entering to that which appeared to offer the greatest advantages at the lowest price. The old pupils had dispersed about in little parties of two or three each, and were amusing themselves according to their different inclinations. Jack Randall had already made friends with all he considered worthy of his esteem, and appeared quite as much at home as if he had been there for years. The ruling powers had covered all the ledges in front of the seats with a thick coating of paint and sand, to prevent, if possible, the perpetration of any more peculiarly anatomical diagrams upon them by wilful students; but this made little difference to Mr. Muff, who was already hard at work with the stump of a scalpel, hacking out a representation of a figure in a state of suspension by the neck, under which he had written the name of the anatomical lecturer.

Manhug and Rapp came in together, and their entrance was greeted with loud applause by their old friends, which courtesy they acknowleded by taking sights, winking their eyes, laying their fingers along their noses, and other familiar demonstrations of affection, previously to taking their places near Muff and Randall. When they were settled Mr. Manhug took a small box from his pocket, made of wood, and shaped like a pear, from which, with great caution, he produced a blue-bottle fly, having a piece of thread tied to one of its legs, terminated by a little square morsel of paper. He then gave the insect his liberty; and provided a fund of amusement for the class, by its ceaseless flights over the bald heads of the governors and old gentlemen below, much to their annoyance, who could not imagine what on earth the

perpetual tickling could be. As for Rapp, he had brought
the whole ceiling into a state of eruption with lumps of masti-
cated paper, to which he had attached little men by long silks
pulled out from the pocket-handkerchief of a new man who
sat below, quite unconscious of the abstraction.

"How d'ye do, sir ?" cried Randall to a perfect stranger,
who came in at the lecturers' door, looking very frightened,
as strangers always do at a medical school—and with some
reason.

"I am very well, I thank you, sir," replied the newcomer,
with much complaisance.

"That's all right," said Randall, "and so am I. I hope
you'll stand a pot of half-and-half after the lecture."

"I shall be very happy," returned the stranger.

"With a cinder in it, of course ?" asked Randall.

The stranger, not exactly comprehending this speech,
looked much confused.

"Never mind him, sir," cried Muff. "He's a very low
young man—quite lost."

"Never care what he says," continued Randall; "you stand
the Hospital Medoc, and then I shall be very happy to show
you the lions of London in return—the Fleet-ditch, Clare-
market, the outside of the Olympic Theatre, and anything
else that won't cost me anything."

All this *badinage* continued until Dr. Wurzel made his appearance. For what he said, how he was received, and other
diverting matters, we refer the reader to the following pages.

THE

LONDON MEDICAL STUDENT.

MR. MUFF'S INTRODUCTORY DISCOURSE TO THE MEDICAL
STUDENTS.

It will be perfectly useless to give any minute report of the
oration delivered by Dr. Wurzel to his pupils, because all introductory lectures, at whatever school they may be given, always end in the same thing, viz., persuading as many students
to enter to the classes as can be talked over. He told them
that they had made choice of a very harassing profession, in
which the pleasure derived from alleviating the sufferings of
their fellow-creatures would be far beyond any pecuniary re-
compense they might expect, which of course he mentally
agreed in, as well as in the following confession, that he and
his colleagues, who formed the teachers of the school, were
actuated solely by a love of their noble calling, and no affection for common-place coin. Moreover, he indulged his hearers
with a history of all the eminent medical men down to the
present time, from the very celebrated people who never ex-
isted except in museum portraits and Lempriere's Dictionary.
And having said all this, and a great deal more which our reporter cannot recollect, inasmuch as he had been fast asleep
for the last half hour, the worthy professor concluded as the
clock of the hospital struck three, to the great relief of his
audience. Of course there was violent applause, although,
generally speaking, medical students are quiet young men,
averse to anything like noise; and then a violent rush took
place to the dissecting-room.

When they had collected therein, Mr. Muff sent Randall
round with the top of an earthen-ware jar, to collect filthy
lucre for half-and-half; and then, having publicly announced
his intention of saying a few words to the new students, he
commenced as follows:—

"Gentlemen! "

"Don't call names," interrupted Manhug.

"Order!" bawled out Mr. Rapp, thumping the table with a stick which he snatched from a new man standing near him, until a glass preparation-jar danced off upon the ground, and broke to pieces, when it was immediately concealed in the flue of the fire-place. "Order! and hear Mr. Muff."

"Gentlemen," continued our friend, by no means disconcerted, "you have heard a very vivacious discourse from Dr. Wurzel, in which he told you all he thought necessary for you to attend to, in your wish to become leading members of the agreeable and not-by-any-means-overdone-by-numbers profession you have decided upon choosing. Now, I have to beg you will forget everything he said, and listen to me; for I am about to tell you what will be of a great deal of use to you in your future career. Jack Randall, be good enough to poke the fire, put on the leg of a stool to make a cheerful blaze, and pass the fermented."

These orders being observed, Mr. Muff continued.

"The knowledge you will gain, gentlemen, during your studies, will be useful, inasmuch as it will enable you to pass the hall and college; but these points once achieved, you will be anxious to forget all you have learned as soon as you can. Your grand study must then be *human nature*, and the *habits of society*. Be assured that at all times a ready tact and a good address will bear down all the opposition that can ever be offered in the shape of professional knowledge and hardly-earned experience. You will do well to take a few private lessons of the nearest undertaker in the necessary art of fixing your looks and assuming a grave demeanor ; and your spare half-hours may be well passed in learning the most abstruse names of the most uncommon diseases; by the display of which you will flabbergaster other practitioners whom you may be, from time to time, called upon to meet in consultation. Leave vulgar common-place affairs, like measles, whooping cough, croup, and colic, to monthly nurses and small apothecaries; but when you have once written a treatise on the exhibition and beneficial effects of Sesquicarburet of Sawdust in the early stages of Megalanthropongenesia, be assured your fame will soon extend. Gentlemen, I beg a moment's pause in order that I may indulge in a modest drain of the commingled, to wash down that last hard word."

The example set by the lecturer was speedily followed by

his hearers, and when he had recovered his breath, after a protracted deglutition, Mr. Muff went on again.

"You will find depreciation of brother practitioners of immense service, but this must be carefully done, to avoid ever being found out. When you are shown their prescriptions, shake your head, and order something else; which take care to make of a different color and taste. In the great world, the term making one's fortune, implies ruining somebody else's; and, as we all attain eminence by clambering over one another's shoulders, do all you can to push down those above you, for stepping-stones. An illustration of this theory may be seen in the Chinese collection at Hyde-Park Corner, only it is a half-a-crown to go in. Wait until it comes to a shilling, and then imbibe the philosophy there taught. There is a picture of a duck-boat, and we are told that the ducks are called in every night in an incredibly short space of time; hustling over one another like the pittites of a theatre on grand nights. This race for superiority is rendered thus animating, because the last bird who goes in is always beaten by the owner. My beloved bricks, recollect that the world is a large poultry-boat, and be careful, even to cracking your fibres and heart-strings with exertion, *never to be the last duck!* Should this happen, the beating will probably maim you, and you will never be able to recover your lost position.

"I shall now bid you adieu until next week, when I propose to continue this important subject."

MR. MUFF'S INTRODUCTORY DISCOURSE.

The diffusion of useful knowledge which Mr. Muff placed at the disposal of the pupils of his own medical school was felt to be so useful by the students at large, that he had a wonderful audience on the following Saturday, when, pursuant to his announcement, he continued his lecture.

Jack Randall was by this time quite at home, and firmly established in the good opinion of all his companions, who looked upon him as an Artesian well of drollery, from the depth of whose inventive genius a spring of unadulterated mischief

was constantly gushing.   He had somewhat added to his pop-
ularity by a bold *coup* on the last board day, when, in the
face of all the old governors, who were standing about the
hall of the hospital, he drove up to the door outside a hack
cab, holding the whip and reins in one hand, and playing
"Jim along, Josey," upon a second-hand *cornet-à-piston* with
the other—an instrument which stood very high in his notions
of surpassing excellence, because it made a great deal of noise
with a very little trouble.

"Hurrah, Manhug!" he exclaimed, seeing our friend at the
door, "I've nailed a victim—capital case—two ribs fractured
and dead-drunk."

The porter came to the door, and by their united efforts,
the patient, who was the real driver of the cab, was taken out.

"How did you contrive to catch him?" asked Manhug.

"Coming through Seven Dials, I saw a row—a fight between two Cabbies, one of whom had thrown a paving-stone
through the other's window.   The aggressor had just been
picked up from his last round, and was beaten to blancmange.
They were going to take him into a doctor's close by."

"And why didn't they?"

"Because I prevented it.   I said, Don't take him there—
blue-bottle shop and flag-of-distress lamp over the door—
sells soda-powders, horse-balls, pitch-plasters, lucifers, and
penny periodicals.   Hospital's the place, you know, for men
of high reputation—accidents admitted day and night, without letters of recommendation.   So I boxed him up all right
in his own hutch, and here he is."

The man was soon settled in a bed of the accident ward;
but being still too much overcome by beer and beating to give
any account of himself, the next point was, how the horse and
cab should be disposed of—a question which Jack Randall
soon made all right by putting Rapp and Manhug inside, and
driving off to Hampstead for a little air.

But all this is an idle digression: we must return to Mr.
Muff, whose stay in town is necessarily limited from his
rapidly-increasing business at Clodpole.   This ingenious gentleman, then, resumed his post of last week; and, having
tapped the ashes from his short pipe, which he returned into
a tin box and put into his pocket, he indulged in a modest
imbibition of the equally commingled, and recommenced as
follows:—

"GENTLEMEN,—There is a portion of your curriculum of

study which carries with it a subject of such vital importance that it deserves especial notice. I allude to the two courses of lectures upon *Botany* which, by the politeness of the Apothecaries' Company, you are permitted to attend. You must be deeply impressed with the importance of thoroughly understanding the physiology of a stinging-nettle in a case of fracture of the skull; and you cannot but laugh at the pretension of a medical man who would attempt to unite a broken bone without first being able to distinguish a daisy from a chamomile. Nor, I am certain, if thrown upon your own skill, would you willingly attend a case of croup or cholera, unless you were clearly aware that the proper name of a *buttercup* was *Ranunculus bulbosus*—an imposing title, well calculated to raise the importance of such an humble vegetable production, and make it think no small sap of itself.

The lecturers upon Botany—with their diagrams of large green leaves that never grew upon any tree in the world, and collections of half-dead garden-stuff which induces a lament that no rabbits or guinea-pigs are kept to devour it—may be looked upon as scientific Jacks-in-the-green. When summer comes and their sessions begin, you will find they will tell you in their first lecture that 'the productions of the teeming vegetable world furnish us with an inexhaustible fund of scientific and gratifying amusement.' This is their idea. Between ourselves, a man must be exceedingly hard up for friends to find recreation in the society of a cowslip; and whenever I hear the lecturers affirm, with respect to vegetables, 'that they rivet our attention by their admirable combinations,' I cannot divest myself of the idea, that they allude merely to lobster-salad and spring soup.

I believe, in the partially-unexplored regions on the banks of the Thames in the neighborhood of Chelsea, there is a large garden of botanical curiosities. I think I have seen its trees from the steamboat, when I have been going to the 'Bells' at Putney to eat stewed eels. I have been told that lectures take place here—at Chelsea, not at the 'Bells' at Putney— at 8 o'clock in the morning. Possibly, if any of you should ever be sufficiently enthusiastic to get up in the middle of the night and go and hear them, you may be talked into a love of 'puff-aways' or 'what's o'clocks,' (I give the vulgar names,) and return perfect enthusiasts. But as medical students do not generally go to bed at half-past nine, I fear you will never get there. They like to retire to rest with a lark, better than rising with one. But connected with these gardens there is one point of great importance, which I wish you to bear in mind. Should you ever find your way there, do not forget to cultivate acquaintances with the gardeners. A few pots of half-and-half will be well distributed in this cause; for you may possibly find out before you go up to 'the Hall' for your examination, what plants have been ordered up for the purpose of testing your botanical capabilities. You have then only to go home and study them well: the examiners, without doubt, are, like thistles, sharp and downy—but medical students are sometimes downier still."

THE CONCLUSION OF MR. MUFF'S LECTURE.

WHETHER it was that the subject was more entertaining, or that the circumstance of allowing pipes and beer during the oration made it more attractive, we cannot exactly state; but decidedly Mr. Muff got a better audience than the professors of the school. Not only the old pupils attended but all the new men also; who, according to the habits of their class in general, brought their note-books with them, and put down everything he said.

He had a famous trumpeter in Jack Randall, who was becoming more popular amongst the students every day, from his great love of fun, and diverting mischievous propensities. He was in the habit of practising the *cornet-à-piston* regularly in the dissecting room at one o'clock, having installed that quiet instrument in his locker on purpose that it might be always handy.

He had much increased the feeling of veneration towards him, prevalent amongst his companions, by an answer he made to Dr. Wurzel, who one day inquiring, half in joke, half in earnest, what he was about, received for a reply, "that he was trying to set Cooper's Surgical Dictionery to music, for performance at the Oxford-street theatre when it opened."

"I think," said Randall, seeing the Professor somewhat flustered, "that much good may be done in this way. I propose opening a medical theatre, where the performances shall be such as may amuse the students, and instruct them at the same time. I would open with 'Concussion,' a tragedy in five acts, to be followed by the 'St. Vitus's Quadrilles;' after which a farce entitled 'Smoke and Toothache;' the whole to conclude with a grand pantomime of action, entitled 'The Imp of Epilepsy, or Harlequin and Delirium Tremens.' I think the proposition a good one, which the Lyceum ought to jump at."

There is a tradition, also, that the matron of the hospital offended him by some severe remarks she made, in conse- quence of having overseen him taking hot potatoes for lunch from the trays which were going up stairs with the dinners for the patients ; and subsequently chucking the servant under the chin, and telling her that she was prettier than her mistress.   Whereupon Mr. Randall first stole a dead monkey which had been bought cheap of a keeper at the Zoological Gardens, to make a skeleton for the Museum of Comparative Anatomy.   Next he painted it green, and having shut it up in a hat-box which belonged to Mr. Widdy—a new man who was very particular about his clothes—sent it by the Parcels' Delivery to the matron, with the united compliments of the life governors and house apothecary—the latter being a pious young man, who had lately published a work about religion and kidneys.   This waggish trick threw the poor woman into a wonderful series of fits, which occupied all the tender assi- duity of the secretary for some hours—indeed there was a slight suspicion that they had a matrimonial design against each other.

Being suspected — and with some plausibility — of this frolic, — everything that occurred in the school, if par- ticularly mischievous, was placed to his account.   And yet, with all this, if there was a prize or honorary certificate to be contested for, Jack Randall always got it, although not a soul ever saw him reading.   The professors could not help this, although they would sooner have bestowed their rewards upon the good young men who "minded their books,"—the sober students with black frock coats and thin legs, who put- tered after them around the wards, like ducks going to a pond, with stethoscopes in their hands, and big books under their arms to look learned.

Previously to Mr. Muff's again commencing his lecture, Randall went around and beat up all the pupils he could find; and then coaxing the old men, and frightening the new ones into subscribers, laid in the usual quantity of Barclay's bar- ley water, (as he termed the commingled), and then told Muff

to begin ; whereupon that talented individual commenced as
follows:—

" Gentlemen,

"Having given you some wholesome advice upon various
portions of the studies you have come up here to pursue, or
which your friends think you have—being all the same thing,
provided they have furnished you with the money—I will
now offer a few remarks upon your education, and I am sure
you will feel wonderfully better after them.

Private lessons in practical chemistry you will find very advantageous, if they only enable you to watch the evaporation
of nothing from watch-glasses on hot sand, or discover arsenic
in stomachs where it is not. I had a course of private instruction myself; when it was finished, I could blow a glass jug almost as well as the man at the Adelaide Gallery, and poison a
sparrow with chlorine gas in a manner marvellous to behold.
All this must be learned to enable you to pass; but when that
triumph is achieved, burn your notes, sell your books, and buy
a grave morning-gown; and a brass door-plate; furnish your
surgery at an expense of five pounds, and have put up a night-
bell that can be heard all over the street; get some convivial
friend, whose habits lead him to be about at unreasonable
hours, to give it occasionally a good pull. If they sold potted
assurance as they do shrimps and bloaters, you would do well
to lay in a good stock; but as it is an article usually manufactured at home, take a few lessons in getting it up, from the
leading members of your profession, and become great, even
amongst the Tritons. But even then do not relax in your endeavors to insure a good practice; but recollect, it is far more
difficult to keep a position than to attain one.

Whether you dissect or not, always tell your friends in the
country that you do; and then, when the tin runs short, you
can often draw upon them for the price of an extremity, varying it as occasion may require. You will not find that minute
knowledge of anatomy which you are expected to acquire of
any use to you. Great accidents, in London, always go to
hospitals; and in the country, are always sent up to London.

Above all, never get off your beer. The archives of Apothecaries' Hall do not present one instance of a man being rejected who stood a pot of half-and-half when he was asked.
And, in commencing life, do not be discouraged; for starting a practice is very like kindling a fire in a Dr. Arnott's
stove—the chief difficulty is to begin. And, with all the as-

surance I wish you to possess, do not be too anxious to be thought brilliant. Dulness and wealth, poverty and genius, are each to each synonymous. No man ever yet rode in his carriage who wrote a poem for his livelihood; and we may estimate talents of intellect in an inverse ratio to talents of gold; namely, that whichever way you take them, as one predominates, the other sinks.

In conclusion, I beg to drink all *your* good healths, and the perpetual indisposition of your patients—if ever you get any."

8

THE MEDICAL STUDENT.

NEW SERIES.

CHAPTER I.

MERELY PRELIMINARY.

For the first time since we have been permitted to supply continuous papers to the columns of PUNCH, we have discarded the term *physiology*, from the head of our articles. It is true we borrowed it from France, and as long as we kept it to ourselves in England, it was all very well; but a crowd of imitators—professors of the sincerest flattery—have scrambled after us, including a contributor to the *New Monthly*.

"The cat may 'μ,' the dog will have his day;" and we now drop the title, not yet considering ourselves quite sunk down to the level of the lady-bird humorists of the pincushion school of literature, who, with one exception, supply that periodical.

With the exception of discarding this word, then (with a full permission for those to make what use they can of it who stand in need), we shall go on precisely as heretofore, in our usual manner; unshaken even by the amusing attempts to 'elevate' our style made in the fashionable morning paper, with its nice affectation of aristocracy—its nervous quivering and sensitive shrinking from the least contact with the everyday and common-place; its pretended ignorance of natural society, and its alleged inability to exist anywhere but in the perfumed boudoirs of May-Fair, with the coarse day-light modified by rose-colored curtains, and the vulgar air overcome by the incense of costly pastilles.

The present period of the year abounds in subjects for the exercise of that genius peculiar to the writers of small poetry for annuals and pocket-books. The fall of the leaf is, of course, the first thing that suggests lyrical effusions to their minds, from the advertisements of Rowland's Kalydor, and cheap tailors, in the newspapers, to "Stanzas on an Autumnal Evening," in a fashion-book; and they write about the brevity of man's life—how one race succeeds another, the return of spring, and other petty and affecting sonnets. We will take an analogy, but in prose, from the same source, in speaking of the medical students—with the exception that they succeed each other, just at the time when the leaves cut their sticks, or, more correctly, their stems and branches; and, in consequence, new faces are always to be met with, about this period, at the medical schools.

Our old friends Muff, Manhug, and Rapp, with their companions, have at last departed—like certain actors, they have had many farewell appearances, but now we shall never see them again. Jack Randall is the only link remaining that connects the chain of new men with the past; in fact, he describes himself "as the last trump card of the hospital pack that has now shuffled and cut itself; and he may be well defined as the Knave of Arts, or Dodges." He is indefatigable in his endeavors to arouse the pupils to a sense of their duties, and a proper degree of spirit in conducting themselves as becomes medical students in general, and those of London in particular.

The first information of the proceedings at the school, with which we can furnish our readers, will be better conveyed in a letter sent by Randall to Mr. Muff, a few weeks after the old party had left the establishment. This invaluable document was written upon several leaves of paper, clandestinely torn out of a note-book belonging to a freshman who sat at his side in the class, and fastened together with pins and wafers. The despatch ran as follows:—

MR. RANDALL'S LETTER.

"To Joseph Muff, Esq., Surgeon, Clodpole.

" Ullow, my Boy!

"Here we are again—how are you? *Scribo has paucas lineas* (you see I am working at my Latin) during the lecture now going on upon "the reflex nervous function;" which, as I merely hope to practice as a surgeon and apothecary, will be of as much use to me hereafter as the minute anatomy of the moon. The subject has now lasted for six weeks, and does not seem likely to finish for as many more. However, old Twaddletongue thinks I am taking copious notes of all he says—so it is just as well.

"I am anxious that you should know how we are getting on, which is pretty well considering, although there has been an immense importation of dummies from the country. They seem, however, very tractable; and I have got them to leave off shoes, wear straps, adopt short pipes whilst they are at work, and subscribe for a set of single-sticks and boxing-gloves, by which, I tell them, they will understand the demonstration, and learn the action of the muscles better than from all the books, lectures, and diagrams ever printed, given, or invented. I have also contrived to dispose of my medical library to them upon very advantageous terms, and I bought a case of scalpels at the pawnbroker's—you remember uncle Balls—which I sold immediately afterwards, for a pound, to a young gentleman red-hot to commence his first dissection. I also put a skull up to be raffled for by twenty members, at a shilling each. I only got nineteen, so I threw the other myself, and won it, as well as all the money. So you see we are going on in the right way.

"We have an immense card here in the shape of a new man —a Mr. Cripps—with whom I think we can have some fun. He has entered the profession rather late in life, and works like a horse, taking in all sorts of lies you choose to tell him, for the sake of information. He bought a box of chemical experiments the other day, and as he chanced to leave it in the pupil's reading-room, we changed all the tests. You cannot think what a hobble it has got into him—all he thinks will be red, turns green, and all the blues are pink, whilst he nearly blew himself up yesterday, through rubbing together some hydro-chlorate of potash and sulphur in a mortar, which of course exploded. This was because we told him it was the best way to make calomel, which they would be certain to ask him about when he went up to 'the Hall.'

"Some of the men here are talking about starting a medical society, to argue about different cases, once a week. I am drawing up a lot that never happened to get the knowing ones into a line, who read long papers which they copy from books, and call their own. Of course all this must be knocked on the head. I shall wait quietly until I get a majority on my side, and then some evening I shall vote that the funds be appropriated to the formation of a harmonic society, at which I have no objection to be the chairman.

"The nice, good, young men of our hospital are very angry with PUNCH, for writing about Medical Students. We have several hungry young physicians, who, having nothing to do, hang about the wards, and potter after the professors, in the hope of one day being sub-officers, or medical attendants, to a gratuitous dispensary. Well—everybody has his object of ambition—this is theirs. They say PUNCH has only shown up the students in their worst light; perhaps they will favor him with their notions upon the subject.

"I am going to have a hammock slung in my room, for any friends who may come to London and want a bed; so when you get mildewed and rusty by staying at Clodpole, run up for an evening and give us a look in. If anybody there should annoy you, let me know, and I will send them down a barrel of oyster-shells, or a two-dozen hamper of cracked bottles, by way of a Christmas present.

"Good-bye, old fellow. Always keep your powder dry, and have plenty of black-draught boiled. Wishing you every epidemic and contagious disorder that can infect the rural districts, believe me to remain,

"Yours, no end of sincerely,

"JOHN RANDALL."

––––––––

CHAPTER II.

OF MR. SIMPSON BRIGGS.

IT is generally the custom of biographers to commence their notice of any individual with a mention of his birth and family, or at least some particulars of his early days; but in the present case it is impossible to do so.

Although Mr. Simpson Briggs was as well known to the pupils of the school as the porter of the hospital, or the bust of John Hunter,—the former personage, however, never recollecting any of them in return, unless they gave him half a-crown at Christmas,—still nobody was aware when he first entered his name as a student of the establishment, or indeed, commenced the caricature of his education generally. Some years back, when a party of medical lecturers out of place, opened a cheap school up some court, as the "Arena of Anatomy," Mr. Simpson Briggs came there to dissect "just before he went up." The concern did not pay, and the classes broke up after two sessions, one or two of its professors instituting the "Metropolitan Theatre of Medical Education," and at the introductory lecture, there was Simpson with the same old black note-book—the same small uncomfortable ink-bottle—and apparently the same old steel pen (contained in the same handle), drawing such diagrams as his inventive genius led him to put down, and fancying that he was taking notes.

Although the new school offered considerable advantages, with the option of entering at once "to all the lectures necessary to pass the College and Hall," for fourteen pounds, or something of the kind; and although one of the professors could lecture on everything, still the "Metropolitan Theatre of Medical Education" did not flourish, and when, at the end of the course, the six lecturers shared forty-five pounds amongst them, they were so disgusted with the little rush of students their talents had induced, that they retired in dignified contempt from the lecture-room. Subsequently some went abroad "for the benefit of their wives' health, which was very delicate," and others, not at all proud, opened blue-bottle shops at the corners of streets in "populous and rapidly-increasing neighborhoods," and one of an aspiring mind christened his establishment the "North South East and West London Self-supporting Dispensary," with vaccination direct from the cow, advice gratis, and shilling tooth-drawing. A very thin young physician, in shoes and spectacles, attends for two hours each day to give the gratuitous advice; and a drudge, at nothing a year, with permission to attend lectures, was stuck in the shop to look after the retail, which included tamarinds, lucifers, and Windsor soap.

When the last-named undertaking tumbled to pieces, Mr. Simpson Briggs was not seen for some time. At length one day at Stanley's lecture some of the Bartholomew's men who knew him well, were delighted to see him make his appearance, with his note-book as heretofore, a new great-coat, and a fresh snuff-box, something about the size and shape of a portable shaving apparatus, with a looking-glass in the lid. In answer to my inquiries, he replied, that he was come there to dissect a little, "just before he went up," and that he had entered as house-pupil to a *grinder* in the neighborhood—a glorious chap, who allowed pipes and half-and-half during his examinations, holding his classes in the parlor of some public house, and knew all the "catch-questions" of Apothecaries' Hall, as well as having copies of all the prescriptions which the men presenting themselves had to translate.

Two winter seasons passed by, and still Mr. Simpson Briggs was at his post. He was perpetually dissecting, or rather marching up and down the room in a black apron and oil-skin sleeves, somewhat resembling a butcher who had been dipped in a tub of ink, overlooking the men who were at work, and fancying himself a pattern of industry. Nor did he neglect attending the grinding classes; but he was principally remarkable for never knowing anything in the world about the subject he was examined upon. With this tardy imbibition of knowledge, it is more than probable that he would have remained there many years; but the grinder got elected to some permanent parochial and medical situation, which being previous to the New Poor Law Union regulations, was worth his acceptance; and Mr. Simpson Briggs was again thrown upon the wide medical world.

It was a short time after this event that he entered to the school; whose students and transactions we have from time to time chronicled in our columns. During the days of Muff, Manhug, and Rapp, he was little known, being naturally of a retiring disposition, although nowise disaffected towards half-and-half. But now they had left; and Jack Randall being rather put to it for acquaintances who harmonized with his own convivial temperament, soon got very friendly with Simpson, both agreeing in their love for everything like leisure, and a distaste for all kinds of hard mental industry.

"I say, Simmykins," said Randall one day to Mr. Briggs, with whom it will be seen he was upon tolerable terms of intimacy, "have you been long at this fun?"

"Above a bit," answered Briggs. "I have seen the rise and fall of a few schools."

"And why don't you go up?"

" Because I don't feel confident. I think, though, I shall
begin to read next Monday."

For seven years had Mr. Simpson Briggs been going to begin to read next Monday.

" Why do you want to know?" he added.

" Because," said Jack, " I'll begin to read with you. I can
study better with another fellow than I can by myself. Is
the heavy good in your neighborhood?"

" Slap—and such prime bird's-eye at the corner shop. When
will you come?"

" Why, whenever you like: I'm always game," replied
Randall.

" Well, then—say to-morrow night."

" Ah—to-morrow night—I can't. I'm going to a concert
in Drury-Lane, and a ball at the Lowther Rooms afterwards;
and I don't think I shall read much after that."

" Well, the next night, then."

" Let's see. The next night a man in Lincoln's Inn has
asked me to punch and rats."

" Punch and rats!"

" Yes; in his rooms—a regular lark—I believe you. He
buys some rats and hires a terrier. We let them all loose in
the room, and then get on the shelves of the book-case to see
the fun."

" Who's your friend?" asked Mr. Briggs.

" Such a brick! his name's Warment. He wants the chambers of the man underneath him, so he has put up a set of
gymnastic poles in his own rooms, and a lot of us meet there
to exercise. I think we shall drive him away soon."

" I should think so," observed Simpson.

" If he don't take the hint, we shall get up quintets for the
cornets-à-pistons."

" Well, I see you won't come this week; I shall begin, however, as soon as I have finished ' Pickwick.' Good bye."

And Mr. Simpson Briggs having put on his apron and
sleeves, and walked about the dissecting-room for a quarter
of an hour with an old scalpel in his hand, singing something
from " Norma," with his own words, finally went home to
dinner, satisfied that he had done his daily work with credit
to himself.

CHAPTER III.

OF THE LODGINGS INHABITED BY MR. SIMPSON BRIGGS.

WHEN Mr. Simpson Briggs first came to town, he took up his abode in a mansion, whose various rooms were dedicated solely to the purpose of lodging medical students; and of course a very quiet, well conducted, and respectable house it was. Here then he pitched his tent, or more properly, pitched his things down, for he was not over tidy in the arrangement of his wardrobe in the drawers, generally choosing to keep his clean shirts in the closet with the candles and bottled porter, and his clothes in his trunk in company with odd bones, short pipes, and scrap leaves of various "Anatomist's Guides," and "Student's Companions."

The rooms on the separate floors were all alike, except in the rents; and by describing one, a just idea may be formed of all. The landlady and the furniture had both seen better days, as landladies and furniture generally have. The bed-curtains were of dark glazed calico to keep clean a long time, and not show the dirt when they ceased to be so; the dingy walls were redolent of tobacco; and there was, in the sitting-room, a dark old-fashioned half-round mahogany table, whereon was to be seen a Quain's Anatomy, a scapula, a broken scalpel, a sixpenny song-book, and sundry circles of evaporated moisture, somewhat about the circumference of the bottom of a quart-pot. The pattern of the carpet had long been obliterated, and its colors had now settled into a very neutral tint, variegated with mud. The looking-glass had been scored all to pieces with diamond rings whenever any of the tenants had been fortunate enough to possess such articles; a few pictures of that elaborate and entertaining kind, only met with in lodging-houses and brokers' shops, adorned the walls, and you have a very fair idea of the apartments which Mr. Simpson Briggs rented at fourteen shillings per week.

Although the house was situated in a very quiet street, yet various internal noises were perpetually occurring to prevent a monotonous tranquillity, depressing the minds of the inmates. The servant was usually called up by a summons over the stairs, from the various floors, as all the bell-pulls had disappeared in times of the most remote antiquity; and occasionally a noisy clattering down stairs agreeably broke the silence, as a student slid down the last flight, a species of descent much in vogue with the tenants, by which the top rail of the banisters had been worn as smooth as polished mahogany, and the mat at the bottom of the stairs lacerated in several places by receiving the first shock of their heels when they landed in the passage.

The spot of earth on which this interesting tenement stood, was in that wide locality commonly known as "over the water," — a territory principally appropriated to medical students and actors, the latter of whom may be seen in crowds upon Waterloo Bridge about six o'clock in the evening, on their way from their mysterious abodes to the theatres; and who may also be met again, if you choose to wait for them, about midnight, retracing their steps homeward. The nearest clue we can give to Mr. Briggs' first abode is, that you went over Waterloo Bridge to get to it; which circumstance afforded great amusement to those gentlemen who honored him with their acquaintance when they came to call upon him. The tolls were not then reduced, and they usually stopped a few seconds to hold a little converse with the pikeman, offering to toss him whether they should pay twopence or nothing apiece to go over. This was always refused very surlily; and then they would ask him which was the lowest he could take for permission to drown themselves from off the bridge, and if it was more expensive to try hanging, by way of variety. And sometimes when Mr. Simpson Briggs had been supping at Evans', and was going home very jolly, he would enquire of the pikeman if he had seen a gentleman go over that evening, in a black coat and short Wellington's, with a cotton handkerchief in his hat, because if he had, he wished his compliments to be given to him when he came back again. And, if he had friends with him, they would make a few remarks upon the flourishing state of the bridge-funds, and the immense fortunes the shareholders were reaping from them; and the last who went through the turnstile generally spun it round as he passed, with a force that sent it turning and clicking for the next two minutes; to the great anger of the toll-keeper, whom the constant revolving of the gate before his eyes had rendered very bilious and irritable.

Well, Mr. Simpson Briggs, located at this lodging for four or five winters, going home every summer for the purpose, as

he assured his friends, of a little country tranquillity to recruit his health, and enable him to work very hard against
the ensuing course, at the end of which he thought about
going up for his examination at Apothecaries' Hall. At
length, as we have before stated, he entered to the school
which Muff and his companions patronized ; and as the present lodging was too far, and his landlady appeared going to
die, or fail, or something of the kind, he packed up his goods,
which were comprised in a carpet-bag and a fishing-basket,
and emigrated to another quarter of the town; having first
written to Jack Randall, to beg if he would see if there were
any cheap apartments in the neighborhood likely to suit him.

"I think I have got a crib that will do for you," said Jack,
when his acquaintance came to the school one morning,
"there's only one thing against it."

"Well, what's that?"

"Only the landlady's a very pious old woman,—all religion
and rheumatism—she don't like much noise, and says she
won't take any medical students to live in her house, because
they are such rackety dogs."

"Well, I don't think so," replied Simpson.—"How people's
opinions do differ ! But I say, Jack !"

"Now then, throw it off."

"She need not know I'm a medical student."

"That's what I was going to recommend. Say you are a
clerk in a bank—the clerks in the bank are always very esti-
mable young men."

"Well, that might do," replied Mr. Briggs, after about a
moment's reflection. "But I say, Jack—suppose she sees any
bones lying about, clerks in the bank don't study osteology."

"But you mustn't let her see any," returned Randall.
"Learn your anatomy from pictures—that's what I always
do. The rooms are cheap enough ; ten shillings a week for
the whole *suite.*"

"And what does it consist of?"

"A parlor and a turn-up bedstead, with a recess to hang
your clothes up in. It is on the first floor, too."

"Now, if I hire it," said Mr. Briggs; "don't you be a fool
and let out that I am a medical student."

"You may trust me," replied Randall. "You certainly
don't look much like one with that old-fashioned mug of
yours. I should take you for forty."

"And you may not come kicking up shindles there the first week or two," continued Simpson.

"You need not be afraid," returned Jack. "I am going out of town for a few weeks. You will see nothing of me until you are firmly settled in the old lady's good graces."

In a few days, Mr. Simpson Briggs having assured the lady of the house that he was an extremely well-conducted young man, of regular habits, and respectable connections, was comfortably installed in his new lodgings; and fearful his father should begin to think it was time he went up for his examination, he wrote him a long letter, telling him how very hard he was working, and what a flattering *finale* he expected to his approaching examination. All this his father was very glad to hear, for Simpson was now approaching his sixth anatomical session; and, moreover, as he had entered the profession rather late in life; it may very readily be imagined that he had not too much time to spare.

He was much astonished, the first night he entered his new house, to see a large chest in the middle of the room, apparently put there for the purpose of being in everybody's way; but he was a great deal more surprised, on lifting up the lid to see what it contained, to discover that it had no bottom, but that he could see right down into the room below. He immediately rang the bell, to inquire the cause and intent of so strange a piece of furniture, and equally singular communication between the first and ground floors. The old lady who kept the house, and who could talk anybody deaf, began a long story in reply, of the state of her affairs upon her husband's death, and finally came to the point, by affirming, that when she first took the house it had been a cook-shop, and the chest was a species of contrivance through which the plates of meat and vegetables were sent up from the shop below to the dining-room, which part of the establishment Mr. Simpson Briggs' room once formed. She added that he had nothing to fear, as there was a very nice gentleman below, who belonged to some house in the city; and he could always lock the chest if he chose, and thus shut off all communication.

Mr. Briggs professed himself perfectly satisfied with this explanation; and in another four-and-twenty hours was quite at home in his new domicile.

CHAPTER IV.

OF THE MANNER IN WHICH JACK RANDALL AND MR. SIMPSON
BRIGGS DISTINGUISHED THEMSELVES IN PUBLIC.

ONE fine afternoon, towards the close of the session, there
was a notice put up on the board where the public information
was generally posted, stating that Mr. Poddy, the anatomical
lecturer, could not meet his class that day at two o'clock as usual.
The reason assigned for his absence was an important post-
mortem examination, some little distance out of town; and
this was subsequently found to be correct, the subject in question being a very fine turkey at a friend's house with an accompanying piece of more minute dissection in the shape of
a saddle of mutton. The question of what they should do
immediately rose among the students.' Some of them, who
were expecting their examination shortly, went home to read;
but the majority, including Jack Randall and Briggs, thought
it best to stop and indulge in a little harmony and half-and-
half in the dissecting-room. People of delicate nerves or fine
feelings might perhaps imagine that a more fitting locality
might be chosen for conviviality than the spot just mentioned,
but as medical students cannot in general afford very fine feelings, and are only conscious of the existence of nerves in the
extremities that come under their hands for dissection, they
are not very particular respecting the scene of their revels.
Accordingly, our friends were in high glee before a quarter of
an hour had elapsed. They had drawn a table towards the
fire, round which they were assembled, the article of furniture being literally a festive board, and a goodly circle they
formed. Jack Randall was, of course, in the chair, or rather
on the highest stool, and was entertaining the company with
the account of a row he once got into at Epsom races, where
he fought four thimble-rig men at once, and was obliged to
sleep all night at some particular part of the Warren, in consequence of being too much overcome by poverty and brandy-
and-water to get back to town. At the same time he illus-
trated the respective localities connected with the event, by
drawing plans on the table in half-and-half with his finger.
Mr. Newcome, who had now arrived at his third session, was
seated on one side of the fire-place, using a fire-shovel to cook

some "brown bait," as Randall termed a bundle of sprats which lay on the mantel-piece. Mr. Beans, a man from the country, next told a story, instead of singing, about some adventures he had when he was an apprentice, which nobody could recollect when he had finished, but which, nevertheless, Mr. Beans took great delight in narrating; quite unconscious that, during the recital, Jack Randall was filling the pocket of his apron with sawdust, cinders, and all the heads and tails of sprats that he could collect. Then after much pressing, Mr. Simpson Briggs indulged the company in the exhibition of various artful problems and keen puzzles, with short bits of tobacco-pipe; and concluded by singing a song—a crime of which he was only guilty after the second pint—involving many curious speculations on the respective comforts enjoyed by the Pope and Sultan; and concluding with the affirmation that he would sooner be himself—Mr. Simpson Briggs—than either of them. Mr. Newcome applauded the performance, by rattling the poker between the bars of the grate; and Mr. Beans, who was getting sentimental at the last verse, contented himself with marking the time, in graceful measure, with his pipe; whilst he threw a glance of mingled interest and affection at a crumb of Abernethy biscuit that lay on the table.

As the contents of the pewters disappeared, the mirth and noise gradually increased. The choruses, which had hitherto been sung in time and tune, grew louder and more prolonged, until every one joined in at the top of his voice, with any particular air or words that came uppermost. Jack Randall took upon himself to conduct the orchestra, which he did à la Jullien, with much satisfaction to himself, using a *humerus* as a baton; and Briggs kept up a pleasing accompaniment by rattling a vertebra and a penny-piece in a quart pot. At last, they kicked up such a tremendous riot, that the lecturer on the Practice of Physic, who had been holding forth to a class of five, in the theatre, since three o'clock, sent in word by the porter, to say, that if the gentleman did not immediately vacate the dissecting-room, and either go home, or come in to his lecture, he would report the whole of them to the Board of Governors. Whereupon, choosing the least of two evils, the majority rose to go home, and Jack Randall and Briggs, feeling somewhat inclined to feed, began to think about dinner, and started for the eating-house they usually patronized, in company with Beans and Newcome. The *restaurateur's* was not far off, and they all entered, one after another, like policemen, stamping on the floor in such regular time, as they marched to the end of the room, and with such energy, that they frightened all the other customers, and caused one gentleman of delicate fibre, to pour his pint of porter into his hat, whilst he looked another way after our friends.

The dinner passed off as most eating-house dinners do, very hastily; and the reckoning being settled, they rose to depart. Previous to this, however, Jack Randall emptied the salt-cellar into the decanter of Preissnitz as he called it; whilst Briggs, who was getting rather jocose, and whose hand very much resembled a shoulder of mutton cut into five strips, squeezed the tops of all the pewter pots together, having first filled them with potato-skins.

Beans and Newcome here left them, for they were working for the anatomical prize, and had each invested a shilling in the purchase of half a pound of coffee, to keep them awake whilst they made out the diagram they had copied at lecture —a series of elaborate drawings, which their landlady presumed to be puzzles, or plans for getting into the Mazes at Hampton Court and Rosherville Gardens. Jack Randall and Briggs therefore were left to themselves, and not feeling much inclined to go home, agreed to wander about for any amusement chance might turn up. At last they got into Clare Market, and this refined quarter of the town offered them no end of subjects for their temporary drolleries; as they indulged in unmitigated chaff with the keepers of the stalls that bordered the pavement; and who had illuminated their wares with tallow candles sheltered in paper bags, that cast a mellow and subdued light over the gasping flounders, consumptive garden-stuff; sleepy pears; and lucifers, whelks, straps, apples, and periwinkles, that are the staple commodities of the district. Jack Randall asked every policeman he met if he was at Waterloo, and Mr. Briggs inquired where he bought his oilskin cape, because he wished one like it; with other pleasant outpourings of great minds giving way to light relaxation from the graver duties of the accident-wards, and the dissecting-rooms.

"I'd like to looshe some monies vid you," said a son of Israel, as they passed his magazine of second-hand clothes.

Jack Randall immediately offered, with extreme politeness, to part with the paper lining of his hat upon very advantageous terms.

"I'll be happy to wait upon you at homesh, if you've got clothes to part vid."

"Oh! I've got lots," replied Randall; "when can you come?"

"Any vensh," was the reply.

Whereupon Jack wrote down the address of Mr. Poddy, the Professor of Anatomy, and told the Jew to go there the next morning, before ten. They then walked on towards Drury Lane, when they were accosted by another barker at the door of a similar establishment, as follows:

"Any things to shell?"

"Do you want a shirt?" asked Briggs.

"I should think you did," returned the Israelite.

"You've got it now," said Randall, laughing; "that was a thorough sell."

"I shan't chaff the peoplesh any more," observed Briggs; but he had evidently been asked the same question before, from the readiness of his reply.

They entered Drury Lane, and were immediately beset by the people with play-bills, from each of whom Jack Randall took a bill with a low bow, and carried it in his hand some little distance, until the vender demanded payment; when he directly returned it, begging their pardon for the mistake, but saying that he thought, from their pressing solicitations, he was doing them a kindness in taking one.

"Did you ever go to a concert, Simmy?" inquired Jack.

"Oh, yes," returned his friend; "very frequently: at the Hanover Square Rooms, and also at the Horns, at Kennington."

"Oh, you mean the ten-and-sixpenny toucher," said Randall.

"To be sure; and don't you?"

"Oh, no, my man. I allude to the penny melody for the million, at a musical tavern."

"I have never had that pleasure."

"Then here we are," said Jack, as they approached the corner of Great Queen Street. "Now, if you don't get value for your money, never trust me again."

And perfectly ready to have accompanied his friend to the infernal regions— via the common sewer and gas-pipes, if he had wished it—Mr. Simpson Briggs begged Jack Randall would forthwith introduce him to the cheap temple of harmony.

9

CHAPTER V.

A FURTHER ACCOUNT OF THE DEBUT OF JACK RANDALL AND MR. SIMPSON BRIGGS IN PUBLIC.

THE mansion of melody, before which Jack Randall and his friend now rested, had the appearance of a small private house which had come to distress, and was now forced to keep a gin-shop for its subsistence. A flaming placard in the window, whose component letters were staggering about as if they had taken a little too much, informed the public that there was a "Concert every Evening" within; and two long bills, wafered to the panes of glass, set forth in attractive display, the programme of the evening's amusement, the principal feature being the gladiatorial posturing of the Syrian Indefatigables.

Upon paying a penny each to a dirty fellow who stood at the bar, Mr. Simpson Briggs and Jack Randall were allowed to ascend an exceedingly unsafe staircase to the first floor of the mansion, the whole of which was appropriated to the "Grand Concert Room." The apartment was decorated with tawdry daubings, which on a minute inspection were discovered to be intended for romantic views of imaginary localities, where mountains, lakes, ships, Gothic ruins, Grecian temples, waterfalls, and Swiss cottages, were grouped together in magnificent confusion, as if the world had been put into a kaleidoscope, and tumbled about all ways to see how it would look perfectly broken to pieces. All the skies were endowed with perpetual sunset, merging from deep orange into dirt; all the water had little boats on its surface sailing any way they chose; and the whole series was mellowed with a *chiaro-oscuro* of gas and tobacco, which had a very fine effect, inasmuch as it softened the outlines, and produced a series of tints which could not be obtained by other means.

A series of rough benches were placed across the room, having ledges in front on which to stand whatever refreshments the company chose to indulge in—pipes and porter apparently forming the staple commodities of the house. The company themselves were rather numerous than fashionable; but experience has proved that it is impossible to command an exclusively aristocratical audience in London for a penny, and so Jack Randall found them quite as select as he expected.

They took their seats; and ordering a pot of half-and-half, awaited the commencement of the entertainment; in the interim reading two placards in the room, one of which conveyed the following announcement:

REMEMBER! DON'T FORGET!
THE TENTH OF DECEMBER IS THE NIGHT!
THE BLOOMSBURY BRAHAM AND THE LITTLE WONDER!
A STUNNER FOR A PENNY!
COME EARLY!

These cabalistical inuendos were as incomprehensible to Randall and Briggs as they doubtless are to our readers; but the *habitués* of the room appeared perfectly to understand the attractions set forth. Another bill stated that "the Judge and Jury Society met there every Sunday evening;" the entertainment in question consisting of mock trials—a species of amusement much relished by the "gents" of London, the whole of the jokes and humor thereunto attached being brought down to the most debased standard of animal intellect.

The commencement of the concert was announced by the waiter, who knocked a wooden hammer against the back of the door; and then some drapery was pulled up with a clothes-line, and discovered the orchestra—a recess about six feet square, part of it being occupied by an old jingling square piano. At the instrument was seated a melancholy-looking female, about five-and-forty years old, attired in a faded shawl and bonnet, of that fashion only to be met with in Drury-Lane on wet evenings. She immediately commenced thumping out some popular air upon the keys, with an enthusiasm which made Mr. Simpson Briggs wonder at the tenacity of the wires; but the piano appeared to have its spirit broken down by years of long unmitigated suffering, and now patiently put up with any infliction it encountered.

"Give your orders, gents," shouted the waiter at the conclusion of the "overture;" "give your orders, gents, and Mr. Lumson will oblige."

The announcement was received with much tabular percussion; and the object of the applause suddenly leapt upon the platform, attired in a dirty frock-coat, dirtier waistcoat, and very dirty shirt indeed. After some masonic communication with the pianiste, he fell into an attitude and sang "The White Squall," throwing such grand expressions into the words, "a hocean grave," that it quite frightened his audi- tors.   When he had finished, the piano suffered another ten minutes' torture, and then, after another request from the waiter that the guests would give their orders, Mr. and Mrs. Simms "obliged"—the singer of the "White Squall" des- cending from the orchestra, and, not at all proud, sitting down amongst some of the company, and, resuming his pipe, just as if he had been a common mortal.

Mr. Simms was a small man with somewhat the air of a journeyman glazier without his apron. He had on a pair of faded black trowsers which had evidently never been made for him, and shady white Berlin gloves with remarkably long fingers, that would have rendered the process of picking up a sixpence from the table a task of extreme perplexity, had he felt inclined to do so. Mrs. Simms had on an elegant cloak, apparently worn inside out to look imposing; and two gaudy silver flowers were stuck in her hair, which had a very bril- liant effect. The lady and gentleman then sang a duet ex- pressive of the minor annoyances and désagrémens attending the married state; and they quarrelled so naturally, that Jack Randall agreed with Mr. Briggs, "the perfection could only have been obtaied by long and unceasing rehearsals at home."

"What may I offer you to drink, ma'am?" said Jack Ran- dall with an air of extreme politeness, as the lady con- cluded. "You must need some little refreshment after your exertion."

"I'll take a draught of your beer, if you please," replied Mrs. Simms.

"Certainly," said Mr. Simpson Briggs, handing the pewter with much reverence to the lady. Then, turning to her hus- band, he continued,—"And you, sir—what will you do me the favor to drink with me?"

"I thank'ee, sir," replied Mr. Simms; "I'll take threepenn- 'orth of cold."

Mr. Simpson Briggs had not the slightest idea what was meant by the professional gentleman, who, to judge from a perpetual short inspiration of air through his nose, and slight huskiness in the upper tones of his voice, had laid in a suf- ficient quantity of cold already; so he told him to give his order to the waiter, and he would have the pleasure of set- tling the account.

The curtain then fell, to prepare for the exhibition of "The Gladiators ; " and when it rose again, the audience beheld two gentlemen in long drawers and cotton "jerseys," with their arms apparently thrust down the legs of stockings, and their hands and faces chalked and floured, who were standing in attitudes expressive of animosity. Then the piano uttered some imposing chords; and one of the gladiators threw his fist out in defiance toward one of the gas-lamps; and the other appeared to invoke the inmates of the second floor, first looking uncommonly savage at a crack in the ceiling, and then knocking his chest three times with his fist, which proceeding enveloped him in a cloud of white dust—no doubt emblematical of glory. Then they showed the audience how the ancient Romans fought—which was apparently, by standing on their heads, getting upon one another's shoulders, hanging out at right angles with their foot around the neck of their adversary, tying themselves into knots, and various other very remarkable feats, which are certainly not adopted in the pugilistic encounters of the present day, but which nevertheless much edified Mr. Simpson Briggs and his friend. They applauded the performance loudly, and declared it could not be surpassed—although a gentleman near them in a shiny hat and shirt-sleeves observed—"They fit a deal better the night as he seed 'em afore."

When this division of the programme concluded, there was a slight hiatus in the amusements, as the gladiators divested themselves of their attire, and put on their every-day clothes, which were also very much after the antique. Taking advantage of a temporary pause, Jack Randall rose from his seat, and, without saying a word about his intentions to his companion, thus addressed the company:—

"Ladies and gentlemen—I have the pleasure to inform you that my esteemed friend on my right—"

"What the devil are you going at?" inquired Mr. Simpson Briggs, half-frightened, as Randall placed his hand upon his shoulder.

"Or-der!" shouted a voice from the end of the room.

"Hush! I'll tell you," replied Randall. "My esteemed friend on my right," he continued, "has commissioned me to inform you, that he is so delighted with the harmony, he wishes to contribute to it himself."

"Jack—hang it!—don't be a fool;" again interrupted Briggs.

"His natural modesty," persevered Jack Randall, "prevents his telling you so himself." And then, looking doubly mysterious, he added—"You little know who he is."

At these words most of the people in the room rose from their seats to peep over one another's shoulders at the illustrious visitor, who, knowing that when Jack Randall had once started upon any subject, you might as soon attempt to stop a mail-train with a turnpike of barley-sugar, gave himself up for lost, and allowed his friend to go on.

"Nephew of the immortal Rubini," continued Jack, "by his uncle's side, he only waits the certain retirement of his gifted relative to appear at the Opera. In the mean time, he delights his friends; and, with your permission, the gentleman on my right—Mr. Allen Harrison Templeton Briggs—will favor us with the celebrated comic song from the opera of 'Semiramide,' or, 'The British Worthy;' and, on this occasion only, he will sing it with the chill off, and a cinder in it."

And amidst the vociferous cheers of the company, who anticipated something immensely grand, Jack Randall seized Mr. Simpson Briggs by the arm, and literally dragged him into the platform—the people taking his resistance for the modesty of real talent, and in consequence redoubling their applause.

CHAPTER VI.

THE CONCLUSION OF THE CONCERT.

"Now, Ladies and Gentlemen, but especially the Ladies," said Jack Randall, as he dragged Mr. Briggs to the front of the stage, with the air of a manager leading forward a *débutant*, who exhibits the pantomimic reluctance at the prompt side of the proscenium usual upon such occasions—"My friend, Mr. Allen Harrison Templeton Briggs, has every song at his command that was ever known, and he wishes you to name your favorite one."

There was an instant of silence after this announcement, no one liking to make the first choice. But presently the gentleman in the shiny hat and shirt-sleeves, begged Briggs would oblige the company with "Spare that 'ere tree." This encouraged others to solicit their favorite ballads; and the whole audience began simultaneously to call out for the songs they most wished to hear, which included "Halice Gray," "The Single Young Man Lodger," "My Art's in the Islands," and "Hot Codlins;" but the popular desire was certainly in favor of a lyrical effusion which appeared very well known to the frequenters of the concert under the title of "O crikey! don't I love my mother?" a burst of natural affection, which in point of intensity could be equalled but by few ballad-writers of the present day.

During this period Mr. Simpson Briggs had been apparently enacting the struggles of "The Gladiators" over again with Jack Randall, in his strenuous efforts to free himself from the grasp of his pertinacious friend. But Jack had seized hold of his collar with the clutch of a cast-iron policeman, and, taking advantage of the violent struggles of Mr. Briggs, turned it to account by calling out,

["Imitation of Messrs. Blanchard and Ellsgood in the drunken combat of the Dumb Girl of Genoa."

This speech he followed up by springing and stamping about in the most approved melodramatic style, nevertheless keeping a firm hold of his friend. The elderly female at the piano, imagining that it was all intended, began to play some of the same wild chords with which she was wont to accompany the evolutions of the Syrian Indefatigables; and at the same time the company, taking it all for granted, came down with thunders of approbation, which increased as Mr. Briggs became more and more energetic in his efforts to get loose. At last he collected all his force, and with a violent spring broke away from Randall, and tumbled off the platform, coming down all in a heap upon the nearest table, which fortunately had only pewter pots upon it, or the damage would have been most extensive. Another cheer greeted this feat, which was also supposed to be part of the performance by the spectators; and then, as a concluding hit, Jack threw himself into a posture of triumph, and informed the company it was a representation of "Achilles slaying the learned Hygeist," being the first words that came uppermost, and having a relation in sound, if not in sense, with the name of some statue he had seen on the terrace-garden at Windsor Castle.

"What a fool you are, Jack," was the salutation with which Mr. Briggs greeted his companion, as Randall, having bowed

to the audience, stepped from the platform and resumed his
seat.

"Hush! hold your tongue," replied Jack.—"Great lark—
immense—they think it was all meant."

"Song! song! song!" cried many voices from different
parts of the room.

"Hear—they insist upon your singing," said Jack—*sotto
voce*, to Mr. Briggs.

"Oh—nonsense! you know I can't. I never sang a note in
my life."

"All right, sir. I'll make an apology, and sing one myself."

Whereupon Jack Randall rose, and, turning to the company, informed them "that the exertions of his friend had
somewhat disabled him from complying with their request,
but that, with their permission, he would attempt, though he
was laboring under a cold, to contribute to the convivial harmony of the evening."

Fresh applause followed his speech; the audience did not
appear particularly to care who the song came from, provided
they got one; and Jack Randall, with all the assurance in the
world, once more ascended the platform. He understood
enough of music, to be able to get through a trifling piano
accompaniment, and having requested "*The pianist*," with
much politeness, to vacate her seat in his favor, he took his
place at the instrument. There was a little confusion created
at first starting off, by the leg of the music-stool getting into
a hole in the floor, that had been made for the insertion of a
post when the wonderful man-monkey exhibited his supernatural performances, which, the bill stated, "placed him at
once on an equality with the animal creation." This little
accident was awkward, inasmuch as it shot Jack Randall off
his perch: but immediately recovering, he favored the company with a ballad which alluded to a young lady passing
through the different stages of maid, wife, and widow, under
the various head-dresses of a wreath of roses, orange flowers,
and weeds; and proving the keen observation of Jack Randall, who made very minute remarks on her appearance,
although he confessed that he saw her but a moment; "but,"
added he, looking at a dirty piece of music before him, upon
which some vivacious predecessor had drawn a lady's profile,
taking a sight, "methinks I see her now."

Had Jack Randall been ambitious, the reception which the
song met with, from all except the regularly engaged profes-

sionals, would have incited him to further displays of his musical and vocal talent. But recollecting the grand secret of success in life, to retire when you have made a good impression, he acknowledged the plaudits of the company by a very magnificent bow, and having requested they would do him the favor to drink his health in a gallon of half-and-half, which he would settle for with the waiter, he resumed his seat.

"I ask your pardon, sir," said a very cadaverous-looking man, approaching him; "I ask your pardon, sir, but my benefit is fixed for the tenth of December. I am the Bloomsbury Braham, what is mentioned in the bill. If you would give me a song, you would greatly oblige me."

"Oh certainly, certainly," replied Jack. "Two or three, any songs, all sorts of songs—comic, Italian, or *mentisental.*" Then raising his voice he added, to the room in general:—

"Ladies and gentlemen,

"The hour is come that we must part; but the remembrance of the happy evening we have passed together, will never be eradicated whilst memory holds her seat in my brain's parliament. In the name of my friend, Mr. Allen Harrison Templeton Briggs, whom you have not heard to-night, but who trusts on some future opportunity, not far distant, to have the pleasure of again contributing to your enjoyment, we respectfully bid you farewell."

And amidst a storm of concussions, in which the tables suffered considerably from the bottoms of the pewter pots, the two students left the room, and sallied out once more into the open air.

The theatres were just over, and all was noise and confusion amongst the carriages assembled, except the vehicles at the private box entrance of Drury Lane, whose drivers and footmen had been quietly sleeping on their boxes for the last hour and a half, and required nothing less than an actual personal insult to arouse them. As soon as they had passed the stage door, and the usual crowd of loungers about it—friends of the drum, cousins of the thunder, and convivial acquaintances of the first citizen and second peasant, Jack quietly informed Mr. Briggs "that it was his intention to arouse the ire of the John Thomases."

From a keen observance of human nature, Jack Randall had observed, in his nightly perambulations, that when coachmen go to sleep upon their box, which is the invariable re-

sult of waiting above twenty minutes in the open air, they
always let their whip drop upon their left arm, towards the
near side of the carriage, and supported in a measure by the
knees of the footmen, who are snoring at their side. Jack
consequently found the thongs of all the whips belonging to
the coachmen of the company in the private boxes hanging
over the pavement, like so many fishing lines. So he tugged
down every one that came in his way, with a sudden jerk,
and then let it fly back again, startling the coachman from his
slumbers, with the general accompaniment of a flick in the
face from the thong, as the lash recoiled. By the time he was
awake, Jack and Mr. Briggs had walked on to another carriage, and this facetious amusement was repeated until the
whole line was in a state of great excitement trying to catch
him with the lash of their whips—which intended punishment
always fell upon the next passer-by—or saluting him with such
jocular speeches as "There goes two tailors!" "Halloo! you
counter-jumpers, here's your master a-coming;" or "Are you
out for the night?" to which last inquiry Jack generally replied that he was, with the key, and that his mother didn't
know it.

After a few more practical jokes, at the expense of the
ham-sandwich men, and the venders of "Frrrruit-pie orrrr-ra
meat!" for gallery consumption, Mr. Briggs avowed his intention of going home, because, as we have stated, his landlady
was religiously rheumatic, and did not like Medical Students
or late lodgers. And Jack Randall, who could not get to
sleep if he went to bed before three in the morning, wan-
dered into the parlors of various taverns, to see if he could
find some acquaintances in any of them to sup with, concluding his evening in a most unexpected manner, to which, in all
probability, we may hereafter refer.

CHAPTER VII.

HOW MR. SIMPSON BRIGGS WAS COMPELLED TO LEAVE HIS LODGINGS.

Soon after the events of the last chapter, the usual placid-
ity of mind which Mr. Simpson Briggs enjoyed, was somewhat startled by a letter he received from home. The epis-
tle, which was from his governor, went to state, that as the

lectures were nearly over, he feared his son would only idle about in London, and had therefore better return to his home; which was somewhere on the line of the Southampton Railway, and rejoiced in a kind of lath-and-plaster omnibus, which ran at all kinds of odd hours to meet the trains; and never started at the same hour two consecutive weeks, after the manner of railway omnibuses in general.

Now this desire on the part of the old gentleman to have his son at home was exceedingly inconvenient to Mr. Simpson Briggs for several reasons. Firstly he had no wish to return; secondly, he owed for three months' lodging, and people lately had got into a nasty habit of expecting to be paid for their goods; and thirdly, if he went, he would be expected to pay his debts. At present, he lived upon credit from his landlady, who, being a pious old lady, as we have stated, thought him a very quiet, steady young man, was ignorant that he was a medical student, and from his noiseless habits, not only trusted him so long, but would even have lent him five pounds had he wanted it.

He was ruminating what he should do, with the letter in his hand on the morning he received it; when his meditations were broken by a most discordant noise in the street below, resembling a tune played backwards on a cracked horn, and followed by shouts of "Yo-he-o!" "Lurli-e-ty!" and other vivacious outbursts of mirth. He immediately, to his extreme horror, recognized Jack Randall's voice, whom he had always studiously avoided asking to his lodgings; for knowing the rather exuberant hilarity of his disposition, he feared that his presence might offend his quiet old landlady, and procure him a notice to pay for and quit his abode at the same time. And Jack Randall had been in general very considerate, and not at all obtrusive; but he was in superabundant spirits this morning, and evidently boiling over with something he wished to tell his companion.

"I say, old fellow, let us up, will you?" was the question that greeted Mr. Briggs as he opened the window, and put his head out to check Randall's hullaballoo.

"Well, come up, if you must," replied Simpson, in a tone of resignation; "but why are you kicking up that awful riot?"

"All right," replied Jack; "I only wanted to see if you were at home." And thereupon he pulled the bell, and knocked at the door, and blew the horn all at once with a perseverance that threw the whole household into convulsion; and no one could have told which was the most alarmed—Mr. Simpson Briggs or his landlady.

In two minutes more Jack Randall had clattered up stairs, and entered the room. He looked exceedingly rakish, and had evidently been knocking about all night; which manner of passing the hours devoted to slumber having rendered him rather thirsty than otherwise, his first speech was an inquiry as to the presence of beer in any of Briggs' secret closets. A bottle of stout was forthwith produced from some mysterious recess, which Jack Randall emptied into a pewter pot he found in the hat-box, stating it was very low to drink beer out of glasses. And having pronounced his state of health to be much better after his imbibition, he proceeded to exhibit an old *cornet-à-piston* he held in his hand, which he had just purchased at a second-hand shed, and then offered to give Briggs a specimen of its tone.

"No, don't—pray don't!" cried Simpson, quite alarmed: "you'll tire yourself."

"Not at all, my dear fellow," said Randall, putting the instrument to his mouth, and producing a serious of sounds seldom equalled and never excelled. "There," he continued, as he stopped for lack of wind, "there! what do you think of that? I mean to play it down to the races—how are you going?"

"I don't think I shall go at all," answered Simpson; "the governor wants me at home. How are *you* going?"

"All right," said Jack, "on a soda-water truck; devilish pleasant way, too, when the corks dont fly with the heat. Look here," he continued, darting off to another subject, as he took a small quill from his pocket; "here's a funny thing?"

And to show the powers of this instrument to his friend, he poured some beer in the inkstand, and inserting one end of the quill into the liquid, blew through the other, when a loud whistle was the result, bearing a close resemblance to the chirp of a bird. "It beats Herr Von Joel hollow, don't it?" he asked, with admiration, as the performance concluded; "I gave a penny for it, as I came along in the Recent Incision."

"The what?" asked Simpson.

"The Recent Incision—it's the polite name for the New Cut. Let's give the people in the street the benefit of it."

"No, don't, Jack," earnestly implored Briggs.

"What prime plants you've got there!" said Randall, heedless of Simpson's petition, and opening the window, on the outside ledge of which were displayed several flower-pots of mignonette and other cockney floricultural favorites. "They look very dry, though—don't you think I had better give them a little beer?"

"No—what are you thinking about?" cried Briggs, in agony; "you'll kill them."

"Devil a bit," returned Jack. "It'll do them good—make them blow all colors at once;" and without another word, he distributed about a pint of stout over the hapless flowers, which running over, dripped down upon the heads of the people who were passing below, and produced a storm of salutations far more expressive of choler than courtesy.

"There!—see what mischief you are doing," said Mr. Briggs. "Now, come and sit down quietly, and tell us what you did last night after the concert. I left you in Covent Garden."

"Well, I went and played billiards, at the rooms we generally patronize, and lost five shillings—all I had, except sixpence."

"I know that table, well," said Briggs; "I ought to; I was locked out one night, and slept upon it. They made me pay nine shillings in the morning for my bed."

"How so?" asked Jack Randall.

"Six hours' use of the table, at eighteen-pence an hour," returned Simpson.

"Well, cut on, and where did you get to next?"

"I went to Evans'! There I had a pint of stout, and sang a song."

"Oh! gammon, Jack!" observed Mr. Briggs, in a tone of disbelief.

"True bill, sir," answered Randall. "I'll sing it now."

"Oh, don't, don't—pray don't!" cried Briggs. "I tell you, you musn't make a noise here."

But Randall did not appear to heed the trouble of his friend, but cleared his throat as if in preparation, and then broke out into a run of such wonderful facility and execution, that there is no knowing where it would have ended, if a knock at the door had not interrupted it, and an accompanying voice, which uttered, "If you please, Mr. Briggs, missus will thank you to be a little quieter, because there's a sick lady in the house."

"There now, Jack!" cried Briggs. "See what a scrape you will get me into. Never mind the song—you can sing it to me another time. Where did you go next?"

"Oh—I forgot to tell you," answered Randall; "I met two of the students at Evans'—Robinson and Parry, with a new man named Hicks, whom they were showing life to, and telling him all the lies they could possibly invent. Poor fellow!"

"What makes you say poor fellow?"

"Because he's in the police-office, and will be brought up at Bow-street this morning."

"How's that?" asked Simpson.

"Why, I think he ate too many poached eggs, and they rather exhilarated him: for when we got into Convent Garden, he would insist upon trying to drag us in a vegetable cart. He lifted up the shafts to do it, when the cart, which was loaded with turnips, was overbalanced, and tipped up backwards. The chain, which went across from one shaft to the other, caught hold of him, and lifted him up like a swing into the air, and there he sat."

"Well, and what did you do?"

"We saw the policeman, and ran away as fast as we could. Hicks was nailed, and I suppose by this time has paid his five shillings—very little lark for five shillings, though—was it not?"

"Uncommon," replied Mr. Briggs. "And where did you go next?"

"Why, I can't exactly remember," said Randall, whose ideas of his subsequent adventures appeared to be rather indistinct. "But you see, here I am, all right and fresh as a lark. I say, what have you got for breakfast?"

Mr. Simpson Briggs was compelled to confess that there was not a great deal in the house. Whereon Randall took upon himself to find out, and having looked into various closets and boxes, at last opened the chest which we have spoken of before as communicating with the floor below.

"Halloo!" he cried, with some astonishment, "What the deuce is this? I can see right down into the room underneath—Halloo!"

"Hush! for goodness' sake, don't kick up that row, Jack. The place was formerly an eating-house, and the dishes used to come up there from the kitchen."

"I know," said Randall, imitating the tone of a waiter, and

bawling down the chest—"One ox, two mocks, three bullies, and a mutton to follow!"

"You will ruin me!" cried in Briggs, in despair. "There's a very quiet man lives down there; and my landlady is so particular, that I shall certainly be told to go if you continue this diabolical uproar."

But the whole affair was so novel, that Jack Randall's excitement rose to the highest pitch; and intimating his wish to treat the gentleman to a little music, he seized the cornet, and blew a blast down it, that might have been heard on the other side of the street, and, in all probability, on the other side of the water.

CHAPTER VIII.

HOW MR. SIMPSON BRIGGS LEFT HIS LODGINGS.

THE only way to keep Jack Randall at all quiet was to give him something to eat and drink. Begging him, therefore, to restrain his musical and harmonic propensities whilst he called for the servant, he sent her out for some coffee and bloaters, which he hoped would keep Jack's mouth somewhat tranquil by completely filling it. He then produced a machine, bearing some resemblance to a tin bandbox, which he placed with great importance on the table.

"What the devil's that?" asked Jack.

"A Bachelor's Despatch," replied Mr. Briggs. "This will roast, boil, bake, stew, steam, heat flat-irons, melt butter, cook eggs, toast bread, and diffuse a genial warmth, all at once, with a ha'porth of brown paper."

"That's your sort," said Jack, "let it off then."

But this was not so easily done; for Randall; in his hilarity, had poured some beer into the box of lucifers which was somewhat against their lighting; and after several vain attempts, he proposed borrowing some of Mr. Spiff underneath. But Mr. Spiff did not chance to be at home, so that Mr. Briggs, who knew he kept his lucifers on the top of a bureau, opened the chest of communication, and fished down it with a pair of tongs, finally producing the desired matches, after having in turns brought up some lobster's shells, a pewter go (which, if

everybody had their own, would possibly have belonged to Mr.
Rhodes), and then something which was very like a woman's
cap. Fire was then produced, and the "despatch" set in action—brown paper being discarded from not having any, and
the want of it clandestinely supplied by Jack, partly from
the notes Mr. Briggs had taken at lectures; and partly from
some hay which he secretly pulled out of the old easy-chair.
The coffee arrived, and the breakfast was made, our friends
laying the cloth on the top of the chest, because the table
was covered with articles of study and recreation—books,
pipes, inkstands, pewter-pots, and tobacco-jars.

"Jack," said Mr. Briggs, mysteriously to his companion,
when their hunger was somewhat appeased, "Jack, I want to
tell you something."

"Out with it, then," replied Randall.

"But you'll laugh?"

"No, I won't—honor."

"Well, then," resumed Briggs, with some hesitation, "I
think I'm in love."

Jack Randall finished cramming the tails of the herrings
into the bowl of Mr. Briggs' pipe, in which occupation he had
been quietly engaged; and, looking the other steadfastly in
the face, exclaimed—

"Gammon, Simmy! Who ever heard of a Medical Student
being in love?"

"I'm afraid I am, though," replied Mr. Briggs, with a sigh.
"Such a nice little girl!—quite well conducted and respectable."

"Oh, of course—of course," replied Jack. "Where did
you meet her?"

"On the top of Primrose-hill, last Sunday; all amongst the
nuts and bull's-eyes. She keeps a bonnet-shop in Cranbourne-
alley. I bought one of her own bonnets, and made her a
present of it."

"More fool you," said Jack, briefly.

"Not at all," replied Simpson, half angry. "I gave her a
handkerchief, besides, with a Union Jack on it—a flag, you
know."

"I know," said Jack. "The wizard at the theatre had
one, that went here, there, everywhere, and nowhere, all at
once."

And here Randall caught up the tea-caddy, and was going
to show Mr. Briggs some necromantic performances thereon,

when the lid of the chest which formed their table was suddenly elevated, the whole of the breakfast equipage shot off upon the ground, and the head of Mr. Spiff, perfectly unconscious of the confusion he had created, appeared in the box, quietly asking—

"I say, Briggs, have you got my lucifers?"

Jack Randall went off at once into a roar of laughter, and Mr. Briggs got exceedingly irate. He thrust the lucifers into Spiff's hand without saying a word—for, indeed, he was somewhat overcome at the sudden *chute;* and, putting down the lid almost before the head of the intruder was out of the way, sat down upon it, and contemplated the ruin around him.

"Never mind," said Jack, with noble philosophy; "let us set to work and pick up the things; we can make all straight in two minutes."

And in his laudable attempt to absorb the coffee spilt on the chest and floor, he pulled out a large flag handkerchief to wipe it up, which he had no sooner displayed, than Briggs uttered a cry of terror, and exclaimed—

"I say, Jack! where did you get that?"

"Oh," said Randall, laughing with the most wicked fun; "A young lady gave it to me—quite well conducted and respectable—keeps a bonnet-shop in Cranbourne-alley. I met her on Primrose-hill."

"What a horrid occurrence!" exclaimed Briggs, pale with astonishment. "That's the very handkerchief I gave my sweetheart!"

"What a joke!" replied Randall, laughing. "Now, come, I don't want to cross your love: we'll toss up who shall pay his addresses to her."

"I'm sure I'll do no such thing," said Briggs, whose dignity was quite offended.

"Well, then, we'll fight for her hand, like the knights of old," continued Jack.

"I can't fight, and I won't," replied Briggs.

"Yes, you can. I don't mean with fists, you know; bolsters are the things."

And in an instant this vivacious gentleman had pulled open the turn-up bedstead, and dragged a pillow and bolster from its depths.

"Now, come on," said Jack. "I'll keep the pillow, and there's the bolster for you. The long odds are on your side."

10

"I tell you I won't fight," said Briggs, getting near the window, which was open.

"Pshaw! come on," cried Randall; and hurling the pillow at Briggs, who stooped to avoid it, it went right through the window, knocking away the regiment of flower-pots, which immediately fell into the street, and an awful smash was the result.

"There—you *have* been and done it," cried Briggs, "that's the last move. The flower-pots have fallen on the china and glass stall ; you've broken a pound's worth of crockery, and we haven't got half-a-crown to pay for it."

"I beg your pardon there," said the imperturbable Randall, "I think we've got a good deal to pay for it."

"Well, this is a settler ! " cried Briggs. "I'm off at all hazards, and seizing a carpet-bag from a peg, he rapidly began to cram his things into it. Two minutes had scarcely elapsed, before a noise was heard of people ascending the stairs, Jack divined their business and immediately bolted the door, as one of the assailants knocked at it.

"Where's Mr. Briggs?" cried a voice from the outside, which sounded very like a policeman's.

"You can't see him," cried Jack in return, "He's ill in bed—I'm putting some leeches on him."

"But I saw this pillow fall down upon the glass, from his room," said the voice.

"No, no," returned Jack. "It's a mistake, it came from the floor above."

At this instant a horn sounded in the street, and Briggs ran to the window. "I knew it," he cried ; "its the Southampton railway bus. If I can but get out, I am saved."

"Get down the chest," said Randall, "I think everybody in the house is up here on the landing."

"Open the door," cried the voices.

"Wait an instant till the leeches come off," said Jack, in reply.

"We will break it open," cried the invaders.

"Do if you dare," said Jack ; and pushing the turn-up bedstead against it, he blew a fearful note of defiance on his cornet.

The crisis had arrived ; Mr. Briggs, in the short interim, had crammed all of his effects into his fishing-basket and carpet-bag; the beauty of which latter article is, that it is never so full but you can put something else in. Begging a rapid pardon for the intrusion, he threw his things down into Spiff's room, and followed by Randall, descended after them, letting the lid close over their heads. In another minute, he had gained the street unopposed; for, as Jack had suspected, all the people of the house were up on the landing outside their door. The omnibus was at the end of the street; a short run enabled him to overtake it, and plunge into the seclusion of its interior; and Jack Randall, after telling Mr. Spiff he should be happy to serve him in a like strait, and begging he would tell the landlady that Mr. Briggs left all effects they could find for the benefit of his creditors, also took a hurried departure.

That same evening Mr. Simpson Briggs was located in safety at home, and Jack Randall having got his certificates signed, of his first course of lectures, was once more domiciled with his old friend Mr. Muff, at Clodpole. Peace, and plenty of patients, be their portion.

MEDICAL ANECDOTES.

FUNNY SAYINGS AND DOINGS OF MEDICAL MEN.

Motto:

"A little nonsense now and then
Is relished by the wisest men."

MEDICAL ANECDOTES.

A PHYSICIAN "POPS THE QUESTION" BY A QUEER PRESCRIPTION.

On one occasion, when I was ill, the General called in Dr. Hunt, his family physician. The doctor was a tall, lank, ugly man—"as good as gold," but with none of the graces that are supposed to win young ladies; yet he was married to one of the loveliest young creatures I ever knew. General Jackson accompanied him to my room, and after my pulse had been duly felt, and my tongue duly inspected, they drew their chairs to the fire and began to talk.

"Hunt," suddenly exclaimed the president, "how came you to get such a young and pretty wife?"

"Well, I'll tell you," replied the doctor. "I was called to attend a young lady at the convent in Georgetown. Her eyes were bad; she had to keep them bandaged. I cured her without her ever having a distinct view of me. She left the institution, and a year afterward she appeared here in society, a belle and a beauty. At a ball I introduced myself without the slightest ulterior design, as the physician who had restored her sight, although I supposed she had never seen me. She instantly expressed the most heartfelt gratitude. It seemed so deep and genuine, that I was touched. That very evening she informed me that she had a severe cold, and that I must again prescribe for her. Well, it didn't look reasonable, but I did it. I wrote my name on a bit of paper, folded it, and handed it to her, telling her she must take that prescription. She read it and laughed. 'It's a bitter pill,' she said, 'and must be well gilded if ever I take it.' But whether it was bitter, or whether it was gilded, we were married."

IN THE HOSPITAL.

SCENE.—Hospital.—Two surgeons in consultation over a man twenty-four hours previously injured about the head in a railroad accident, and still rather stupid.

First Surgeon.—"Nurse, has he passed any urine?"

Nurse.—" No."

Second Surgeon.—" We had better catheterize him."

First Surgeon.—" Yes, at once.   (Gets catheter ready, calls for oil bottle, and attempts to introduce the instrument.)

Patient resists quite vigorously, without speaking.

Second Surgeon.—Let us stand him up and see if he cannot make water himself.

Patient is raised up and passes water in a full stream quite easily.

Patient (loq.)—"If I had known that was what you wanted, I could have saved you all that trouble."   (Tableau.)

First Surgeon.—" Wonder why he resisted the catheter so strenuously?"

Nurse.—"Let me see the oil bottle."

Bottle is brought, and found labelled "Acid Carbolic, 95 per cent."   (Tableau and exeunt.)

IN THE AMPHITHEATRE.

Professor in Quiz.—"What do you understand as a plastic operation?"

Student.—"Why—why—I think it is an operation with plasters."

ADDISON'S COMPARISON.

DOCTORS were humorously compared by Addison to the army of ancient Britons, described by Julius Cæsar: "Some slay on foot, and some in chariots; but those in the chariots do the most execution."

THE SMALL CHILD.

A' LADY visiting a friend just confined, remarked to the grandmother: "How small the child is!" The old lady replied, " Well, we had a Homœopathic doctor."

JOHN HUNTER AT HIS WIFE'S PARTY.

JOHN Hunter had no sympathy with his wife's poetical aspirations, still less with the society, which those aspirations led her to cultivate.   Grudging the time, which the labors of practice prevented him from devoting to the pursuits of his museum and laboratory, he could not restrain his too irritable temper, when Mrs. Hunter's frivolous amusements deprived him of the quiet requisite for study.   Even the fee of a patient who called him from his dissecting instruments could not reconcile him him to the interruption. "I must go," he would say, reluctantly, to his friend Lynn, when the living summoned him from his investigations among the dead, "and earn this d—d guinea, or I shall be sure to want it to-morrow." Imagine the wrath of such a man, finding, on his return from a long day's work his house full of musical professors, connoisseurs and fashionable idlers, in fact, all the confusion and hubbub, and heat of a grand party, which his wife had forgotten to inform him, was that evening to come off.   Walking straight into the middle of the drawing room, he faced round and surveyed his unwelcome guests, who were not a little surprised to see him—dusty, toil-worn and grim, so unlike what "the man of the house" ought to be on such an occasion "I knew nothing," was his brief address to the astounded crowd.   "I knew nothing of this kickup, and I ought to have been informed of it beforehand; but, as I have now returned home to study, I hope the present company will retire."

Mrs. Hunter's drawing-rooms were speedily empty.

PREFERRED TO DIE.

A physician fell into a fit, while making his round of visits and was carried into a drug store.

"Send for Dr. X," says somebody:

"No, no," says the dying man feebly, at the mention of his rival's name, "if he brought me round, it would advertise him, I prefer to die."

DR. JEPHSON'S REPLY.

Dr. Jephson was a distinguished physician of Leamington, fifty years ago.   The doctor was noted for being brusque and unceremonious.   A great London lady, a high and mighty leader of society, who was taken suddenly ill, sent for him. Jephson was so off hand with her grace, that she turned on him angrily and asked:

"Do you know to whom you speak?"

"Oh, yes," replied Dr. Jephson, quietly, "to an old woman with the stomach-ache."

OBJECTIONABLE ANÆSTHESIA.

Western women are sharp but the Plattsmouth (Neb.), female is entitled to the premium for smartness. The other day she went into a shoe store to buy a pair of shoes. The clerk was in the act of sprinkling some chalk-powder inside, so they might slip on easily. She glanced furtively at him, and remarked: "I know what you are doing." The genial clerk smiled acquiescence. She slid toward the door, and said, in tones that startled his nerves: "You can't chloroform me, mister; I was fooled once before, and I'm blamed if I'll be again." And she left without the shoes.

PASSING THE EXAMINATION.

"Well," said the narrator, putting down his empty glass, and filling it again with Madeira, "I was shown into the examination room. Large table, and half-a-dozen old gentlemen at it. Big-wigs, no doubt," thought I, "and sure as my name is Symonds, they will pluck me like a pigeon."

"Well, sir, what do you know about the science of your profession?" asked the stout man in the chair.

"More than he does of the practice, I will be bound," tittered a little wasp of a dandy—a West End ladies' doctor.

I trembled in my shoes.

"Well, sir," continued the stout man, "what would you do if a man was brought to you during action, with his arms and legs shot off? Now, sir, don't keep the board waiting! What would you do! Make haste!"

"By jove, sir!" I answered—a thought just striking me— "I should pitch him overboard, and go on to some one else I could be of more service to."

"By ——! every one present burst out laughing; and they passed me directly, sir; passed me directly."

GOOD-BYE TO THE DOCTOR.

Bouvart, on entering one morning the chamber of a French marquis, whom he had attended through a very dangerous illness, was accosted by his noble patient in the following terms:

"Good day, Mr. Bouvart; I feel quite in spirits, and think my fever has left me."

"I am sure it has," replied Bouvart, dryly. "The very first expression you used convinces me of it."

"Pray, explain yourself."

"Nothing is easier. In the first days of your illness, when your life was in danger, I was your dearest friend; as you began to get better, I was your good Bouvart; and now I am Mr. Bouvart. Depend upon it, you are quite recovered."

THE OLD ROMAN GOD.

"I wouldn't be in Egypt," said Mrs. McGill last week, "for all the wealth of Creosote." Seeing a look of astonishment in the face of her auditors, she added: "Creosote, you know, was an old Roman god, and everything he touched turned into gold."

QUACKERY YEARS AGO.

In a French work entitled "The Art of Medicine, or, The True Means of Succeeding in Medicine," published in Paris in 1843, we find the following amusing anecdote, which tends to show that the quackery of to-day is no new thing:

"During a journey which Barthez was making in the South of France, he resolved to visit Bordeaux. Arriving in that city, he put up at the Hotel d'Angleterre, which was the rendezvous for all the travelers of distinction.

The morning after his arrival, very early, his sleep was broken by a confusion and noise which was going on upon the stairs. It sounded like a crowd of people coming and going, ascending and descending without cessation. Barthez rose in haste and quietly half-opened his door to find out the reason of all this commotion, and to know if they were not patients who wished to consult him; they certainly were patients, but alas! they passed his door as if scorning him and repaired to an apartment opposite his own, on which was a large placard above the door, bearing the inscription:

"Consultation gratis!
Medicines only charged for."

Barthez closed his door in confusion; during the whole day and the following one, the mob never ceased.

Lucky confrère! said he to himself; he takes them all and does not leave even the most trifling consultation to a physician, who, without doubt, is in no sense his inferior, (Barthez had good cause to pay himself the tribute). "Who is this man who is in such vogue?" he inquired of the servants in the hotel; the doctor was only known there by name: his name was Dr. Laurent, and every one repeated:

"It is Dr. Laurent."

One day Barthez, being at the head of the stairs, his unknown confrère emerged from his apartment, muffled in a rich dressing gown and wearing a black velvet cap fringed with gold. He saluted Barthez humbly, who, utterly astonished, suddenly exclaimed: "What, is it you Laurent?" In fact, it was Laurent, his old servant!

"Yes, sir, it is I."

"But how? Since when? Who the deuce made you a doctor?"

"You, sir, and I owe you my fortune. You remember, without doubt, that when I was in your service, I accompanied you everywhere, in your professional visits, and that you employed me to convey your opinions to your numerous patients. Well, I listened to all that you said, read all that you wrote, and with all this and the help of a few good formulæ, that I had stolen from you, I made a science of my own, which you see has produced me something handsome."

"You astonish me, Laurent; but your success surprises me still more; and I am so much the more astonished that I, who have been here fifteen days, and whose presence in Bordeaux ought to be known, have not had a patient, while you," he added smilingly, "but what kind of a city is this?"

"It does not differ from others, sir, and fools are plentiful here, as everywhere else. Your astonishment, permit me to tell you, does not become a man of talent, like yourself. Answer me; how many sensible people do you suppose there are in a population of 120,000 souls? 500? 1,000? 1,500? I will grant you 2,000. Well, these 2,000 are your property; but the remaining 118,000, who are fools, are mine, and you can look to them for nothing. Hence, you need not be surprised at my numerous clièntèle."

Barthez reddened, said farewell to Laurent, and left Bordeaux the same evening, promising himself in future, not to have such great confidence in his profound wisdom.

This anecdote proves that the supply of quacks will fail the fools, before the supply of fools will fail the quacks.

JOHANNES CABALLUS, M. D.

In the early part of the sixteenth century, the old University of Montpelier, France, was reputed to be given to the crooked ways of Buchanan. It sold diplomas extensively, in many instances even dispensing with the presence of the buyer, presumably making use of ye ancient mails in the fraudulent practice. *Rabelais*, satirist that he was, as well as physician and philosopher, put up a practical joke on the venerable Faculty. He addressed them a formal application on behalf of a young friend, dwelling on his profound learning and wonderful skill in medicine. Enclosing the customary fee, he ended with the request that the degree of M. D. be conferred on this friend, whose name was Johannes Caballus. In due course of time the precious sheepskin arrived, but the rage of the Faculty may be better imagined than expressed, when the report reached them that they had made a jackass a doctor; M. Johannes Caballus being none other than Rabelais' favorite jackass.

HAHNEMANN AND THE LORD.

Hahnemann, the founder of the homœopathic school, was one day consulted by a wealthy English lord. The doctor listened patiently to the patient. He took a small phial, opened it, and held it under his lordship's nose. "Smell! Well, you are cured." The lord asked, in surprise, "How much do I owe?" "A thousand francs," was the reply. The lord immediately pulled out a bank note, and held it under the doctor's nose. "Smell! Well, you are paid."

THE STUDENT'S COLD.

Student.—"How is it, doctor, that I always take cold in my head?"

Doctor.—"It is a well-known principle, sir, that a cold is most likely to settle in the weakest part."

DISINFECTANTS.

"What is the action of disinfectants?" was asked of a medical student.

" They smell so bad that people open the door, and fresh air gets in," was the reply.

SILK AND TAPE-WORMS.

An Irish woman needing some silk and some tape, sent her husband for them. The silk was shown, but the buyer thought the price too great. The clerk explained that all silk goods were dear, owing to some disease at this time prevalent among the silkworms. The tape was next examined, and the Irishman thought that a little stiff as to price. "And indade, sir," says he, "is there likewise a dezase a-prevailin' among the tape-worms ?"

VIVAT SEQUENS.

Not long since a doctor was attending a case of labor. About the time the baby arrived, an older chick of two years had found its way into the sick room, and watched the operation of tying the cord, and separating and handing over to the nurse, with marked interest. The doctor supposed the little chap was now busy with the nurse, and proceeded to remove the after-birth, and just as this was about completed, the little gentleman peeped over the opposite bed-rail, and piped out, "*More babies*, doctor ?"

A KINDLY INQUIRY.

" What acid do we get from iodine?" asked the medical professor. "We get–a–n–usually get idiotic acid," yawned the student. "Have you been taking some?" quietly asked the professor.

THE SHARP REJOINDER.

A sharp rejoinder is an arrow that buries itself in the target. A gentleman who took to medicine late in life, said to a friend, "You know the old proverb, that 'at forty a man must be either a fool or a physician?'" "Yes," was the reply; "but, doctor, don't you think he can be both ?"

A DIABOLICAL JOKE.

The following diabolical joke is laid at the door of Dr. Oliver Wendell Holmes. A druggist in introducing his son,

asked the physician-poet if he did not see a resemblance between the offspring and his sire?" "Well, yes," was the
reply, "I think I can see some of your liniments in his face."
At last reports, the poet was doing as well as could be expected.

SHE WOULD NOT HAVE COME.

A NOTED Philadelphia laryngologist, on examining a girl
with a relaxed uvula and mucous membrane of the throat, concluded that the cause of the difficulty was some uterine
trouble, for which he advised her to place herself under the
care of her family physician. Her reply was: "Doctor, if I
had known that you could see all the way down, I should not
have come to you."

THE OPIUM HABIT.

A DOCTOR in a certain town, advertised to cure the "opium
habit," and had acquired considerable repute in that direction. A little miss said to her ma, the other day: "Oh! I
say, mother, Dr. S., over there, cures people of the habit of
eating Ethiopians."

A SLIGHT MISTAKE.

ONE cannot be too particular with his directions. A messenger came to B., saying that one of his lady patients was
suffering horribly from a bug which had gotten into her ear.
B. was engaged at the time, and could not go to the patient,
but sent word to "pour some oil in her ear." In a short time
back came the messenger to ask, "Which ear?"

GOOD ADVICE.

"WHAT ought I to take or do when my feelings of exhaus-
tion come on?" asked a patient of his physician, who was a
sensible man, as his reply indicates. "Go and lie down, like
any other beast."

NO HURRY.

AT THE Kit-Kat, Dr. Garth once stayed to drink long after he had said that he must be off to see his patients. Sir Richard, more humane than the physician, or possibly like the rest of the world, not disinclined to be virtuous at another's expense, observed: "Really, Garth, you ought to have no more wine, but be off to see those poor devils." "It's no great matter," Garth replied, "whether I see them to-night or not, for nine of them have such bad constitutions that all the physicians in the world can't save them ; and the other six have such good constitutions, that all the physicians in the world can't kill them."—*J. C. Jeaffreson.*

HEALTHY OYSTERS.

"ARE oysters healthy ?" inquired an ancient dame of her physician. "I am inclined to believe that they are remarkably so," was the reply, "as I have never yet met with a single one that complained of being unwell."

THE MUSICIAN'S ILLNESS.

PROFESSOR (with his class in a French hospital), to patient: "What is your occupation ?" Patient (who has pulmonary disease)—"Musician, sir." (Professor to class—"There, gentlemen, at last I have the opportunity of demonstrating what I have often told you in the lecture-room, that the wear and tear on the respiratory tract, caused by the blowing of musical instruments, is a fertile source of just such difficulty as our patient here labors under." To patient—"What instrument do you play, sir?" Patient—"The violoncello, sir."

SAILORS' LANGUAGE.

DOCTOR (looking learned and speaking slowly)—"Well, mariner, what tooth do you want extracted ? Is it a molar or an incisor ?" Jack (short and sharp, replies)—"It is in the upper tier, on the larboard side. Bear a hand, you swab, for its nipping my jaw like a lobster."

THE NEVADA TRAMP.

A NEVADA tramp applied to a doctor for work, and on being asked what he could do, replied, "Well I could dig graves!"

THE BIRTH RETURN.

IN filling out a "birth return" in a case in which the name of the father was doubtful, a Chicago doctor, with prompt exhibition of forethought equal to any emergency, filled in the blank E Pluribus Unum.

THE DULL STUDENT'S INQUIRY.

IN lecturing on the recognition of the sex of the child in utero, a noted professor was expatiating on the theory of the pulse rate, claiming that if the pulse beat 120 per minute the child was a boy; if 140 per minute, the sex was female. A terribly dull student electrified the class by inquiring "whether, if the pulse rate was 130 would the result be a hermaphrodite?"

IT WAS TOO MUCH FOR HIM.

Doctor—" Well, are you better? Have you taken your medicine regularly, and eaten plenty of animal food?"

Patient—" Yes, sir, I tried it; and so long as it were be-ans and o-ats I could manage pretty well, sir, but when it came to that there chopped hay, that right down choked me, sir."

THE BEST REMEDY.

A LADY brought a child to old Dr. F. to consult him about its health. Among other things, she inquired if he did not think the springs would be useful. "Certainly, madam," replied the doctor, as he eyed the child, and then took a large pinch of snuff. "I haven't the least hesitation in recommending the springs—and the sooner you apply the remedy the better!" "You really think it would be good for the dear little thing, don't you?" "Upon my word, it's the best remedy

11

I know of." "What springs would you recommend, doctor ?"
"Any will do, madam, where you can get plenty of soap and
water?"

RADCLIFFE'S OPINION.

RADCLIFFE tells us that on one occasion a miserly old mer-
chant attempted to steal his opinion with regard to his own
case. "What shall I do?" said the patient to him. "Why,
sir, I should advise you to take advice."

NOT THE ONLY ONE.

DR. RADCLIFFE was not endowed with a kindly nature.
"Mead, I love you," said he to this fascinating adulator; "and
I'll tell you a sure secret to make your fortune.—Use all man-
kind ill." Radcliffe carried out his rule by ringing as much
as possible from, and returning as little as possible to his
fellow men. He could not pay a tradesman's bill without a
sense of keen suffering. Even a poor pavior, who had been
employed to do a job to the stones before the doctor's house
in Bloomsbury Square, could not get his money without a
contest. "Why, you rascal !" cried the debtor as he alighted
from his chariot, "Do you pretend to be paid for such a piece
of work? Why, you have spoiled my pavement and then covered it over with earth to hide the bad work." "Doctor," responded the man, dryly, "*mine is not the only bad work the
earth hides.*"—*J. C. Jeaffreson.*

A MAID'S INTUITION.

A LADY's maid visiting with her mistress at the residence of
a celebrated surgeon, then deceased, noticed the classic invitation, "salve," upon the hall floor, and in the parlor a picture
of Cleopatra applying the asp to her beautiful bosom. Whereupon, with that quick but not always correct woman's intui-
tion about which we hear so much now-a-days, she confidently, but in all innocence inquired: "Dr. — was a physician,
was he not? I felt sure he was when I saw salve on the entry floor, and then that poor thing in the parlor, with her

broken breast, and the leech in her hand. I knew he must have been a doctor."

THE STUDENT'S PREDICAMENT.

" GIVE me the names of the bones of the cranium ?"
" I've got them all in my head, professor, but I can't give them."

A PATIENT'S MERIT.

A PHYSICIAN, much attached to his profession and his own skill, during his attendance on a man of letters, observing that the patient was very punctual in taking all his medicines and following his rules, exclaimed, in the pride of his heart, " Ah, my dear sir, now you deserve to be sick."

THE FOUNTAINS OF CONSOLATION.

" Do you think I shall recover, doctor ?"   " Certainly, madam; no possible doubt of it.   The statistics show that one per cent. of those afflicted with your disease recover.   Yours is my hundredth case, and as the ninety and nine have gone before, I can confidently promise you that you will be left."   Statistics are fountains of consolation.

A STARTLING ANSWER.

Professor of Chemistry—" Suppose you were called to a patient who had swallowed a heavy dose of oxalic acid, what would you administer ?"
Student (who is preparing for the ministry, and who takes chemistry because it is obligatory)—" I would administer the sacrament."

DOCTOR'S PAY.

"SAVE me, doctor and I'll give you a thousand dollars."
The doctor gave him a remedy that eased him, and he called out, "Keep at it, doctor, and I'll give you a check for five hundred dollars."   In half an hour more he was able to sit up,

and he calmly remarked,—"Doctor, I feel like giving you a fifty-dollar bill." When the doctor was ready to go, the sick man, by this time up and dressed, followed him to the door and said:

"Say, doctor, send in your bill the first of the month." When six months had been gathered to time's bosom, the doctor sent in a bill for five dollars. He was pressed to cut it down to three, and after so doing was obliged to sue to get it, and after he got judgment the patient put in a stay of execution.

TIME IS MONEY.

ABERNETHY's time was precious, and he rightly considered that his business was to set his patients in the way of recovering their lost health—not to listen to their fatuous prosings about their maladies. He was therefore prompt and decided in checking the egotistic garrulity of valetudinarians. This candid expression of his dislike to unnecessary talk had one good result. People who came to consult him took care not to offend him by bootless prating. A lady on one occasion entered his consulting-room, and put before him an injured finger without saying a word. In silence Abernethy dressed the wound, when instantly and silently the lady put the usual fee on the table and retired. In a few days she called again and offered her finger for inspection. "Better?" asked the surgeon. "Better," answered the lady, speaking to him for the first time. Not another word followed during the rest of the interview. Three or four similar visits were made, at the last of which the patient held out her finger free from bandages and perfectly healed. "Well?" was Abernethy's monosyllabic inquiry. "Well," was the lady's equally brief answer. "Upon my soul, madame," exclaimed the delighted surgeon, "you are the most rational woman I ever met with!" —*J. C. Jeaffreson.*

OUGHT TO BE TAKEN INTO ACCOUNT.

A YOUNG widow, whose aged husband had died, becomingly appeared two months afterward at the Paris Mairie, to announce her forthcoming marriage to her cousin. "Pardon me, madame," observed the clerk, "but the law peremptorily forbids a woman to marry within ten months of her husband's death." "Yes, truly," replied she, "but are not those eight months of paralysis to be taken into consideration?"

WANTED A REDUCTION.

A GENTLEMAN recently about to pay his doctor's bill, said: "Well, doctor, as my little boy gave the measles to all my neighbors' children, and as they were attended by you, I think you can afford, at the very least, to deduct ten per cent. from the amount of my bill for the increase of business we gave you."

THE NEW BABY.

Nurse—"Is it a Cherman or an Enklish papy?"

Lady—"Well, I don't know. You see she was born in England, but my husband is German."

Nurse—"Ach, so. Zen ve vill vait to see vat lenkvetch she vill schbeak, and zen ve vill know."

A SURE SIGN.

L'UNION MEDICALE gives the following conversation between a physician and nurse in a Paris hospital:

Physician—"Be sure and test the water by the thermometer before using it to bathe the child."

Nurse—"I can tell whether it is right or not without using the thermometer."

Physician—"How?"

Nurse—"Put the child in, if it gets blue, the water is too cold; if it gets red, the water is too hot."

"LA VIE OU LA BOURSE."

A RICH man upon whom a surgeon has just performed a serious operation; received from the latter a demand for an enormous sum. "You ought to have warned me said the sufferer, "that your way of carrying on your trade is to demand 'your money or your life.'"

A PROMPT ANSWER.

A SOCIETY lady, noted for her levity, asked her physician how many doctors it would take to make a scholar. He replied, "just as many as it would take of lovers to satisfy a coquette."

THE DELIGHTED SURGEON.

WILLIAM COOPER was, like Abernethy, a most tender-hearted man. He was about to amputate a man's leg, in the hospital theatre, when the poor fellow, terrified at the display of instruments and apparatus, suddenly jumped off the table, and hobbled away. The students burst out laughing ; and the surgeon, much pleased at being excused from the performance of a painful duty, exclaimed, "By God, I am glad he's gone!" —*J. C. Jeaffreson.*

AT LEAST ONE CONSOLATION.

Surgeon Cox, who recently died at Chattanooga, was an eccentric man as well as an able surgeon. After the battle of Antietam he amputated the leg of a Connecticut soldier, but became so absorbed in the operation that he failed to notice that his patient was dying. While he was sewing up the stump the hospital steward chanced along and remarked: "Doctor, there is no use going on; the man is dead." The doctor looked up in surprise and replied: "I am sorry the poor fellow is dead, but there is one consolation about the matter, he has gone to heaven with a flap that he can be proud of."

KEEP IT UP.

Dr. L. is cautiously treating a sick man concerning the nature of whose disease he is quite in the dark. "Well," he says to the nurse, on making his usual morning visit, "how do we find ourselves to-day? Did he sleep well? Did the medicine act?" "Yes, sir, he slept, but I left the gas burning, turned down very low." "Ah, he slept well, did he? I thought he would. And you left the gas burning turned down low? Very good, very good ; all is growing very nicely." And he takes his hat. "What, doctor! have you no instruction, no prescription, nothing?" The doctor, (sagely, and after mature deliberation), "Yes; keep the gas burning, turned down very low."

THE PHYSICIAN.

A London correspondent visited a doctor, and after consultation asked, "What is your fee?" He replied: "Specialists and extortionists charge two guineas, quacks ask half a guinea, but a physician's fee is a guinea. I am a physician."

MOSQUITOES AS A STIMULANT TO REPRODUCTION.

A gentleman traveling in the low lands of Arkansas, was surprised to find a great number of children at the different houses which he passed. Stopping at a house where a numerous progeny seemed to abound, he enquired of its maternal guardian for the cause of this universal prolificness. "Oh! my dear sir," she answered, "the mosquitoes are so bad in this country that we folks can't sleep at night."

TWO PHILADELPHIA DOCTORS.

Doctor X. is an eminent physician of Philadelphia: in manner he is brusque and overbearing. Among his office patients one morning was a gentleman, who after occupying exactly five minutes of the great man's time, took a ten dollar note from his pocket and enquired the fee. "Fifty dollars," said the impatient medical man. The patient demurred a little, whereupon the physician rudely remarked, "Well, what do you expect to pay? Give me what you have," and on receiving the ten dollar bill, turned scornfully to his negro servant, and handing him the money said, "That's for you, Jim," but lost his temper still more when his patient coolly said, "I did not know you had a partner. Good morning, doctor."—*New Remedies*, August, 1881.

Mrs. Y., the wife of an eminent and amiable physician of Philadelphia discovering that her husband received far more patients into his office than the cash realized, or the charges made would indicate, set about to mend matters.   Unfortunately for the inauguration of the scheme, Dr. Y. had invited a friend to spend the evening with him, and Mrs. Y. discovered his prolonged presence in the office, scored the friend for an office consultation, and sent the bill.   A few weeks after, the doctor met his friend on the street and enquired why he had not been around again, remarking that he enjoyed his visit very much.   Whereupon his friend replied, "What are you going to charge me *this* time?"   Y. not knowing about the Madame's transactions was chagrined to see his visitor produce a receipt for office consultation.

ANECDOTE OF SIR THOMAS WATSON.

When attending Lawrence, the great surgeon, when he had hemiplegia with aphasia, it was thought desirable to give the patient some sedative.   Lawrence knowing this and wishing to indicate what remedy he desired, was unable to find the word he wanted, and became greatly agitated in consequence. Sir Thomas Watson got pen, paper and ink, and asked him to write the word.   This he could not do, but taking the pen full of ink, made a large splash on the paper, and offering it to those at his side.   Sir Thomas Watson at once perceived the drift of this, and saw that his patient wished for the "black drop," a discovery which greatly delighted and satisfied Lawrence.

THE BELL-HANGER.

Dr. Latham was a very eminent, learned, and accomplished physician of St. Bartholomew's Hospital, but he had published more on the diseases of the heart and lungs than upon any other subject.   A patient of his, who had recently recovered from some pulmonary affection, one day said to him, "I feel that as regards my lungs I am quite well, and now think of going to consult Dr. Watson about my general health." To which Dr. Lapham replied, "Yes, I see; in your estimation Dr. Watson is an architect, and me, I suppose, you look upon as a bell-hanger."—*J. C. Jeaffreson.*

SEDATIVE REMARKS.

Patient.—" Do you mean to say my complaint is a danger-ous one?"

Doctor.—" A very dangerous one, my dear friend. Still, people have been known to recover from it; so you must not give up all hope. But recollect one thing; your only chance is to keep in a cheerful frame of mind, and avoid anything like a depression of spirits!"

COULD HAVE DONE NO MORE.

A MAN falls on the street in a fit. As the doctor hastens up, a bystander exclaims: " Oh! if he'd only come sooner!" But the doctor looks up from the fallen man, and remarks, " He is dead; I myself could have done nothing more."

HOMŒOPATHIC PIES.

THE *Boston Traveler* tells the following on the authority of a truth-telling auctioneer of that city: "A year or more ago, the auctioneer had for sale a lot of homœopathic med-icines. All these medicines were dumped into one pile, and disposed of in one lot, there being various kinds of medicines in the mass. A boarding-house keeper bought the lot, and some days after the purchase, the auctioneer asked her, " What did you do with that homœopathic medi-cine, Mrs. ——?" She replied, " I thought I could use it, and it was cheap and so I crushed it under the roller and then filled my sugar-bowls with it. The boarders seemed to like it, and especially when powdered over pies."

A FORTUNATE ERROR.

A PHYSICIAN wrote on a prescription for a foreign patient, " One pill to be taken three times a day in any convenient vehicle." " Vehicle " was a word which the patient did not understand, and on consulting a dictionary, found it to mean " cart, wagon, carriage, buggy, wheelbarrow." He therefore concluded that the doctor intended that he should ride out, and while in the vehicle swallow the pill. This he did to the letter, and the fresh air, exercise, and pills combined, brought relief, which either taken alone might not have done.

THE PATIENT'S GRATITUDE.

THE gratitude of the patient to his physician! I know that. It is part of the disease. It is declared during the fever, cools down in convalescence, and is cured when health returns.—*Jean Baudry.*

A DESERVED REBUKE.

DR. ABERNETHY was often brusque and harsh, and more than once was properly reproved for his hastiness and want of consideration. "I have heard of your rudeness before I came, sir," one lady said, taking his prescription, "but I was not prepared for such treatment. What am I to do with this?" "Anything you like," the surgeon roughly answered. "Put it on the fire, if you please." Taking him at his word, the lady put her fee on the table, and the prescription on the fire, and, making a bow, left the room. Abernethy followed her into the hall, apologizing, and begging her to take back the fee, or let him write another prescription; but the lady would not yield her vantage-ground.—*J. C. Jeaffreson.*

CALLING THE DOCTOR.

The following item from the *Louisville Medical News* illustrates one of the ways in which medicine is practiced in that city: "The other morning, as a belated member of the Owl Club was steering home through the dense fog, which the writer is reliably informed, hangs over the city at three A. M., he passed the house of a well-known physician. The vestibule of this residence was open, and on its side the dim rays of the moon, struggling through the gloom produced by the efforts of the city gas company, disclosed the mouth of an acoustic tube, underneath which was the inscription: 'Whistle for Dr. Potts.' Not wishing to be disobliging about so small a matter, the Owl stumbled up the steps, and steadying himself against the wall, blew into the pipe with all the strength of his lungs. The physician, who was awakened by the resultant shrill whistle near his head, arose, and after wondering at the singular odor of whisky in the room, groped his way to the tube, and shouted, 'Well!' 'Glad to know you're well,' was the reply; but being a doctor, I s'pose you can keep well at cost price, can't you?' 'What do you want?' said the man of pills, not caring to joke in the airy nothing of his night-gown. 'Well,' said the party at the other end of the tube, after a moment's meditation, 'Oh,' by the way, are you young Potts, or old Potts?' 'I am Dr. Potts; there is no young Potts.' 'Not dead, I hope?' 'There never was any. I have no son.' 'Then you are young Potts and old Potts too. Dear, dear, how singular.' "

"What do you want?" snapped the doctor, who was beginning to feel as though his legs were a pair of elongated icicles.

"You know old Mrs. Peavine, who lives in the next block?"

"Yes, is she sick. What's the matter?"

"Do you know her nephew, too—Bill Briggs?"

"Yes. Well?"

"Well, he went up to Bridgeport, shooting this morning, and—"

"And he had an accident? Hold up a minute. I'll be right down."

"No, he's all right; but he got sixty-two ducks—eighteen of 'em mallards. I thought you might like to hear it."

And the joker hung on to the nozzle, and laughed like a hyena digging up a fat missionary.

"I say," came down from the exasperated M. D., "that's a jolly good joke, my friend. Won't you take something?"

"What?" said the surprised humorist, pausing for breath.

"Why, take something. Take this." And before the disgusted funny man could withdraw his mouth, a hastily compounded mixture of ink, ipecac and asafœtida squirted from the pipe, and deluged him from head to foot, about a pint monopolizing his shirt-front and collar.

And while he danced frantically around, sponging himself off with his handkerchief, and swearing like a pirate in the last act he could hear an angel voice from above sweetly murmur: "Have some more? No? Well, good night. Come again soon, you funny dog, you. By-bye."

THE WONDERFUL CURE.

SIR HUMPHREY DAVY in his young days assisted Dr. Beddoes, who at that time was bent on curing all diseases by the inhalation of gases. It so happened that Davy was accustomed before applying the inhaler, to ascertain the temperature by placing a thermometer under the tongue. While thus employed on a countryman, who fancied this was the wonderful process he had heard of, the man exclaimed that he already felt better. Davy took the hint, left the thermometer in its place some time, and reapplied it every morning. His patient improved in health, and ultimately got quite well without any other treatment.

FOUND HIS MASTER.

ABERNETHY at one time had to examine a medical student. "What would you do," bluntly inquired the surgeon, "if a man was brought to you with a broken leg?" "Set it, sir," was the reply. "Good, very good, you're a very pleasant, witty young man; and doubtless you can tell me what muscles of my body I should set in motion, if I kicked you, as you deserve to be kicked, for your impertinence?" "You would set in motion," responded the youth, with perfect coolness, "the flexors and extensors of my right arm; for I should immediately knock you down."—*J. C. Jeaffreson.*

THE TWA SIMPLES.

SIR WALTER SCOTT once had a colloquy with a grave sagacious-looking doctor, attired in black, for whom, in a small English town, Scott had sent on behalf of his sick servant. In the doctor, Scott, to his amazement, recognized a Scottish blacksmith, who had formerly practiced as a veterinary operator. "How in the world," exclaimed Sir Walter, "came you here? Can it be possible this is John Lundie?"

"In truth it is, your honor, just a' that's of him."

"Well, let us hear, you were a horse doctor before; now it seems you are are a man doctor; how do you get on?'

"Oh, just extraordinar' well, for your honor maun ken that

my practice is vera sure and orthodox. I depend entirely on twa simples."

"And what may their names be? Perhaps it's a secret."

"I'll tell your honor (in a low voice); my twa simples are just laudamy and calamy."

"Simples with a vengeance!" replied Sir Walter, "but John, do you never happen to kill any of your patients?"

"Kill, on ay, may be sae, whiles they dee, and whiles no; but it's the will o' Providence. Ony oo, your honor, it will be lang before it maks up for Flodden!"

ONLY 2,000 FRANCS.

The Lyon Medicale says a young nobleman, while skating fell and broke his leg. He was attended by a medical celebrity, who sent him a bill of 2,000 francs. The youngster enclosed two bills of 1,000 francs each with the following brief note—"My Dear Doctor——you are perfect in reducing a fracture. There is but one thing more that you have to learn, viz., to reduce a —— facture."

CHILD-BIRTH IN THE AIR.

THE Rappel, of Paris, announces the birth of a boy, a few days since under very novel circumstances. In the "captive balloon," a young lady was taken ill. A doctor from Tarbes, who happened to be in the car, saw her safely delivered of a boy before the balloon reached the ground, when a cab took the mother and child to a hotel. The husband (son of one of the leading Manchester manufacturers) presented the doctor with five hundred francs for his services; and the Rappel commends balloon-ascents to doctors in want of patients.

THE IMBECILE.

ONE day an Englishman, upon whom Prof. Blandin had operated for anal fistula, came into the latter's office and said to him: "I have come to thank you for your good care, and to ask how much I owe you!"

Three thousand francs," answered Blandin. The Englishman opened a great pocket-book and took out five bills, each of one thousand francs, pinned together, took out the pin and put two of the bills into his pocket-book, gave the other three to Blandin, saluted and left.

"I am an imbecile!" said Blandin, smiting his forehead. "This Englishman wanted to pay me five thousand francs, and I only asked three thousand of him. I am an imbecile a true imbecile!"

DR. LETTSOM'S INHERITANCE.

Dr. Lettsom, who was the founder of the Sea Bathing Infirmary at Margate, and of the General Dispensary, was left by his father what, in the language of some parts of the world, is called *property;* but which happened to consist almost entirely of a number of slaves, on an estate in Jamaica. When the benevolent Doctor went out to the West Indies, to take possession of his inheritance, he is said to have emancipated every one of the slaves on his arrival; so that, in the words of his biographer, "he became a voluntary beggar at the age of twenty-three." The Doctor went afterwards to Tortola, where, by his practice as a physician, he amassed a considerable sum of money, with which he returned to England in 1768.—*J. C. Jeaffreson.*

CAUSE AND EFFECT.

A lady, during pregnancy, carried with her a pocket edition of Moore's Poetical Works, which she read almost constantly. Her child, at three years of age, exhibited a most wonderful gift of putting sentences into rhyme; in fact, naturally expressed his little ideas and thoughts in flowing measure! Blame not the bard—but a case like this shows how important is a well-assorted library to a gravid uterus.

IT DIDN'T TAKE.

Georgie M., aged four, asked why his little cousin, Sarah, was being taken to church, and on being answered that she was to be baptized, said: "I want to be baptized too." His mother replied that he had been baptized already. "Yes, I know," said he, "but it didn't take." Georgie had been vaccinated unsuccessfully a while before, and got baptism and vaccination mixed.

THE DOUBLE DIAGNOSIS.

An amusing story is told, in Le Practicien, of a distinguished savant at the dinner of the Anthropological society, Paris. It was not delivered publicly, but whispered in the ear. "I visited," said the narrator, "a young man aged 15, who, without any apparent cause, was getting weaker from day to day. Suspecting albuminuria or diabetes, I asked for the urine of my young client for examination. What was my surprise to find in it a quantity of kiesteine. Assuredly this was not the urine of my patient. On my next visit, in presence of the family, I said you are trying to humbug me. I asked for the urine of this patient, and you have sent me that of a pregnant woman. Scarcely had I pronounced these words, when two persons fainted: the young man and the bonne who had opened the door.

She cried out, 'Oh, M. Earnest, you have done for me.' Light was thrown at once on my mind. The maid knew why the young man had fainted. She sent me her own urine, so that unconsciously I had made a double diagnosis."

CORRECT.

Professor hands a femur to a candidate.—"Will you tell me, please, which bone this is?" Student, after meditating and turning and re-turning the bone in his hands, with much confidence:—"Sir, this is the bone of a dead person."

BOUND TO STAY WELL.

On the night before his execution a French prisoner of rank sent for the celebrated M. Villette, and informed him that he was greatly troubled by the state of his health. The physician examined him and prescribed for him, and the medicine was taken as gravely as though the invalid expected to live for years. Memoirs of M. Villette.

DR. RATCLIFFE'S REVENGE.

ONE evening as Dr. Ratcliffe was sacrificing in a tavern to the purple god, to whom he was as much devoted as to the god of physic, a gentleman entered the room in great haste, and almost breathless, "Doctor, my wife is at the point of death! make haste; come with me." "Not till I have finished my bottle, however," replied the doctor. The man, who happened to be a fine athletic fellow, finding entreaty useless, snatched up the doctor, and carried him out of the tavern. The moment he set the doctor upon his legs, he received from him, in a very emphatic manner, the following threat: "Now, you rascal, I'll cure your wife in revenge." The doctor kept his word.—*J. C. Jeaffreson.*

A WISE DECISION.

A LITIGATION once arose in the University of Cambridge whether doctors in law or doctors in medicine should hold precedence. The chancellor asked whether the thief or the hangman preceded at the execution, and on being told that the thief usually took the lead, "Well then, let the doctors of the law have the precedence, and let the doctors in medicine be next in rank."

AN EYE-OPENER.

"DOCTOR, my daughter seems to be going blind, and she's just getting ready for wedding, too. Oh, dear me, what is to be done?" "Let her go on with the wedding, madam, by all means. If anything can open her eyes, marriage will."

THE NEW POULTICE.

A CINCINNATI woman, speaking of her sick husband, said, "you see, I gave him a great deal of bread and milk—the doctor tells me to. I don't know why he prescribes it; but I suppose it flies to the part, and acts as a kind of poultice, you know!"

HOW TO DIFFERENTIATE.

"Doctor, how is a man to tell a mushroom from a toad-stool?" Scientific authority: "By eating it: if you live, it is a mushroom; if you die, it is a toadstool."

KEEP 'EM ALIVE.

"Keep 'em alive, boy—keep 'em alive!" said an old physician to his brother practitioner. "Dead men pay no bills."

ABSENT-MINDED.

An absent-minded doctor, on calling upon a gentleman, who had been some time ailing, put a fee into the patient's hand, and took the medicine himself—which he had prepared for the sick man. The medical man was not made sensible of his error till he found himself getting ill and the patient getting better.

SCIENTIFIC AFFECTION.

A French chemist is said to have condensed the body of his deceased wife into the space of an ordinary seal, and had her highly polished and set in a ring. He made a nice income by betting with lapidaries and others that they could not tell the material of the seal in three guesses, and after pocketing the money, would burst into tears and say, "It is my dear, dear wife."

NEVER CAME AGAIN.

Some time since a young lady, by some strange fatality, stumbled on the word "gonorrhœa." She innocently asked the family physician its meaning. He told her that it was the technical name for head-ache! Being visited by a medical student regularly, who seemed very much pleased with her, she, doubtless to show her aptitude at medical technicalities (when at their meeting he asked after her health) informed

12

him that she had had a "slight gonorrhœa for the last four
or five days!" He never came again, and she wonders.

THE NEW LIP.

"WONDERFUL things are done now-a-days," says Timmins;
"the doctor has given Flack's boy a new lip from his cheek."
"Ah," said the lady, "many's the time I have known a
pair taken from mine, and not a painful operation either."

THE DOCTOR'S LITTLE FRIENDS.

WHILE a doctor was visiting a woman in Rowlandsville,
Pa., two children poured a pint of molasses into his silk hat,
which he didn't notice till he put the tile on his head. Language cannot describe his feelings, but it is said that he will
petition the next legislature to pass a bill making it a criminal offence for a child to be born under twelve years of age.

THE FLORENTINE QUACK.

DR. PARIS in his Pharmacologia tells a story of a Floren-
tine quack, who gave a countryman six pills, which were to
enable him to find his lost ass; the pills beginning to operate,
obliged him to retire into a wood, where he found his ass.
The clown soon spread a report of the wonderful success of
the quack, who in consequence, reaped an ample reward
from the proprietors of strayed cattle.

AT HIS REQUEST.

ABERNETHY being actively engaged in inserting a cervical
séton in "a noble patient," who had requested that this should
be done, his patient exclaimed, "Sir, you give me excessive
torture; will your seton do good?" "No sir," said the doctor. "Then why do you insert it?" screamed the patient.
"Because," said the doctor, "you told me to do so, and I will
get five pounds for my work."—*J. C. Jeaffreson.*

UNDER THEM.

A PHYSICIAN finding a lady reading "Twelfth Night," said: "When Shakespeare wrote about patience on a monument, did he mean doctor's patients?" "No," she answered, "you don't find them on monuments, but under them!"

SOUNDS FROM THE CONSULTATION-ROOM.

"How long will it take you to cure me, doctor?" "Well, Mr. Blank, I think you can get back to your desk at the bank in about a month, but you will have to remain under treatment for several years." "But you mistake; I am not Mr. Blank the banker, but Mr. Blank the letter-carrier." "Oh, that alters the case. There is nothing the matter with you but a little biliousness. You will be well in a month."

A NEW ARTERY.

A CANDIDATE was lately plucked because he answered the question: "How would you treat post-partum hemorrhage?" —"I would tie the post-partum artery."

RESULT OF A CONSULTATION.

THREE medical celebrities met together to consult, at the sick bed of General X. After they go, the General rings for his man-servant: "Well, Jacques, you showed those gentlemen out; what did they say?" "Ah, General, they seemed to differ with each other; the big fat one said that they must have a little patience, and at the autopsy—whatever that may be—they would find out what the matter was."

DR. HARVEY'S REWARD.

DR. S. V. CLEVENGER makes the following citation from John Aubrey's "Lives of Eminent Persons:" "I have heard *Dr. Harvey* say that after his booke of the circulation of the blood came out, he fell mightily in his practice; it was believed by the vulgar that he was cracked and all the physitians were agaynst his opinions and enveyed him." Aubrey was at Harvey's funeral, and "helpt carry him into the vault."

THAT SETTLED IT.

A LADY complaining to her attending physician, during an attack of severe illness, that the taste of an important prescription which she was taking, was disagreeable, received, in reply the rather emphatic declaration: "Madam, we are not confectioners." This explanation was, apparently, satisfactory, as no further dissatisfaction with the flavor of the drug was expressed.

CURRAN'S SARCASM.

CURRAN being at a party at the seat of an Irish nobleman, one of the company, who was a physician, strolled out into the churchyard. Dinner being served up, and the doctor not returned, some of the company were expressing their surprise where he could have gone to. "Oh," says Curran, "he has just stepped out to pay a visit to some of his old patients."

ON DERBY DAY.

SIR WILLIAM JENNER went one day into the pathological laboratory, and remarked how few students were present. "It's Derby Day," said his house physician. "Derby Day, sir!" said Jenner, with unconcealed surprise, "when I was a student, I knew as little when it was Derby Day as when it was Trinity Sunday."—*J. C. Jeaffreson.*

PLUCKED AGAIN.

A GROUP of young students were around the dissecting-room fire, cross-examining Tomkins, who had been up for his primary college the day before, as to the nature of the questions, and how he had done, etc. Tompkins, who had been rejected three times previously, answered that he had done very fairly, and thought it very likely he had "stumped" the examiners at last. "By-the-bye," proceeded the hero of many examinations, "there was one question I couldn't understand; when I was leaving the hall he asked me if I knew '*how many blue beans made five*?' can any of you fellows tell me?" The roar of laughter which followed this recital was something terrific. I need hardly say that Tompkins was plucked again.

LITERARY PHYSICIANS.

It is remarkable that of all men of letters who pursue any profession, none so willingly quit their avocations, to write on other matters, as physicians. Ficinnius has given a Latin version of Plato, and explained his system. Julius Scaliger, who was a doctor in physic, has written much criticism. Perrault, the antagonist of Boileau, translated Vitruvius, and gave public lectures on geometry and architecture. Akenside and Armstrong are celebrated for their poetry, and Doctor Smollett had more frequently his pen than the pulse of a patient in his hand.

MEDICAL HONESTY.

"You may say what you please," remarked the old doctor, "physicians are not all humbugs. There are some honest men among them." "Unfortunately, yes," replied Fogg; "of course you refer to their patients, doctor."

STOCK-JOBBING DOCTOR.

As Chirac, a celebrated physician, was going to the house of a lady, who sent for him in a great hurry, he received intelligence that the stocks had fallen. Having a considerable property embarked in the Mississippi scheme, the news made so strong an impression on his mind, that while he was feeling his patient's pulse, he exclaimed, "Mercy upon me, how they fall! lower, lower, lower!" The lady in alarm flew to the bell, crying out, "I am dying; M. de Chirac says that my pulse gets lower and lower; so that it is impossible I should live!" "You are dreaming, madam!" replied the physician, rousing himself from his reverie; "your pulse is very good, and nothing ails you; it was the stocks I was talking of."

WHAT A DOCTOR IS.

A DOCTOR is a *piller* of society. His enemies say that he can kill with *powder* without shot, and that his *drops* are almost as dangerous as the hangman's.

INCORRIGIBLE,

Medical Adviser.—"Now, first of all, you must not drink beer in the morning."

Patient.—"No more I should, old fellow, but it so happens there's not a drop of brandy in the house!"

TYSON, THE MISER.

TYSON, the miser, being near his last hour, magnanimously resolved to pay two of his 3,000,000 guineas to Dr. Radcliffe, to learn if anything could be done for his malady. The miserable old man came up with his wife from Hackney, and tottered into the consulting-room in Bloomsbury-square, with two guineas in his hand. "You may go, sir," exclaimed Radcliffe to the astonished wretch, who trusted he was unknown—"You may go home, and die, and be d——d, without a speedy repentance; for both the grave and the devil are ready for Tyson of Hackney, who has grown rich out of the spoils of the public, and the tears of orphans and widows; you'll be a dead man, sir, in ten days.—*J. C. Jeaffreson.*

LIKE DOCTOR, LIKE PATIENT.

A VERY eminent physician happened to be sent for one evening, after having indulged at a convivial meeting; so that by the time he had been whirled to his patient's door, he was very ill-qualified to decide in a case of difficulty. Having made shift to reach the drawing-room, and seeing a lady extended on a sofa, assisted by a female attendant, he, by a sort of mechanical impulse, seized her hand; but finding himself utterly unable to form an opinion on the case, he exclaimed, "Drunk, drunk, upon my honor!" (meaning that *he* was in that unfit state) and immediately made the best retreat he was able. Feeling rather awkwardly at this adventure, he was not impatient to renew his visit, but being sent for on some other occasion, he took courage, and was preparing an apology, when the lady presently removed his apprehensions, by whispering in his ear—"My dear doctor, how could you find out my case so immediately the other evening? It was certainly a great proof of your skill! but pray not a word more on the subject."

THE DUKE OF NORFOLK'S TOAST.

AFTER the funeral of Lord Brougham's grandfather in 1782, the then Duke of Norfolk who acted as chief mourner, took the chair at the feast. Dinner over, the Duke rose and said: "Friends and neighbors, before I give you the toast of the day—the memory of the deceased—I ask you to drink to the health of the founder of the feast—the family physician."

PISCATORIAL.

THIS, to his assistant, from one of our prominent physicians, who is off on a little fishing excursion:

Doctor.—"Tell everybody I am off to the country in attendance upon a bad case."

"But patients are so curious," was the response, "what shall I say of the case; give it a name."

"Well, call it, let me see—yes, call it a case of *ichthyosis.*"

PHYSICIAN AND CLERGYMAN.

A CLERGYMAN and a physician lived in the same village, on terms of great intimacy. The former was attacked by a violent fit of the gout, and the latter attended his reverend friend *gratuitously*, with unabating success.

The medical gentleman soon after called upon his neighbor, the parson, to perform the matrimonial service; and the call was promptly and cheerfully obeyed.

The clergyman took an early opportunity of withdrawing himself from the assembled company, alone and unobserved; but he was soon followed to his home by a brother of the physician, requesting his acceptance of a rouleau of guineas as a marriage fee. The divine retired for two minutes to his study, and returned the rouleau to the bearer, with a note containing the following

IMPROMPTU.

To the doctor, the parson's a sort of a brother!
And a good turn from one, deserves one of the other;
So take back your guineas, dear doctor, again,
Nor give—what you so well can remedy—*pain.*
Permit me to wish you all joy and delight
On the occasion that brought us together to-night.
May health, fame, and wealth, attend you thro' life,
And every day add to the bliss of your *wife.*

THE AFFRONT.

The largest fee Sir Astley Cooper ever received was paid him by a West Indian millionaire, named Hyatt. This gentleman having occasion to undergo a painful and perilous operation, was attended by Drs. Lettsom and Nelson, as physicians, and Sir Astley as chirurgeon. The wealthy patient, his treatment having resulted most successfully, was so delighted that he feed his physicians with 300 guineas each. "But you, sir," cried the grateful old man, sitting up in his bed, and speaking to his surgeon, "shall have something better; there, sir—take that." The *that* was the convalescent's nightcap, which he flung at the dexterous operator. "Sir," replied Sir Astley, picking up the cap, "I'll pocket the affront." It was well he did so, for on reaching home he found in the cap a draft for 1,000 guineas. This story has been told in various ways, but all its tellers agree as to the amount of the prize.—*J. C. Jeaffreson.*

GRAND CURE FOR THE TOOTHACHE.

A man some time ago entered into a coffee-house at Vienna with his hand pressed close to his cheek, groaning, stamping, and exhibiting every symptom of violent indisposition. He took a seat, called for some punch, and made useless efforts to swallow it. Several people collected around him, and inquired the cause of his illness; he replied, that he was tormented by a violent fit of the toothache, which resisted every remedy. Various things were prescribed for him, but without effect. At length a man who was playing at billiards in an adjoining room, stepped forward, and said,

"Allow me to prescribe for the gentleman; I possess a remedy, which I am certain, will cure him in five minutes." He drew from his pocket a box, filled with small chips of a yellow kind of wood. "Here, sir," said he, " apply this to your tooth."

The patient did as he was directed, and to the astonishment of every one present, he immediately experienced a diminution of pain; the remedy operated as if by enchantment, and in less than a quarter of an hour he was completely relieved, and drank his bowl of punch to the health of his deliverer.

"Sir," said he, "you have performed a most wonderful cure, and I shall be eternally grateful to you, if you will inform me, where your valuable remedy can be purchased."

"Nowhere," replied the billiard-player: "I procured it during my last visit to South America, and brought it home with me for my own private use; the Indians of *Oya Poc* never use any other remedy."

"Well, surely you will not refuse to let me have a few pieces of the wood."

"Impossible."

"I only ask for twenty pieces, and I will give you a ducat for each."

"Well, I consent out of pure humanity; but mind, you are the only person to whom I can grant such a favor."

Every one present now wished to have some portion of the divine wood of *Oya Poc*; all were subject to the toothache; all claimed the sacred rights of humanity, and the compassionate traveler was obliged to part with nearly all his chips of wood, and to fill his box with ducats. The master of the coffee-house himself, unwilling to suffer such an opportunity to escape him, had the good fortune to purchase ten pieces. When occasion came for putting the virtue of the wonderful wood to the test, however, it was soon found that it had none of those effects on the good people of Vienna, which it had on the savages of *Oya Poc*. Had it lost its virtues by carriage and keeping? So the happy few who had got bits of the rarity insisted; for, as usual, the greatly hoaxed were the last to acknowledge the ingenuity by which they had been fooled and cheated.

SHOULD HAVE STAYED AT HOME.

Wife (to a doctor just home from a week's hunting): "Well, James, did you shoot anything?"

Doctor (sadly): "No. Awfully bad luck; never killed a thing."

Wife (who knows him, sweetly): "My dear, you would have done better if you had stayed at home."

HIS BITTEREST ENEMY.

A visiting committee to a hospital came to the second bed from the door of a ward.

"Well, my man, how are you getting on? Can we do anything to make you more comfortable?"

The patient expressed a wish to exchange beds with the one next to the door, and on being pressed for the reason, said:

"That man is my bitterest enemy. The doctors always come in at that door, and they put the same thermometer in my mouth that has just been in that man's stern."

DR. CADOGAN'S FRIGHTFUL SUGGESTION ABOUT HIS WIFE.

DR. CADOGAN, of Charles the Second's time, was a favorite with the ladies. He secured as his wife a wealthy lady, over whose property he had unfettered control. Against the money, however, there were two important points, figuring under the head of "set-off"—the bride was old and querulous. Of course, such a woman was unfitted to live with an eminent physician, on whom bevies of court ladies smiled, whenever he went west of Charing Cross. After spending a few months in alternate fits of jealous hate and fondness, the poor creature conceived the terrible fancy, that her husband was bent on destroying her with poison, and so ridding his life of her execrable temper. One day when surrounded by her friends, and in the presence of her lord and master, she fell on her back in a state of hysterical spasms exclaiming: "Ah! he has killed me at last. I am poisoned."

"Poisoned!" cried the lady friends, turning up the whites of their eyes. "Oh! gracious goodness!—you have done it, doctor!"

"What do you accuse me of?" asked the doctor, with surprise.

"I accuse you—of—killing me—ee," responded the wife, doing her best to imitate a death struggle.

"Ladies," answered the doctor, with admirable nonchalance, bowing to Mrs. Cadogan's bosom associates, "it is perfectly false. You are quite welcome to open her at once, and then you'll discover the calumny."—*J. C. Jeaffreson.*

ANOTHER CURE FOR STERILITY.

A PROFESSOR stated in a lecture that he had noticed that in sterile women the hair on the Mons Veneris was always straight. The professor was rather surprised by the inquiry of a student, whether curling the hair would cure the sterility.

A NEW WAY FOR SURGEONS TO OBTAIN THEIR FEES.

A GOOD story is told in the Journ. des Conn. Méd. A medical man having made a rectal examination, asked the moderate fee of five francs from the gentleman(!). The latter quietly put down a forty sous piece on the mantel-shelf, and began to walk out, whereupon the doctor first, to the astonishment of his patient, divested himself of his coat, then his waistcoat, and lastly began to remove his indispensables, saying at the same time: "If you will now do to me the operation I have just performed for you, I will at once hand you twenty francs." The abashed patient, stuttering some excuses, at once paid the remaining sixty sous and left.

THE PECULIAR FIT.

"Doctor, doctor," panted a messenger, "come down the street, quick; there's a man in a fit."

"In an apoplectic?" questioned the doctor.

"No, sir; he's in an ulster," answered the messenger.

KNEW ITS FATHER.

At his own expense, a physician tells a story about a small donkey he sent to his country-house for the use of his children. One of his little daughters going out with the nurse to admire the animal in the paddock, was distressed when the donkey brayed dolefully.

"Poor thing, poor thing!" she exclaimed, and then turned to her nurse and said : "Oh, I am so glad! Papa will be here on Saturday, and then it won't feel so lonesome."

DR. MESSINGER MOUSEY.

Dr. Messinger Mousey, who was many years physician to Chelsea College, and known all over London for his eccentricities, used, by way of ridiculing family pride, to say, that the first of his ancestors, of any note, was a baker, and dealer in hops ; a trade which enabled him with some difficulty to support a large family.   To procure a present sum of money, he robbed the feather-beds of their contents ; and supplied the deficiency with unsalable hops.   In a few years, hops became very scarce, and enormously dear ; and the hoarded treasure was ripped out, and a good sum procured for hops, which, in a plentiful season, would not have been salable : "and thus," the doctor used to add, "our family *hopped* from obscurity."

The doctor enjoyed the office of physician to Chelsea Hospital for so long a period, for he lived to the great age of ninety-six, that the reversion of the place was successively promised to many persons who never lived to see it vacant. The gentleman for whom it was last intended, having gone out to Chelsea to take a view of his land of promise, the doctor saw him from his window examining very curiously the house and gardens ; and guessing the purpose of his visit, he went out, and thus accosted him : "Well, sir, I see you are examining your house and gardens that are to be, and I can assure you they are both very pleasant, and very convenient: but I must tell you one circumstance ; you are the fifth man that has had the reversion of the place, and I have buried them all ; and what is more, there is something in your face that tells me I shall bury you, too!" Not only was the doctor's prediction verified ; but of such bad omen did the reversions to the physicianship of Chelsea become at last, that nobody would accept of it; and at the doctor's death, there was no one who had the promise of the situation. Although the doctor was a man of great whimsicality, he possessed a very comprehensive understanding, and no small share of wit and genius. He numbered among his most intimate friends some of the greatest men of his time, among others, the great statesman, Lord Godolphin. Of Mousey's skill in his professional capacity, the proofs on record are not so satisfactory. He is said to have adopted a very singular mode of drawing his own teeth : It consisted in fastening a strong piece of cat-gut firmly around the affected tooth; the other end was fixed to a perforated bullet ; and with this a pistol was charged, and when held in a proper direction, by touching the trigger, a troublesome companion and tedious operation were got rid of. A person whom the doctor fancied he had persuaded to adopt this new mode of operation, went so far as to let him fasten the cat-gut to his tooth ; his resolution then failed, and he loudly cried out that he had altered his mind. "But I have not," said Mousey, holding fast to the string and giving it a smart pull, "you are a fool and a coward for your pains."

The doctor had a taste for mechanics; and to this, his mode of tooth-drawing may with probability be ascribed. An apartment of his house he had converted into a workshop, and filled with a confused collection of wheels, pendulums, nails, saws, hammers, chisels, and other instruments of handicraft. As long as age and eyesight permitted, he would amuse himself here the whole day long, and took particular pleasure in executing all sorts of joiner's work, either for himself, or any of his friends. In his habits, the doctor was penurious and saving; and like all misers, one of his chief cares was the care of his treasures; he was often at a loss to know which place was the safest to deposit his cash in; for bureaus and strong boxes, he knew were not always secure.

Previous to a journey into Norfolk, one summer, he selected the fire-place of his sitting-room, for his treasury; and placed the bank-notes and cash under the cinders and shavings. On his return, after a month's absence, he found his old woman preparing to treat a friend or two with tea, and in order to show the more respect to her guests, the parlor fire-place was selected for boiling the kettle, as she never expected her master until she saw him. The fire had just been lighted, when the doctor arrived at the critical moment: he rushed, without speaking, to the pump, where luckily a pail of water was standing: he threw the whole over the fire and the poor old woman, who was diligently employed in removing it. His money was safe; for, although some of the notes were partially burnt, sufficient fragments remained to enable the doctor, with some official trouble, to get paid at the bank.— *J. C. Jeaffreson.*

THUNDER AND LIGHTNING.

"So you have twins at your house, Johnnie."

"Yes'm, two of 'em."

"What have you named them?"

"Thunder and Lightning, ma'am."

"Why, what very singular names."

"Yes'm, that's what pa called 'em soon's the doctor brought 'em."

BY THE FIRST WIFE.

A VISITOR at asylums relates an incident almost unparalleled in its incomprehensibility. He went to a private lunatic asylum which he had previously visited, and seeing there a distinguished looking man sitting moodily alone, went up and said to him :

"How do you do? I think I have seen you before. May I ask your name?"

"My name," returned the man fiercely, "I am Alexander the Great !"

"Why," said the visitor, who suddenly remembered having already had a discussion with the man, "the last time I was here you were St. Paul !"

"Yes, of course," the man rejoined quickly, "but that was by my first wife."

SAVED HIS LIFE.

THE following compliment was paid to Dr. Ferry by an Irishman, who credited the doctor with saving his life:

"You see, sur, I had a complication of diseases, an' two

other doctors did be working on me for some time, an' I was in a mighty bad way, an' the two doctors they gave me up an' wint away, an' thin me friends they sint for Dr. Ferry, but he had another engagement an' didn't come."

KILLING TWO BIRDS WITH ONE STONE.

A GOOD story is told of a physician of a suburban town. After he had continued his calls on a lady patient for some weeks, she expressed her fears that it would be inconvenient for him to come so far on her account. "Oh, madam," replied the doctor, innocently, "I have another patient in the neighborhood, aud thus I can kill two birds with one stone!"

ABOUT CREMATION.

IN a discussion on cremation at a London club, a member is credited with the argument, "We earn our living, why should we not urn our dead?"

URINOSCOPY.

IN the biography of the celebrated *Dr.John Radcliffe,* the following incident is narrated: Among many of the artifices by which the credulous have been imposed upon, the pretentions of the urinoscopists of former days were not the least significant. A foolish woman, provided with the infallible indication of disease, came to Radcliffe, and, dropping a courtesy, told him that having heard of his great fame, she made bold to bring him a fee, by which she hoped his worship would be prevailed upon to tell her the distemper her husband lay sick of, and to prescribe the means for his relief.

"Where is he?" cries the doctor.

"Sick in bed, four miles off," replies the woman.

Taking the vessel, and casting an eye upon its contents, he inquired of the woman what trade the patient was of; and learning that he was a bootmaker, "Very well," replied the doctor, and having retired for a moment to make the requisite substitution, "Take this home with you, and if your husband will undertake to fit me with a pair of boots by its inspection, I will make no question of prescribing for his distemper by a similar examination."—*J. C. Jeaffreson.*

PHYSICIAN AND CURER.

The Fortnightly Review tells of an orthodox physician who said disparagingly of an irregular practitioner, " Ce n'est pas un médecin *c'est un guérissiêr*," which, being translated, might be rendered, "He is not a physician, he is a curer." The anecdote serves to illustrate the difference which actually exists between your "scientific" physician, so-called and the intelligent general practitioner.

A KIND SUGGESTION.

An undertaker having advertised that he was prepared to furnish all the requirements for a funeral, a malicious wit suggested that he must combine the practice of medicine with his undertaking business.

WHERE WAS HE STABBED?

We find the following passage in the speech of an Elko (Nevada) lawyer to a jury:

"Here we have a physician, a man who, from his high and noble calling, should be regarded as one who would scorn to stain his soul with perjury. But what did he testify, gentlemen? I put the question to him plainly, 'Where was this man stabbed?' And what was his reply? Unblushingly he replied that the man was stabbed about an inch to the left of the median line, and yet we have proved, by three unimpeachable witnesses, that he was stabbed just below the Young America hoisting works."

THE POWERFUL CATHARTIC.

The following is probably the most thoroughly drastic effect ever produced by a medicine: The professor bowed courteously to the lady whom he had seen the night before on her debarkation from the ocean steamer, and for whom he had ordered a compound cathartic pill.

"What sort of a passage did you have, madam?"

"Perfectly beautiful, doctor," replied madam, "passed two schooners and a sloop."

PLAGUING THE DOCTORS.

MR. COOKE, the miser of Pentonville, as he was called, was a great annoyance to gentlemen of the faculty. He used to put on ragged clothes and go as a pauper to Mr. Saunders and other gentlemen, to have gratuitous advice for his eyes; get a letter for the dispensary, and attend there as a decayed tradesman, for several weeks, until detected. Having a wound in his leg, he employed a Mr. Pigeon, who lived nearly opposite to him, in White Lion Street, Pentonville, to cure it.

"How long do you think it will be, before you can cure it?"

"A month."

"And how much must I give you?"

Mr. Pigeon, who saw the wound was not of any great importance, answered, "A guinea."

"Very well," replied Cooke; "but mark this: A guinea is an immense sum of money, and when I agree upon sums of such magnitude, I go upon the system of *no cure, no pay;* so, if I am not cured by the expiration of the month, I pay you nothing."

This was agreed to. After diligent attention, the wound was so near being healed, that Cooke expressed himself satisfied, and would not let Pigeon see it any more. However, within two or three days of the month being completed, the old fellow got some sort of plaster, with euphorbium on it, from a farrier, and made a new wound on the place where the former had been, and sending for Pigeon the last day of the month, showed him that his leg was not well, and that of course the guinea he had agreed for was *forfeited*. This story the old fellow used to tell of himself with great satisfaction, and call it, "Plucking a Pigeon."—*J. C. Jeaffreson.*

18

DIDN'T LIKE THEM RAW.

OH, horror! "Well, madam, how's your husband to-day?"
"Doctor, he's no better."

"Did you get the leeches?"

"Yes, doctor, but he could only take three of them raw; I had to fry the rest."

ALSO AND LIKEWISE.

A SURGEON once jeeringly asked a Quaker if he could tell the difference between "also" and "likewise."

"Oh, yes," said the Quaker, "Sir William Fergusson was a great surgeon—his skill as an operator was admitted by almost every one. You are a surgeon 'also' but not 'likewise.'"

NEVER ASKED AGAIN.

A YOUNG lady at home from boarding school for the holidays was asked if she would have some roast beef, when she replied:

"No, I thank you; gastronomical satiety admonishes me that I have arrived at the ultimate stage of deglutition consistent with dietetic integrity."

She was never asked if she'd have anything more again.

TIMELY WARNING.

A PLACARD in the window of a patent medicine man in Paris reads as follows:

"The public are requested not to mistake this shop for that of another quack just opposite."

A FEVER TEST.

DR. HOLMES relates the following to illustrate the significance of small things in the sick room:

"Will you have an orange or a fig?" said Dr. James Jackson to a fine little boy now grown up to goodly stature.

"A fig," answered Master Theodore, with alacrity.

"No fever there," said the good doctor, "or he would certainly have said an orange."

MRS. PARTINGTON'S CONSTERNATION.

"Diseases is very various," said Mrs. Partington, as she returned from a street-door conversation with Dr. Bolus. "The doctor tells me that poor old Mrs. Haze has got two buckles on her lungs! It is dreadful to think of, I declare. The diseases is *so* various! One way we hear of people's dying of hermitage of the lungs; another way of the brown creatures; here they tell us of the elementary canal being out of order, and there about tonsors of the throat; here we hear of neurology in the head, there of an embargo; one side of us we hear of men being killed by getting a pound of tough beef in the sarcofagus, and there another kills himself by discovering his jocular vein. Things change so, that I declare I don't know how to subscribe for any diseases nowadays. New names and new nostrils takes the place of the old, and I might as well throw my old herb-bag away." Fifteen minutes afterwards Isaac had that herb-bag for a target, and broke three squares of glass in the cellar window in trying to hit it, before the old lady knew what he was about. She didn't mean exactly what she said.—*B. P. Shillabeer.*

THE GREAT DEBT.

"My dear sir," said the doctor to a disconsolate husband, whose wife had just died, "I sympathize with you from the depths of my heart, in this sad affliction. The case, however, was a hopeless one from the beginning, and, as I told you, medicine was, necessarily, powerless to do more than to ease your dear wife's suffering."

"I know, doctor, you did all that could have been done, and that fact is a consolation to me. You were very kind and devoted, and I feel that I owe you a great debt—"

"Oh, my dear sir," returned the kind-hearted man of medicine, "please don't mention such a thing just now. It will be quite time enough after the funeral, when I will let you have my bill."

CURIOUS EFFECT OF MAGNESIA.

THE barber who shaved me in this village (Madison, Ga.), a very black negro, had a light mulatto wife. They had several children of the proper shade of color, and one, the youngest, almost *white.* Being asked the reason of the last child's being so much whiter than the others, the barber very innocently answered that "it was all owing to his wife having followed the advice of a white lady during her pregnancy, and taken *a great deal of magnesia and chalk, to cure the dyspepsia.*"

THAT ENDED THE LECTURE.

Doctor, advising young lady to have her clothing suspended from her shoulders instead of from her waist. To illustrate, he said:

"See how the men are supported."

"Yes," retorted the young lady, that's so, see how many poor women have to support their husbands!"

And that ended that lecture.

IN COURT.

"PRISONER," said the presiding judge, "tell the gentlemen of the jury, why you threw your wife into the river. What was your motive?"

"It was for her own good," responded the prisoner. "My poor late wife was very sick, therefore the doctors ordered hydrotherapy, and I carried out their advice."

HYGIENE AT A BALL.

AT the last ball given by the countess of L., the son of Lord C——, a jolly blonde young man made his entry into the Parisian world.

The lady of the house introduced her guest to all of her friends in succession, but the *Anglais* persisted in paying his attention to a fat old lady whom he finally invited to dance a waltz, although bewitching young damsels were abounding.

The waltz was followed by a quadrille, and this by a polka;

the Englishman did not quit his corpulent and matronly partner, who enjoyed herself famously in spite of her obesity, for
a second.

Taking him aside, during an interval, the countess whispered, "But, my dear sir, why are you obstinately dancing
with that enormous dame, when the walls are lined with so
many pleasant young ladies who would be most happy to
dance with you."

"Oh! well, well, pardon," said the young lord, while big
drops of sweat trickled down his forehead, "I really didn't
mean any offence, but the doctors advised me to perspire as
much as possible."

MEDICAL UNSELFISHNESS.

A HYSTERICAL female sends for her physician at 2 A. M.,
with a message that she is dying. It is raining cats and dogs,
but the man of medicine does not stand on the order of his
going. Arrived at the bedside, he makes a hasty examination
and, with much simulated agitation, he advises that the clergyman and the lawyer be also sent for. The patient now becomes
really alarmed, and wants to know whether she is really about
to depart. "Oh, doctor? can't you save me? Am I really going to die?" "No, madam," returns the disgusted doctor, "I
don't think you are to die for several years yet." "Then why
send for the clergyman and lawyer?" "Well, I don't know
of any reason, why you should especially pick out your doctor,
to make a fool of him."—*Tableau.*

SOUND HOMŒOPATHY.

OF the late Dr. Gray, homœopathist, of New York, it is
said that a poor sewing girl went to him for advice, and was
given a vial of medicine, and told to go home and go to bed.
"I can't do that, doctor," the girl replied, "for I am depen-
dent on what I earn for my living." "If that is so," said Dr.
Gray, "I'll change the medicine a little; give me back the
vial." He then wrapped around it a 10-dollar bill, and re-
turning it to her, reiterated his order, "Go home and go to
bed," adding, "Take the medicine, cover and all."

DISFRANCHISED.

Two ladies had a conversation on the subject of the late war. One of them was quite indignant over the fact that Mr. Jefferson Davis is disfranchised. "Disfranchised, did you say?" exclaimed the other. "How long has he been disfranchised?"

"Why, ever since the war."

"Well, now, I never heard that before, and don't understand how it can be. I am sure Mrs. Davis has had one or two children since the war."

A WRONG GUESS.

Dr. Dosem, an Austin physician, was called on to attend old Uncle Mose, who drives a dray. "You have been gorging yourself with green water-melons for dinner," said the physician, feeling the patient's pulse. "How de mischief did yer find dat out—by feelin' my pulses?" "No, but by seeing the water-melon rinds under the bed." Said the old man, raising himself up in bed: "You am de knowiuist man in Austin. Heah, old 'oman, take dat old harness from under de bed, or dis heah medicinal gemman am gwine to treat me for eatin' a mule for dessert to settle my stomach. I aint touched a water-melon for a month."

IN THE PARK.

In a park at night. She: "How horrid the mosquitoes are." He: "Yes, they are fearful." She: "Don't you know of any remedy, Harry, that will keep the insects off?" He: "Oh, yes, there are —" She: "I hear oil of tansy is good to keep them off." He remained silent for the next quarter of an hour. Those New York girls are evidently well up in materia medica, but why did Harry preserve that long silence? It was ominous, to say the least.

WHAT A MISER IS.

A miser and his wealth impress a student imbued with the knowledge of chemistry as follows: "He is a molecule consisting of one atom of soul, one hundred of body, and one thousand of gold. Now, death, the greatest decomposer, precipitates the body, the soul evaporates, and leaves the gold in a free and uncombined state."

PAID BACK.

IN his cross-examination of the surgeon, the lawyer said that a doctor ought to be able to give an opinion without making a mistake. The surgeon replied:

"They are as capable as lawyers."

"The lawyer said, "A doctor's mistakes are buried six feet. under the ground, a lawyer's are not."

"No," said the surgeon, "but they are sometimes hung as many feet above the ground."

THE INQUISITORIAL PROFESSOR.

THE *Independent Practitioner* tells of a brow-beating professor who, after giving a lecture on the facial and other expressions of gout insisted that the patient before the class was a victim of the disease. The patient denied ever having had it.

"But your father must have had it."

"No, sir," said the man, "nor my mother either."

"Ah, very strange," said the professor to his class, "I am still convinced, however, that this is a gouty subject. I see that his front teeth show all the characters, which we are accustomed to note in gout.

"Front teeth!" ejaculated the patient. "Well that beats everything. It's the first time I ever heard of false teeth having the gout. I've had this set for ten years."

The inquisitorial professor was, as may be imagined, quite discomfited by this sally.

ANECDOTE OF CLOT BEY.

THE following anecdote is related of this French surgeon, who attained eminence in the service of Mehemet Ali, and died in 1868. For about 1,700 years there had been no public lectures on anatomy delivered in Alexandria, the very birthplace of human anatomy; and so strong were Mussulman fanaticism and prejudice, that although he had the authority of the Pasha to institute a school and commence demonstrations, when, forceps and scalpel in hand, he opened the thorax of a body, a student rushed upon him with a poignard. The blade slipped over the ribs, and Clot Bey, perceiving that he was not dangerously hurt, took a piece of plaster from his dressing-case, and, applying it to the wound, coolly observed to the class: "We were speaking, gentlemen, of the disposition of the ribs and sternum, and I now have the opportunity of showing how a blow directed from above has so little chance of penetrating the thorax," and went calmly on with his lecture. This piece of *sang-froid* gave him an incontestable moral supremacy over his pupils, and he continued his instructions, meeting with success, and turning out some skilful surgeons.

A MODEL STUDENT.

A young American, who had been in Paris a year studying medicine, was visited by his father. He paraded the old gentleman through the city, and pointed out its architectural lions. Finally they halted in front of a many-pillared building.

"What is that lordly pile?" asked the old man.

"I don't know," replied the youth, "but there is a sergeant-de-ville."

They crossed over, and put the question.

"That, gentlemen," said the official, "is the Medical School."

THE MEAN DRUGGIST.

An elderly Scotch woman went one day to an apothecary's shop with a prescription for two grains of calomel for a child. Seeing the druggist weigh the medicine with scrupulous exactness, and not thinking he did this from anxiety not to get an overdose, but from his penuriousness to give as little as possible for the money, she said:

"Dinna be sae mean wi't man; it's for a puir faitherless bairn."

TOLD THE TRUTH.

It is not often that the doctor tells the truth about the results of his practice, but a German physician was lately surprised into doing so by the winning voice of childhood.

"Papa," said the little one, "do people pay you for those patients who die as well as for those who get well?"

"God be thanked they do," was his fervent reply; "otherwise we should all be reduced to beggary at once."

THE GRATEFUL DOCTOR.

One day while the once famous syphilographer, Thierry de Hery, was sauntering through the crypts of St. Denis, paying little attention to the various royal tombs about him, he suddenly precipitated himself before an effigy and began to pray; the berger who was standing near by, called out to him:

"You mistake, sir, that is not a saint's tomb, but that of our late king Charles VIII."

"Simpleton," replied de Hery, "learn that the good king Charles VIII is more than a saint to me, as he imported the pox from Italy, and has been my benefactor to the amount of thirty thousand pounds a year."

MRS. MIXER'S ELOQUENCE.

"How flagrant it is!" said Mrs. Mixer as she sniffed the odor of a bottle of Jamaica ginger. "It is as pleasant to the oil factories as it is warming to the diagram, and so accelerating to the cistern that it makes one forget all pain, like the ox hide gas that people take for the toothache. It should have a place in every home where people are subject to bucolics and such like melodies. Besides, a spoonful is so salubrious that when run down, like a boot at the heel in walking, one feels like a new creature."

HIS FAVORITE.

"Doctor, whom of your professional friends do you prefer to meet in consultation?"

"Oh, my favorite is Dr. B.; he tells such funny stories."

P. P. P. P.

Small boy to rustic parent:

"I say, pa, what kind of medicine is P. P. P. P., which I see painted on the fence."

Parent: "Well, I don't 'zactly know, but I suppose it is something to act on the kidneys."

SENATOR CARPENTER'S LAST PUN.

THE bright, mirthful soul of the late Senator Carpenter was not overawed even by the shadow of death. The evening before he died he suffered excruciating pain, and in his agony wanted an explanation of the cause. "The pain is caused, Senator," replied a physician, "by the stoppage of the colon." "Stoppage of the colon, eh?" and again the sense of humor overcame pain itself—"Well, then, of course *it isn't a full stop.*"

BIRTH MARKS.

THE following good story is told of a physician of Dayton, Ohio: The doctor was recently attending a case of labor in the family of one of his patrons, who, though a very excellent man, is a little slow in the payment of his medical bills. Immediately after the birth of the babe, the father nervously asked, "Doctor, is the baby marked?" "Yes," quietly remarked the doctor, "It is marked 'C. O. D.'"

It is needless to remark that the bill for that baby was promptly settled.

FALSE CONCEPTION.

MR. ADDISON in the House of Commons, three times attempted to make a speech upon a pending question, and each time stopped, after uttering the words, "Mr. Speaker, I conceive." A witty member after the third attempt arose and remarked: "I regret exceedingly that my friend has conceived three times and has yet brought forth nothing. It is a manifest case of false conception."

SHE WAS ILL.

A DOCTOR who had continued his visits on a wealthy lady for an inordinate time after convalescence had set in, was somewhat surprised one day, at being told by the servant that madame could not see him that day as she was ill.

NO USE.

"ARE you feeling very ill? Let me see your tongue, please." "It's no use, doctor; no tongue can tell how bad I feel."

AN ANECDOTE OF SIR WM. FERGUSON.

THE British Medical Journal gives a characteristic anecdote of the late Sir William Ferguson, who, after a successful operation on a Manchester millionaire, was asked by the patient to name his fee. "Two hundred guineas." "Two hundred guineas!" exclaimed the patient. "Yes," said Sir William; "you forget the life-long experience required to give the proper skill, the time and toil of the journey, and the loss of practice in London." "But you have only been ten minutes about it," said old Dives. "Oh, if that is your only objection," said Sir William, in his broad Scotch, "the next time I come I'll keep ye an 'oor under the knife."

THE PROTUBERANT FOREHEAD.

"WHAT a fine 'protuberant forehead your baby has, Mrs. Jones! Did he get it from his father?" "No," replied Mrs. Jones, "he got it from a fall down stairs."

NELATON AND HEMORRHAGE.

THE saying of Nelaton is often quoted: "If you have the misfortune to cut a carotid when performing an operation, remember it takes two minutes for syncope to supervene, and as many more before death occurs. Now, four minutes are four times the time required for a ligature, provided you don't hurry yourself. Never hurry yourself."

WILL GIVE THE SAVAGE DYSPEPSIA.

An English physician with whom Sidney Smith always had a controversy when they met, received an appointment to go to Australia, in its early savage days. When taking his leave of him, the wit said: "Good bye, doctor; you have never failed to disagree with me, and I verily believe you will disagree with the savage who eats you."

A DOCTOR'S DIPLOMA BEFORE A JURY.

A doctor named Royston had sued Peter Bennett for his bill, long over due, for attending the wife of the latter. Alexander H. Stephens was on the Bennett side, and Robert

Toombs, then in the United States Senate, was for the doctor. The doctor proved the number of his visits, their value according to local custom, and his own authority to do medical practice. Mr. Stephens told his client that the doctor had made out his case, and there was nothing wherewith to rebut or offset the claim, and the only thing left to do was to pay it. "No," said Peter, "I hired you to speak in my case, and now speak." Mr. Stephens told him there was nothing to say; he had looked on to see that it was made out, and it was. Peter was obstinate, and at last Mr. Stephens told Peter to make a speech himself, if he thought one could be made. "I will," said Peter, "if Bobby Toombs won't be too hard on me." Senator Toombs promised he would not, and Peter began:

"Gentlemen of the Jury, you and I is plain farmers, and if we don't stick together these 'ere lawyers and doctors will get the advantage of us. I ain't no lawyer or doctor, and I ain't no objections to them in their proper place; but they ain't farmers, gentlemen of the jury. Now, this man Royston was no doctor, and I went for him to come and doctor my wife's sore leg, and he come and put some salve truck onto it, and some rags, but never done it a bit of good. Gentlemen of the jury, I don't believe he is a doctor any way. There are doctors as is doctors, sure enough, but this man don't earn his money, and if you send for him as Mrs. Sarah Atkinson did for a negro boy as was worth $1,000, he just kills him and wants you to pay it."

"I don't!" thundered the doctor.

"Did you cure him?" asked Peter, with the slow accents of a judge with a black cap on. The doctor was silent, and Peter proceeded:

"As I was saying, gentlemen of the jury, we farmers, when we sell our cotton, has got to give vally for the money we ask, and doctors ain't none too good to be put to the same rule. And I don't believe this 'ere Sam Royston is a doctor nohow."

"Look at my diploma, if you think I am no doctor."

"His diploma!" exclaimed the orator, with great contempt. "His diploma! Gentleman, that is a big word for printed sheepskin, and it don't make no doctor of the sheep as first wore it, nor does it of the man as now carries it; a good newspaper has more in it, and I pint out to ye that he ain't no doctor at all."

The doctor was now in a fury, and screamed out:

"Ask my patients if I am not a doctor."

"I asked my wife," retorted Peter. "She said she thought he was not."

"Ask my other patients," said the doctor.

"This seemed to be the straw that broke the camel's back; for Peter replied with look and tone of unutterable sadness: "That is a hard saying, gentlemen of the jury, and one that requires me to die, or to have powers as I have hearn tell ceased to be exercised since the Apostles. Does he expect me to bring the angel Gabriel down to toot his horn before his time, and cry aloud: 'Awake, ye dead, and tell this court and jury your opinion of Sam Royston's practice?'"

"Am I to go to the lonely churchyard and rap on the silent tomb, and say to 'um as is at last at rest from physic and doctor's bills, 'Git up here, you, and state if you died a natural death, or was hurried up some by doctors?' He says ask his patients, and, gentlemen of the jury, *they are all dead!* Where is Mrs. Beasley's man, Sam! Go ask the worms in the graveyard, where he lies. Mr. Peak's woman, Sarah, was attended by him, and her funeral was appointed, and he, the doctor, had the corpse ready. Where is the likely Bill, as belonged to Mr. Mitchell? Now in glory, expressing his opinion of Royston's doctoring. Where is that baby gal of Harry Stephens? She is where the doctors cease to trouble, and the infants are at rest. Gentlemen, he has eaten enough chicken at my house to pay for this salve. I found the rags, and I don't suppose he charges for making her worse, and even he don't pretend to charge for curing her; and I am humbly thankful he never give her nothing for her innards, as he did his other patients, for something made 'um all die mighty sudden."

The applause was great. The doctor lost and Peter won. —*Sanitarian.*

THE HYPOCHONDRIAC.

A RICH patient of hypochondriacal disposition, detailed his imaginery woes and symptoms to his doctor. "My dear fellow," said the witty physician, "I can do nothing for you. The man who listens to himself living hears himself dying."

MRS. NICKLEBY'S REMEDY FOR A COLD.

" I HAD a cold once," said Mrs. Nickleby. "I think it was in the year eighteen hundred and seventeen; let me see, four and five are nine, and, yes, eighteen hundred and seventeen, that I thought I never should get rid of. I was only cured at last by a remedy that I don't know whether you ever happened to hear of, Mr. Pluck. You have a gallon of water as hot as you can possibly bear it, with a pound of salt, and six-pen'orth of the finest bran, and sit with your head in it for twenty minutes every night before going to bed; at least, I don't mean your head—your feet. It's a most extraordinary cure—a most extraordinary cure. I used it for the first time, I recollect, the day after Christmas-day, and by the middle of April following, the cold was gone. It seems quite a miracle, when you come to think of it, for I had had it ever since the beginning of September."—*Charles Dickens.*

ORDERING BY TELEPHONE.

One of the dangers of the employment of women as drug clerks is the consequences which are prone to follow questions like the following, which the "Drug Exchange" says was recently asked a female drug clerk in Chicago: "Have you large black nipples?"

WHO WOULD NOT BE A DOCTOR.

Quite a number of our young men are studying for the medical profession. We do not wish to deter them from this laudable pursuit, for a physician's calling is one of the most honorable, ennobling, humanizing, and useful in the world. But all is not gold that glitters, and the following are some of the sweets of a doctor's life: If he visits a few of his patients when they are well, it is to get his dinner; and if he does not do so, it is because he cares more for the fleece than the flock. If he goes to synagogue regularly, it is because he has nothing else to do; if he doesn't go, it is because he has no respect for the Sabbath nor religion. If he speaks reverently of Judaism, he is a hypocrite; if he doesn't, he is a materialist. If he dresses neatly, he is proud; if he does not, he is wanting in self-respect. If his wife does not visit you, she is "stuck up;" if she does, she is fishing for patients for her husband. If he has a good turnout, he is extravagant; if he uses a poor one on the score of economy, he is deficient in necessary pride. If he does not write a prescription for every trifling ailment, he is careless; if he does, "he deluges one with medicine." If he makes parties, it is to soft-soap the people to get their money; if he does not make them, he is afraid of a *cent.* If his horse is fat it is because he has nothing to do, if he is lean, it is because he isn't taken care of. If he drives fast, it is to make people believe somebody is very sick; if he drives slowly, he has no interest in the welfare of his patients. If the patient recovers, it is owing to the good nursing he received; if he dies, "the doctor did not understand his sickness." If he talks much, "we don't like a doctor to tell everything he knows," or, "he is altogether too familiar;" if he don't talk, *"we like to see a doctor sociable."* If he says anything about politics "he had better let it alone;" if he don't say anything about it, "we like to see a man show his colors." If he does not come immediately when sent for, "he takes things too easy;" if he sends in his bill "he is in a terrible hurry for his money." If he visits his patients every day, it is to run up a bill; if he don't, it is unjustifiable negligence. If he orders the same medicine, it does no good; if he changes the prescription, he is in league with the druggist. If he uses any of the popular remedies of the day, it is to cater to the whims and prejudice of the people, to fill his pockets; if he don't use them, it is from professional selfishness. If he is in the habit of having frequent consultations, it is because he knows nothing; if he objects to having them, on the ground that he understands his own business, "he is afraid of exposing his ignorance to his superiors." *If he gets pay for one-half his services* he deserves to be canonized. Who wouldn't be an M. D.?—*The Hebrew Standard.*

AT THE END.

The doctor's jokes are all very plain. There is a Holmes-pun look about 'em.—*Boston Post.*